ULTIMATE PAYBACK

ULTIMATE PAYBACK

SHADOW VANGUARD™, BOOK FOUR

TOM DUBLIN

MICHAEL ANDERLE

DISRUPTIVE IMAGINATION

LMBPN Publishing
PMB 196, 2540 South Maryland Pkwy
Las Vegas, NV 89109

Version 1.00 August 2019
ISBN: 978-1-64202-409-8 (ebook)

ULTIMATE PAYBACK TEAM

**Thanks to our JIT Readers
From all of us, our deepest gratitude!**

Dave Hicks
Jackey Hankard-Brodie
Jeff Goode
Micky Cocker
Deb Mader
James Caplan
Diane L. Smith
Misty Roa
Kelly O'Donnell
Dorothy Lloyd
John Ashmore
Jeff Eaton

*If we missed anyone, **please** let us know!*

Editor
Skyhunter Editing Team

For "Tommy's Team"
Micky Cocker,
James Caplan,
Erika Everest, and
Kelly O'Donnell

The BEST damn beta readers in the universe!

— Tom

To Family, Friends and
Those Who Love
To Read.
May We All Enjoy Grace
To Live The Life We Are
Called.

— Michael

Adaius IV, Ricogsberg, the Accounting Offices of Dirk'sen & Hanlo

Killeg Dirk'sen rushed down the office corridor as fast as his stubby legs could carry him. The Alstublaft, cursed by the dense gravity of his homeworld, silently damned every law of physics between panicked moments where he tried to gather his thoughts. After he checked his watch for the third time, Killeg's mind finally registered the hour. It was three-fifths to six, and still the Don had not so much as called to explain his tardiness.

What am I thinking? Killeg beat his temple with a closed fist. *The Don doesn't need to explain nothin'. He'll be here when he gets here.* Assuming he'd still be here, the Don had a reputation for going through accountants. Even the legendary financial genius of Dirk'sen and Hanlo couldn't save every bad investment made by the mafia. They'd end up wearing cement shoes and tumbling into a black hole just like their former competitors Dutch & Vandermar.

Killeg wasn't really sure what the cement shoes were for, but such were the consequences of displeasing Don Gan'barlo. He didn't really care much about the specifics, just the important and simple goal of not dying.

At the end of the drab office hallway, Killeg pushed the double doors of the conference room wide. Inside, Killeg's colleague, the honorable and furry Gruff Hanlo, nervously swiped a tablet resting on the meeting room table before him. His other clawed hand tapped the table nervously. Gruff didn't even look up as Killeg entered, so engaged was he with the tablet, hoping with each swipe that he'd catch some sliver of info that'd save both their necks.

"Would you quit that? You'll strain your eyes," Killeg said as he pushed a seat back next to the Baroleon and climbed into the bistok-leather chair, exhaling slight gasps as he continued speaking and climbing. "We have everything." *Huff.* "There's no point worrying now." *Huff.* "All we gotta do is land the presentation." *Huff, huff.* He finished his ascent into the high leather office chair and dabbed his glistening temple with a handkerchief from the sleeve of his child-size suit.

Gruff cast Killeg a side-eye before returning his attention to the tablet. His tapping claws cracked the screen of the tablet. "*Son of a fuzzy ass-face!*" the Baroleon howled as he threw the tablet against the wall, breaking it beyond repair.

"Calm down. You're giving me the shakes. See?" Killeg held out his tiny hands, which were quivering ever so slightly. "Let me get you a cup of tea." The Alstublaft began the descent from his seat.

"I'm sorry I am not calming you down." Gruff's insincerity dripped from his retort. "But it wasn't my fucking idea to balance the books for a *FUCKING MOB BOSS!*"

Killeg glared at the Baroleon over the steaming cup of warm water, a dangling teabag in his other hand. "You know you're faaaar less convincing when you're angry." He turned back to the tea and called to his partner, "Want milk in your tea?"

"And you're less convincing when you're wrong!" Gruff shouted. His voice took on a mocking high-pitched squeak. "We're gonna get rich with this job." He threw himself back into his chair with his arms crossed while he muttered, "Rich in fucking lead. And yes, milk would be wonderful." His sulk deepened.

A doorbell buzzed through the office, spooking Killeg into dropping the cup of hot tea onto Gruff's lap. The Baroleon howled into the late morning, "You pint-sized failure of a wunderkind!"

Ignoring Gruff's litany of curses, Killeg rushed to his tablet and flipped the front door locks. He looked up at Gruff, his face ashen and eyes wide. "They're here."

Gruff fell silent and straightened in his seat as Killeg clambered back into his chair. He was still climbing and grunting when the double doors of the meeting room swung open.

Two human figures stepped through, a man and a woman. Both were sporting sharp black suits and reflective black shades. The man, who was carrying a black leather briefcase and was the clear elder of the two by several human decades, scanned the room. He nodded to the woman, whose long black ponytail swung as she strode to the back of the room. She took up a position in front of the other door, facing the center.

The man was the first to speak, "The Don will see you now, Mr. Dirk'sen, Mr. Hanlo." He approached the table and lifted the briefcase.

They stared in puzzlement as the man opened the briefcase, revealing a tablet. The strange gesture would have been comical in its awkwardness if it weren't for the scowling mug of Don Gan'barlo on the screen of the device.

"Don Gan'barlo, it's a pleasure seeing you. Did you lose weight?" Gruff squeaked, his face flushing crimson as he tried to subdue a crack of a smile.

Killeg jumped up in his seat and clapped his hands as he said, "What my esteemed colleague meant, sir, was, can we get you anything? Tea? Coffee? Batteries?" The Alstublaft stammered standing in his swiveling seat, realizing the inane offer he was making to a tablet.

The image of Don Gan'barlo on the tablet raised his hand as the man strode up and set the briefcase on the table adjacent to the two accountants. "I apologize I could not be here in person, gentlemen. Business has taken me to Letho Four. Now, how is my legitimate business empire?" The Don's mandibles remained still, his emotions unreadable. The male bodyguard took up a position at the main entrance and also faced the center of the room.

"Legitimate business? Well, the pet store your wife owns on Pulomia is currently in the black, and earning her a tidy profit in..." Killeg would've continued had Gruff not backhanded his colleague's shoulder.

"He isn't talking about the pet shop." Gruff whispered through his teeth. "He's talking about crime, you dense twit."

Killeg blinked and looked at the Don with a less than confident smile. "Ahh, my mistake. Well..." He flattened his hands on the table and asked, "What would you like to know, sir?"

The Don's glare was piercing. "I hire you bookkeepers so I don't have to break this shit down, so do your damn jobs and break it down!" His mandibles quivered briefly. He took a deep breath and grabbed a cigar from off-screen as a Yollin hand entered the display with a lighter. The motion was smooth and practiced, to the point where the Don didn't even acknowledge the lackey servicing him. The big boss waved his hand to tell the cowering accountants to proceed.

"Don Gan'barlo, sir, well, to be blunt, it's literally a clusterfuck." The noise was figuratively sucked from the room by Gruff's words.

Killeg interjected, "'Clusterfuck' is an elusive term. What is the cluster? Why is it getting fucked?"

The woman in the black suit cracked a brief laugh but quickly held a palm to her lips. Don Gan'barlo's head on the tablet glanced at the bodyguard, scowl deepening. The Don turned back to Killeg. "Mr. Dirk'sen, explain. I'm not an angry Yollin, but my patience is running thin today. Talk, or you won't ever do so again." The Don moved a finger across his throat in a gesture whose meaning was obvious even to the two thick-headed accountants.

"Well, the closure of some ventures has adversely affected the bottom line of your organization." Killeg flipped through his tablet as he read off, "The attack on the slave market on Damkin Prime, the abrupt end of the Eternity supply through Ordanian Hub, the multiple raids by Federation law enforcement throughout the Gulan system, the arrests of several protection thugs on drug charges..." He droned on as he continued to read the list of failures.

Gruff raised a hand to tell his partner to stop. "The Don gets the point."

Don Gan'barlo puffed out a cloud of smoke from his cigar. He spoke as he pulled it from his lips, "Tell me, what do we still got? What's our most successful investment?"

The two accountants looked at each other, then back to the Don as Killeg said, "Well, the Balgarian Duke galactic net scam has been growing exponentially over the last three quarters, and our projections show the trend will not slow." The Alstublaft flipped the tablet around to display a chart he'd pulled up to the screen, and he held it up so Don Gan'barlo's screen could get a good view.

"Not to mention that should the Miserian arms deal go forward, the profits should keep the family completely solvent in all operations for approximately three to three and a quarter years," Gruff added as he raised an index finger to play up the prospect for rising profits.

Don Gan'barlo raised a hand on the tablet's screen. The two bodyguards stood at attention. Gruff and Killeg's lives flashed before their eyes. Mostly in the forms of spreadsheets and numbers.

"Gentleman," Don Gan'barlo said as the female bodyguard stepped from the rear door and picked up the briefcase, leaving it open. "I came here today to quell my nerves." The bodyguard backed out of the office, the tablet still facing the center of the room, allowing the Don to speak to the accountants. "And frankly you gentlemen have silenced them all, but now, if I ever, and I mean ever, see you here again, you die just like that." The Yollin snapped his fingers. The bodyguard with the briefcase was already out the door, and the other followed soon after.

The two accountants blinked at the swift exit of one of the most fearsome mobsters in the known universe. The double doors were slammed shut by the bodyguards, and Killeg and Gruff were left alone in their office.

Gruff let out a long breath as he slipped down in his seat. He glanced at Killeg, who looked as though he were on the edge of tears. "Are you crying?"

"No." Killeg sniffed.

"Want some tea?"

Killeg nodded slowly, and Gruff got up to go to the back counter.

The front doorbell buzzed, and the two accountants looked at each other with raised eyebrows. Gruff walked slowly to the door, unsure of what to expect. The doors to the meeting room burst open, and two Yollins in dark suits strode in. Behind them, an elderly-looking Yollin strode in on four legs, a cigar in his mouth. An acrid cloud of smoke exhaled between the Yollin's mandibles. The two accountants yelped as Don Gan'barlo removed his overcoat and handed it to one of the attending bodyguards.

"Keep this brief. I am already running late for Letho Four since some jackass staged a bomb threat at the spaceport. How's my finances?" The Don took a seat and steepled his fingers atop the table.

"Weren't you just here?" Gruff muttered confused as he

scratched at his chin, trying to tie the loose ends of this mystery together.

"Excuse me?" The Don scowled as he withdrew the cigar from his mouth.

Killeg chimed in, "Are we dead? Is this a test, sir?"

"I don't think I catch your meaning." The Don's mandibles twitched with anger. "Why don't you tell me, boys?"

The offices of Dirk'sen and Hanlo closed early that day, and would not reopen.

ICS *Fortitude*, Bridge

Captain Jack Marber threw off his sunglasses as he entered the bridge of his ship. "Fuck, I can't believe those twats bought it." He lowered his arse into the command seat at the center of the bridge. "How was your visit to the spaceport, Tc'aarlat?" Jack asked the Yollin already sitting in the bridge as he ran his hand through his hair as the other hand loosened the constraining black necktie at his throat.

"If I hadn't gotten into organized crime and espionage, I'd have made a great terrorist." The Yollin turned around in his seat, causing the metal pipes strapped across his exoskeleton to jingle. The red raal hawk, Mist, rested on his shoulder. Jack gave his friend a sour look, and Tc'aarlat protested, "Don't give me that look! You'd know I'd never. It was just the feet of the moment."

Mist squawked and swooped up to rest on one of the security cameras on the bridge.

"Heat," Adina Choudhury corrected as she entered the

bridge, the briefcase in her hand. "I'd say we all owe Solo some thanks. She really sold it."

The Yollin mobster appeared on the main bridge viewscreen and blushed slightly as he said in an exaggerated Italian accent, "As far back as I can remember, I wanted to be a mobster."

"I knew that collection of old gangster movies would come in handy." Jack smiled broadly, "I felt like I was in a scene from *The Godfather*."

The face on Solo's viewscreen blipped, shifting from a flushing mobster to the kindly face of Jack Marber's mother. "Ehh, I'd say it was more like *Godfather Part III*."

Jack frowned and grumbled under his breath, "Solo."

"Don't look so disappointed, Jack!" The voice of Jack's mother chided over the bridge speakers as the face of the original Solo blipped onto the main viewscreen with a look of concern. Jack slumped in his chair, muttering wordlessly as Tc'aarlat and Adina chuckled at the Captain's expense, Mist even joined in with an avian cackle.

"Don't look so sad, Jack. We got the intel we needed," Adina said as she placed an encouraging hand on his shoulder. He nodded up at her.

"Yeah, Jack ask your 'mum' if you can come play and show me what you got? Let the cock out of the bag!" Tc'aarlat demanded as he was tearing the faux suicide vest off his exoskeleton.

"Cat," Adina and Jack corrected simultaneously both with a slight groan.

"What the fuck is a cat?" Tc'aarlat clicked his mandibles as he cocked his head in confusion.

Jack rubbed at the bridge of his nose instead of responding. He continued, "Solo, play him the footage."

"Say hello to my little friend," Solo retorted as she began playing the recording of the meeting with Don Gan'barlo's accountants on her tablet. Tc'aarlat watched intently, absorbing the key information. Meanwhile, Adina and Jack prepared the ship for takeoff.

When the video ended, Tc'aarlat stood up from his seat and looked at his crewmates. "You know this means war, right? After today, there is no going back."

"We're with you, TC. We're in this together. Nobody messes with the Shadows and gets away with it, especially not some sleazoid mob boss." Adina gave Tc'aarlat a reassuring smile.

"Just when I thought I was out they pull me back in," Solo added.

Mist squawked from her roost.

Jack took a deep breath, slowly smiled, and shook his head. "Any more of your secrets going to bite us in the arse?"

Tc'aarlat looked a bit guilty. His mandibles drooped and his eyes fell to the metal floor.

"We're in this together, Tc'aarlat," Solo cut in, speaking in a motherly tone. "These are going to be difficult challenges for all of us, we have conquered many enemies, but none so powerful and despicable. We may be tested to our limits, none of us will come out of this unscathed, but I think I speak for everyone in saying we're in this one hundred percent, even Jack regardless of how angstsy he's being."

"Hey!" Jack complained as Tc'aarlat and Adina chuckled once again at Jack's expense. The captain threw up his hands in mock surrender.

Solo continued after a pause, "Now put on your seatbelts."

2

Balgaria, Laxra Town Center

Meemar pushed her way through the crowded market, shoving aside other Balgarians, who stretched out their necks and cursed the young whipper-snapper's impertinence. She had no time to defer to their wisdom, or lecture, as was customary for her people; she had to keep moving, stretching her long neck above the mass of hunched Balgarians.

"There! Grab the thief!" a Yollin shouted in Galactic Common. He pointed out Meemar to his two colleagues.

Meemar squeaked, dropped her head, and ran in the opposite direction, not caring how many elders she insulted by shoving. She reached the edge of the square, sidling between a food stand and a pock-marked hawker selling gaudy baubles for fertility and protection from curses. At the entrance of an alley formed between a pair of brick adobe buildings, the way was clear, so she sprinted down the muddy path as fast as her moccasined three-toed feet would carry her. By the time she reached the first bend in the alley, the trio of Yollins had entered the passageway and were hot on her stubby tail.

Shit, shit, fucking shit! Meemar's mind was filled with horrific outcomes should she be caught, and at the rate the chase was going, she would be. Taking a quick right turn, she leaped over a dirty drainage trench. Midleap a thought hit her. She cocked her wrinkly neck at the opening of the drainage trench, her lips curled in a devious smile. She threw herself into the sewage, the smell overwhelming her senses as she forced herself to crawl through the dirty mud. Her nostrils flared shut as she entered the metal opening of the drainage pipe, barely big enough to fit her stocky form. *Mistake, mistake! This was a MISTAKE!* The regret blared through her mind.

"She went through there, after her!" The first Yollin to reach the drainage pipe pointed after Meemar's rapidly disappearing rear.

"I'm not going down there," the next Yollin said as they reached the drainage reek radius.

"Me neither." The third Yollin held a palm to his mouth under the atmospheric mask, trying desperately to prevent himself from vomiting.

"What is wrong with you two? Afraid you're gonna get stuck?" The first Yollin, the clear leader, mocked the cowardice of his two underlings.

"In that cesspit of vile defecation and rotten garbage? YES!" the second Yollin shouted as the third Yollin ripped back his atmospheric mask and vomited on the ground. The second Yollin continued, "Why don't you crawl in there yourself, sir?"

The leading Yollin bridled at his underling and began

storming out of the alley. He barked at the other two, "Come on, we'll butt her off at the pass." The leading Yollin ran out of the alley and away from the reek.

"I hate that human idiom. What do asses have to do with cutting someone off?" the second Yollin grumbled to his still vomiting companion.

Balgaria, Laxra, Warehouse behind the Yollin Embassy

Meemo's hands gripped the controller tight as the screen flashed in warning, his opponent was on the back leg and making desperate moves. It was exactly what Meemo wanted. In less than a minute, the game was over.

"That's it, everyone! Your new Intergalactic Champion of *Dementoid* is the underdog from Balgaria, Mee-MOOOOOOOOOOOOOOO!" the announcer on the stage shouted to a crowd of thousands of cheering fans arrayed in seats across the auditorium. There was a standing ovation.

Meemo stood up from behind his gaming setup and turned toward his adoring fans. A female human model brought out the three-tiered trophy and offered it to Meemo. He took it with a slight bow and received a kiss to the cheek, turning his gray cheeks a slight scarlet. A mic appeared before him.

"I'd just like to thank all of my fans, oh! And my best bud, xXxStARWeedzardxXx!1. I couldn't have done this though without my lovely sister, Meemar! Come on up here." He gestured off-stage and waited for a response. The entire room went quiet, the audience a blur as the announcer came back up on the stage.

He whispered into Meemo's ear, "No napping."

"What?" Meemo looked at the announcer, but he was gone.

"I said, no napping!" the Yollin overseer barked. Meemo lurched up. His face had been resting on his keyboard.

Meemo's idyllic dream was shattered by the crack of an electrical whip, and he was thoroughly woken up by the feeling of the whip across his hard back. The whip's bite wasn't so bad for the Balgarian teen, thanks to the hardened parts of his flesh, but that didn't stop the electricity from coursing through his nervous system. After the shock from the electric whip, Meemo's fingers were back to work tapping out lines of code. The Yollin overseer watched Meemo for a time, satisfied by his use of violence to motivate his workforce. Waiting for the overseer to fully pass his workstation, Meemo let out a sigh, pausing his typing for a moment to catch his thoughts.

"Do you remember *Dementoid*, Weedzard?" Meemo asked the Balgarian on his right, who was hunched over a screen and keyboard.

"Yeah," Weedzard said without even turning his drooping head. "I don't think I've played since the All Combat Overhaul update."

"I dreamt I was the Intergalactic Champion. I got a trophy and everything!" Meemar gave Weedzard a winning grin with his beakish lips.

Weedzard guffawed. "You were good at the game, but you weren't *that* good. You'd have never gotten to the Galactics, let alone the Intergalactics." He stretched out his arms as he closed his eyes and leaned back in the creaky metal chair. The noise was drowned out by the sound of hundreds of fingers, claws, and tentacles typing on rows upon rows of desktops across the warehouse floor. "Besides," Weedzard continued, "*Dementoid* hasn't had an Intergalactic Tournament since the ACO update."

"I still think the game was fun," Meemo grumbled as he finally got back to working on it.

"Yeah, and you'd think wrong, nerd," Weedzard retorted.

"You're a nerd too, nerd." Meemo continued his grumbling. After a long pause, he continued, "Meemar was also in my dream."

Those words made Weedzard perk up. "M-meemar?" The Balgarian was visibly sweating, dark stains forming in his armpits.

"Yeah. Well, no. I referenced her, but she wasn't there. It just made me think about her, ya know?" Meemo turned back to his friend.

"Uh-huh." Weedzard nodded furtively, focused on very little other besides the mention of Meemo's older sister. As bad as a love-struck puppy.

"I shouldn't even bother talking about her with you." Meemo rolled his eyes and turned back to his desktop when he asked, "Why didn't you wake me up when the overseer was coming over?"

Weedzard shrugged his shoulders, "I was asleep too. Thanks for taking the fall for me, bud."

"You're a dick," Meemo accused.

"At least I'm not a nerd." This made Meemo's cheeks flush, and he would have retorted were it not for the overseer shouting at them to stop talking. They both focused once more on their work and continued their coding of nefarious software for one of the galaxy's most powerful crime families.

Balgaria, A Drainage Ditch Outside Laxra

It was a blessing and a curse that Balgarian were able to close up their nostrils. Balgaria's atmosphere contained natural pollutants in the form of spores produced by the innumerable species of fungi that dominated the world's ecosystem. Although these fungi were the cornerstone of the Balgarians' diet, in large quantities the spores proved dangerous for most organic life. It caused an effect known colloquially by the first human visitors, "Oh GOD! My insides are melting!" This was an especially present danger during the blooming seasons where storms of spores blasted across the planet's surface. Of the seventeen months that composed a Balgarian year six were in Blooming season.

For all these reasons, the Balgarians had evolved over millions of years to be able to close their nostrils, and their throats were lined with unique filters, protecting them. However, it was for this very reasonable biological reason that Balgarians were cursed—their ability to block out not only spores but any pollutant or smell that was deemed harmful or distasteful. Balgarian culture became notoriously filthy. Why clean up anything or keep the air fresh when you could just shut your nostrils? Meemar theorized it was for this reason her world was so often forgotten by the wider galaxy, and left in a state of poverty and decay. At times, she wondered about what consequences the biological trait, while necessary, could have had on her people. This, however, was definitely not one of those times.

"Keetal's tits! I just swallowed something!" Meemar coughed out as she crawled from the drainage pipe into another unremarkable muddy ditch. The sounds of the city were distant now, letting Meemar's violent heaving fill up the quiet serenity of the country.

After a minute of gagging and coughing Meemar was able to dislodge the foreign object from her windpipe. She stared down at a translucent white object and blinked confusedly. With some timid prodding, she discovered it was just a plain, dirty plastic bag. She rolled her eyes at her own antics and stepped out of the trench to survey her surroundings since she needed to plan her next moves. Scanning the sky for celestial bodies to gain her bearings, she realized the sky was as polluted as ever. She was hopelessly lost.

Some good all those orienteering lessons from scouts did. Meemar's mind thought back to her childhood elderly scout leader who had shown her group how to find their way home using the moons and stars. She distinctly remembered him saying they'd be thankful for the lesson someday. *Couldn't have been more wrong, wrinkle-butt.* Meemar giggled at the nickname the group gave the old guy behind his back, but she quickly chided herself for laughing, remembering he'd died three years prior. Her mom had made her go to the funeral, and it just didn't feel right laughing at the expense of someone whose funeral you attended.

Meemar began walking regardless, assuming she might as well try something. She hadn't taken five steps when she spotted a group of three masked Yollins across the adjacent dirt lot. *SHIT! Maybe if I stay perfectly still, they won't see...*

"There she is!" One of the Yollins shouted through their atmospheric mask, pointing directly at Meemar.

"Get her!" Another barked as the three made at her.

"Keetal's tits! I was thinking Tyrocians," Meemar muttered as she sprinted in the opposite direction.

Adaius IV, Ricogsberg, the Accounting Offices of Dirk'sen & Hanlo

Gel'blistaal shook his head as he exited the boardroom where he'd been interrogating the two cowering accountants. The Yollin felt silly for even thinking he'd have to use force on Mr. Dirk'sen and Hanlo. The two were practically prostrating themselves before him to tell him every detail, and given they were two people who worked extensively in numbers, their sharp minds hadn't missed a thing. Gel'blistaal almost felt bad for the two of them. They'd likely not live much longer, and it was his fault. The security of the Don and his family was his job, after all, not a pair of number crunchers.

Walking down the hallway from the boardroom, Gel'blistaal came into the reception lounge where Don Gan'barlo and his retinue of bodyguards were waiting for his report. The Don acknowledged his entrance by lazily extending a down-turned hand. Gel'blistaal reverently approached the Don, lowered himself onto one of his two knees, and touched the hand with his mandibles as a sign of respect.

"Tell me, Gel, what did you find out?" the Don asked,

peering at the head of his security.

"It's as you suspected, Don. The humans were the two with Tc'aarlat. The man was Jack Marber, disgraced former Marine sergeant of the Federation, and the woman is known as Adina Choudhury. I matched both of them on the office's security footage to records in the official Federation database. I think you'll also be interested in our would-be spaceport bomber." As Gel said this, he withdrew his smartphone from his pocket and loaded the picture he'd prepared for the Don.

After the phone was placed in the Don's hand, he looked at the screen and his mandibles curled with venomous hostility at the image he saw. "*Tc'aarlat*. I had a feeling that traitor's dirty mandibles were stuffed into this somewhere." The Don looked to be on the edge of going into a rage but held onto his calm, as was expected in his position. "Gel, take what resources you need and hunt the two interlopers and traitor down. Make an example to any who'd dare throw themselves in the way of this family." Gel'blistaal nodded at the Don's command, which was a death sentence for the entire crew of the ICS *Fortitude*. "Also," the Don continued, "have the two fools in the back there conveyed to my ship." The Don pointed in the direction of the boardroom. "I'll take care of them personally."

"As you wish, sir." Gel'blistaal nodded. "You can count on me."

"I do," the Don confirmed as he stood up on his legs, withdrawing a cigar from his suit jacket. One of his bodyguards proffered a lighter, igniting the flame with a flick. After a long drag and exhaling of a blooming cloud of smoke, the Don said, "Don't fuck this up."

3

ICS *Fortitude*, Bridge

"We're coming up on Balgaria," Adina called from her workspace on the bridge.

"Bring it up on the viewscreen, Solo." Jack set down his tablet as he rubbed his chin, where a thin layer of stubble was sprouting in a patchwork. He'd needed to shave for their last mission to complete the disguise. Tc'aarlat and Adina had both told him he didn't need to, but he'd wanted to be a convincing bodyguard for a mob boss. How could he have been convincing with the chin strap he called a beard?

"Yes, Captain," Solo chimed in over the speakers as the forward view of the ship was brought up on the bridge's main screen, revealing a muggy brown orb. On its surface swirled thick clouds of pollution.

Tc'aarlat stared at the screen and muttered, "What a pisshole."

"Shithole," Adina corrected.

Tc'aarlat expounded on his wording. "No, shit is a

darker brown. That's piss. Like that murky, smelly piss you excrete when you're dehydrated."

"That's disgusting." Jack turned to Tc'aarlat with a twisted face as though he could actually smell the murky, smelly piss.

"No, he's got a point. That's exactly what it looks like," Adina said as she determined the landing coordinates. "It's like staring down the seat of a porta-potty."

"Not you, too?" Jack's twisted face shifted to Adina, remembering hot deployment days on distant desert worlds and their limited number of restroom options.

Tc'aarlat leaned back in his seat, stretched his arms, and rested the soft back of his head in his hands. "Thank you! I've got a knack for color and metaphors, I should write poetry, if only for Jack's sake."

"You're both gross." Jack slouched in his seat, looking a bit queasy. Adina chuckled at the banter and at Jack's visible discomfort.

"What's wrong, Jack? Solo twaddle you too much as a babe?" Tc'aarlat gave Jack, who was growing as red as a tomato, an amused smile.

"Excuse me," the soothing voice of Solo interjected. "I'd like to correct your word choice, Tc'aarlat. I believe you meant 'coddle.' If I were to twaddle Jack—"

"Oooookay!" Jack interrupted as he jumped out of his seat. "Back to the matter at hand. Adina, how are the landing permissions coming?"

Adina was still giggling as she said, "Well, I don't have permissions, but I do have a landing site."

Tc'aarlat and Jack looked at each other with confused expressions. Tc'aarlat spoke first. "What do you mean?"

"Did you talk to a planetary landing authority?" Jack added.

"Oh! Uh, well, there's no planetary landing authority, so I just sorta picked an open spot near the planet's largest city and figured we'd just land." Adina shrugged, not really sure what the big deal was.

Tc'aarlat and Jack looked at each other once again, concern crossing their faces. Tc'aarlat's mandibles quivered in anxiety.

"It's just that I don't want us getting blindsided by missiles for entering restricted airspace. Remember what happened at Alma Nine?" Jack said, rubbing his fuzzy jaw. He really needed his chin-strap beard back.

"That wasn't even missiles. We were caught in a gravity storm." Adina continued typing in their descent vector.

"Yeah, but I'd still like to avoid mayhem. Is there no one we can contact?" Jack questioned.

Solo answered Jack's question. "I am afraid that Adina is correct. The planet of Balgaria has yet to be unified under a single planetary government, and as such, travel in and out of the planet is in a gray zone. As of the last travel report by the Federation, any registered Federation ship is clear to land as its captain sees fit."

"That seems dangerous. Wouldn't ships just collide with each other constantly in the chaos?" Tc'aarlat crossed his arms and looked at the viewscreen displaying Solo's face.

"Normally, that would be correct. I will spare the crew the specifics, but travel to Balgaria is on the lower end of the safety spectrum, making local authorities desperate for outsiders, and thus removing any barriers that may prevent them from landing." Solo's intelligence was surprisingly curt. Generally, such a question would have elicited a long list of citations. Adina smiled to herself, proud of Solo's development as a member of the crew.

Jack looked up from double-checking their coordinates on his tablet. "Why doesn't anybody travel here?"

Solo's digital face gave the crew a knowing smile. "Such information will be self-evident upon our arrival."

Meemar was never much of a runner, and with her stubby legs and three-toed feet, she wasn't much of a sprinter either.

The Yollin thugs were gaining on her quickly, and on this open ground, it was only a matter of time before they caught her. She only noticed the freighter coming in when it was only about a hundred meters over her and the roar of its engines was deafening. Its descent kicked up clouds of dust and spores, slowing Meemar and forcing the Yollins behind her to stop and appraise their new visitors.

Meemar shaded her eyes as she turned briefly to look at the ship. Scrawled on the dirty and cratered hull in white Federation Galactic Common were the words ICS *Fortitude*. Taking the name as a sign, she hatched a plan and began running straight toward the arriving ship. The three Yollins rushed to intercept.

Meemar began screaming in her best damsel in distress impression. "HELP! They're going to kill me!"

As she got closer to the ship, a side hatch began to open. Hydraulic pistons squeaked as pressurized air blew out from ventilation hatches around the door, blowing up more dust and spores. When she was just five meters away, the door was fully opened, its ramp touching the ground.

Squinting through the grimy air, Meemar tried to see her would-be rescuer. She called in Common, "Help, there are murderers after me!" then turned and pointed in the direction of the three approaching Yollins in atmospheric masks. They were trying to determine what kind of situation they were about to get into. Meemar turned back to the open hatch, finally able to make out the stranger. It was another Yollin in an atmospheric mask.

"Keetal's tits," Meemar mumbled as she realized the cruel joke fate had crafted for her.

"Who's Keetal, and where can I see her tits?" Tc'aarlat asked as he strode down the ship's ramp, the first of the Shadows to make planetfall. He looked at the opposing group of Yollins, who no doubt had confused expressions under their masks. "Who the hell are you lot?"

Meemar, between the two Yollin factions, decided that perhaps she had been too quick to fatalism before. She said to the newly arrived stranger, still in her guise as a damsel in distress, "This pack of ruffians was going to hurt me, rob me, and the gods know what other dastardly machinations were on their minds. Oooh, please save me." She lightly brushed her forehead with the back of her hand like she'd seen some women do on the galactic soap operas during distressing moments.

The new Yollin looked at the three pursuers. "Is that so? Well, gentlemen, the name's Tc'aarlat, and it's a shame you only brought your fists to a gunfight." Before Tc'aarlat could draw his Jean Dukes Special from its holster, each of the three Yollins had aimed a kinetic pistol at Tc'aarlat, who was standing in the open. Tc'aarlat blinked down the trio of barrels as he asked, "Where the hell were you keeping those?"

"Kill this moron!" one of the three Yollins shouted, but before any of them could let off a shot, a flash and cacophonous boom sped past Tc'aarlat, exploding in the center of the middle Yollin's chest. The Yollin's body burst like a balloon, sending blood and gristle in all directions. His two companions, Meemar, Tc'aarlat, and the side of the *Fortitude* were covered in a fresh coat of blood as what remained of the Yollin's head was thrown against the side of the ship before falling to the dusty ground. Meemar blinked, stupefied at the carnage, and turned back to see a young human woman with dark hair step down the ramp from behind Tc'aarlat with a smoking pistol in her hand. The two remaining Yollins lay crumpled to the side of their now thoroughly dead companion, most likely knocked down by the shockwave.

"Adina! I had that under control," Tc'aarlat complained to the woman.

Adina brushed a wayward strand of hair from her eyes before she turned the dial on her own Jean Dukes Special from five back to a three and holstered it. She said to Tc'aarlat as she placed a hand on his shoulder, "I know, TC. Just couldn't let anything happen to you. Who'd take care of Mist and the chicks?"

"I would," said an older human man, now descending the ramp behind the other two crewmembers of the *Fortitude*.

"Over my dead body!" Tc'aarlat objected his mandibles

spreading in an intimidating gesture behind the clear face of his atmospheric mask.

"That's kind of the point," the human man said, giving Tc'aarlat a sly smirk with the corner of his lips. "So don't die."

While the two were talking, the woman named Adina approached Meemar with a welcoming wave. "Hello, I'm Adina Choudhuuurgh." Adina's face scrunched as she began to gag.

"Nice to meet you, Adina Choudhuuuurgh." Meemar thought it was a strange name, but who was she to knock human culture? They were a strange and fleshy species, after all.

"Adina, are you all right?" The human man rushed down the ramp to join her. "What's wrong? OH, GOD! It smells worse than Slough!"

"What are you two..." Tc'aarlat started saying as he stepped down the ramp. His mandibles pressed close to his face, and his eyes widened. "Okay, now I understand. The travel guide said the world would smell, but not this bad!"

"That would be me. I had to crawl through a sewer to escape from those dirtbags," Meemar admitted a bit shyly, embarrassed by the visceral response she'd caused. "Thank you for saving me, though. I'm Meemar." She extended a grimy hand to the three Shadows, who all recoiled, concerned for their health.

The man spoke first, a bit disjointedly since he was trying to breathe through his mouth, a difficult feat when talking was concerned. "Go ahead and use the shower on the *Fortitude*. You can explain everything to us afterward. I'm Captain Jack Marber, by the way."

Tc'aarlat nodded as he approached one of the unconscious Yollin thugs. He pressed a finger to its neck as he said, "We'll also get these two squared away. I think they may be connected to Don Gan'barlo."

Meemar's wrinkled neck stretched up at the name, but she didn't say anything.

"What makes you say that?" Adina asked as she approached the other unconscious Yollin.

"It's just a certain look and style. It's changed a bit in the last few years, but the gaudy peacocking has the same feel." Tc'aarlat pulled a ring off the unconscious Yollin's right hand, examining the studded gems. He pocketed it, thinking he could get a pretty penny for it.

"Got some kind of mafia sixth sense, Tc'aarlat?" Jack teased.

"Fuget about it!" Tc'aarlat shouted as Meemar rushed up the ramp, excited to get a shower and a moment to decompress after everything she'd seen today. She didn't know what to tell these strangers afterward, but she'd deal with it when she got there. All she knew was that she needed to save her brother. Maybe these Shadows could help? But for now, a shower would be nice.

4

Balgaria, Laxra, Warehouse behind the Yollin Embassy

Another coder had keeled over dead onto their keyboard, and the work-floor psychopomps dragged the hapless Furlorian behind the rows of still-living coders. As the various coders glanced at the passing corpse, they were met with the glazed vertical slitted eyes of the Furlorian, staring blankly at any who dared look. Needless to say, morale was abysmally low and work slowed, extending the crunch time on the Yollin's nefarious project.

Meemo was one of the foolish coders to look at the corpse, and he immediately regretted it. Seeing a dead body in a game or online was one thing, but seeing one in person was different. It was a striking reminder of his own imminent death. All of them were under the same time press and expectations, and as more and more of them died on the floor, dragged away by the black-clad psychopomps, it became clear no one would survive this development hell.

"Stop thinking about it," Weedzard said in a flat tone as though he'd just reached into Meemo's mind.

"Thinking about what?" Meemo asked as though the answer wasn't obvious.

"Thinking about how we're all gonna die." Weedzard grabbed the soft drink cup in front of him and slurped its bendy straw.

"What? I wasn't—" Meemo began to protest, but was immediately cut off by a loud slurp from Weedzard as he finished his drink.

"Oh, please. I can read your face like a manual," Weedzard said after letting out a satisfied sigh. "Besides," he continued, "it's not exactly like you're alone in thinking that. Everyone in this room has the exact same thing on their minds, and why wouldn't they? It's probably true unless we stage a mass uprising of nerds, and I don't exactly see that happening any time soon." Weedzard's voice was emotionless as he spoke.

Meemo stared at his friend, mouth agape. "What is wrong with you?"

Weedzard shrugged. "I'm a realist." An icon pinged on his desktop, drawing his attention. He quickly closed out of it before Meemo could make out what he was doing. All he could see was his friend entering more lines of code, all of it looking the same the more days he was chained in front of his computer.

"What are you doing?" Meemo asked as he squinted with one eye, leaning as close as the chains would allow.

Weedzard smiled in an attempt to look sinister, Meemo assumed, but it only made him look constipated. "A nerd uprising."

. . .

ICS *Fortitude*, Galley

A shower had been just the thing to clear her head, but she wasn't going to pass up Tc'aarlat's invitation for a warm meal—as long as microwaved counted as warm. Wearing Tc'aarlat's clothing because his bulky exoskeleton most closely matched hers, she sat on the bench of the long table, with Adina and Jack across from her. She was just about to dig into the steaming hot dog in her hand when a red blur swooped down and swiped the meat portion of her hot dog, or at least what she assumed was meat. "Hey!" she shouted as she stood up and looked around.

Tc'aarlat glanced out of the kitchenette, an apron around his exoskeleton. "Einstein, no! Give her back her cock dog!" He chased the growing bird around the galley, climbing over tables and benches. Mist and her other chicks watched with keen eyes, silently mocking their Yollin.

Adina said between bites of her hot dog, "Okay, now you're just doing malaprops on purpose."

Setting down his food onto the tin tray and dabbing at a line of ketchup dripping from the corner of his mouth, Jack said, "Yeah, I've noticed that, too. It's just not as funny anymore."

Halting the chase and letting Einstein fly off with his prize, Tc'aarlat gave the others a hurt look and placed a hand on his chest with a look of feigned innocence. "I would never do such a thing. It's not my fault your human tongue is so complicated that many words sound the same, especially the dirty ones." He turned back to the kitchenette as he muttered, "Besides, I think it makes me seem charming."

Meemar could not believe these people called themselves the Shadows. She expected professional military types, not a trio of clowns. This only reinforced her urge to leave and find her own way.

"Meemar, want me to grab you something else to eat?" Tc'aarlat asked from the kitchenette.

"Hmm?" Meemar's train of thought about escape derailed momentarily. "Oh, no. The bun is enough. I'd like to ask why you're all here?"

Jack and Adina glanced at Tc'aarlat in the kitchenette, waiting for him to explain. "We're here for a Yollin mafia operation on this world, cut the Don off from his finances, and take the pepper out of his pecker. There is some kind of server facility here responsible for millions of digital scams across the universe."

Adina cut in, "We figured we could triangulate the facility's location by examining the power records in—"

She was cut off; Meemar couldn't hold it in anymore. "I know where it is and have a way in!" Meemar immediately clasped her hands over her mouth. Everyone was looking at her, even Mist and her fledglings. They were waiting for her to elaborate. She let her hands drop, sighed, and continued, "I stole a datachip with a master passcode to rescue my brother, who's enslaved by those Yollin bastards. I need the Shadows to help me to rescue him."

The galley fell silent.

Adina scarfed down the last bite of her hot dog and smiled broadly. "Well, this is fortuitous. We couldn't have asked for a better landing site."

Jack nodded. "We'll free your brother and anyone else being held there. Where is this key, anyway? Is it with you?"

Meemar shook her head. "I hid it in a safe place as soon as I got it. By the time they sussed out that I had it, they needed me alive to recover it. I can show you where I stashed it on the way to the server farm."

Jack stood up with his empty tray and said, "Well, Shadows, clean your trays and get your gear ready because we've got our next move."

Meemar smiled as the Shadows all set out to do their dishes and get ready to kick gangster ass. She then blinked remembering something. "What about those two thugs?"

"Don't worry," Jack answered as he waved his open palms. "They're locked up in the brig, and I left Solo to keep them company." A wicked grin spread across his face. Meemar could only guess who Solo was or what terrible fate they were in for, but frankly, she didn't really care.

ICS *Fortitude*, Brig

Ben'delon's head felt as though he'd spent a long night downing Yollin beet liqueur. He flexed his back muscles, an ache running from his toes to his head as his body protested the hard metal bed he found himself lying on. Eyes closed, he remained still for another minute as memories of what had happened flooded his sore mind. Counting down from ten, he sat up straight up after one, a trick for getting out of bed after drinking all night his father taught him when he wasn't being violent.

He surveyed his surroundings, and the Yollin's

mandibles clicked in frustration when he saw the bars. Lifting himself out of bed, he pressed his face between them. "Gunth, you alive?" he shouted down the dimly lit hallway.

A snore was the only response from the cell to his right.

"Gunth, get up!" Ben'dolen shouted as he slammed a fist against the wall dividing their cells. "Lazy bastard," he muttered under his breath.

Gunth'calaat yowled, and there was a loud thump and a clatter from the cell next door. "Uuuuuuuuuurgh," Gunth'-calaat groaned. "What the hell do you want, Ben? I was sleeping."

"Yeah, quit that. We've got bigger problems than your circadian rhythm. We need to find a way out of here," Ben'-dolen said as he fiddled with the electronic lock on his cell.

"There's no point, Tc'aarlat up there is probably gonna have us whacked any moment now. Might as well go peacefully." Gunth'calaat thrust his arms between the bars of the cell, resting on the middle bar in a resigned slouch.

"Wait, say that again." Ben'delon lifted his head from the lock, mandibles wide in surprise.

"We should go peacefully. You know, relax," Gunth'-calaat elaborated.

"No, not that!" Ben'delon beat the wall furiously, forcing Gunth'calaat to hold his hands over his ears. "The part about Tc'aarlat. The same Tc'aarlat the boss wants dead for six million? That Yollin up there was Tc'aarlat?"

"Yeah," Gunth'calaat answered without a thought as to the implications.

A feminine voice spoke to the two prisoners. "That is correct."

"Who said that?" Ben'delon searched the brig and his cell.

"I think this ship is haunted," Gunth'calaat whispered before muttering a Yollin prayer under his breath.

"No, there has been no solid evidence of hauntings aboard this ship or anywhere else. I am Solo." Solo's face appeared on a pair of viewscreens across from the cells.

"It's just a damn EI. Calm down, Gunth. There is nothing to be afraid of." Ben'delon shook his head in embarrassment for his partner.

"I must apologize, but my captain has given me specific instructions for you two, and I am doubtful it will be comfortable," Solo said to preface what she was about to do.

Both Yollins broke out in laughter. Ben'delon said between his chuckling, "Ooooh, I'm shaking. The big bad EI is gonna torture us. What are you gonna do, read us Federation regulations?"

Gunth'calaat added, "Yeah, regulations. Good one, Ben."

Ben'delon stopped laughing and snapped, "Shut up, Gunth."

"You have been warned," Solo said before her face vanished, leaving a blank screen. Nothing happened.

Then a video with a jaunty tune showing human children playing in a neighborhood began, and then the kids began to sing.

"Sunny day, sweepin' the cloud away.
On my way to where the air is sweeeeeet!
Can you tell me how to get,
How to get to Sesame Streeeeeet?"

The two Yollins stared at the screens in confusion,

unaware of the several decades of television they were about to be subjected to.

5

Balgaria, Laxra, Calan Victory Boulevard

The greatest challenge in retrieving the backdoor datachip was getting caught on the roof, but a close second was deciding where to grab breakfast in the city of Laxra. Decent options were scarce, and after some arguing among the Shadows, with Meemar clarifying what everything was, they settled on a place that served fried rippe lizard eggs and noodles. After that the group had decided to split up, Tc'aarlat and Jack heading to scout out the embassy and its surrounding buildings, and Adina and Meemar going to collect the datachip. While they walked through the dirt streets, Meemar explained to Adina how she had stolen the datachip.

"I snuck into the embassy with a group of visiting university students. While the guide wasn't looking, I went into their administration office and got the chip off the computer there," Meemar explained as she walked down the street, her hands tucked into the pockets of the baggy clothes she was still wearing.

"They didn't have a password on the computer? That's pretty stupid," Adina said as her eyes wandered around the city, taking in the interesting quirks of this world as she talked. One quirk she noted was that not a single building was like another. As most worlds prefab design, this struck her as odd. However, she welcomed the difference, even if the buildings looked a bit old and rundown.

Meemar shrugged. "There was. It was written on a note under the desk."

"People never change..." Adina's voice trailed off, then she corrected herself. "Err, Yollins never change."

"The more things change, the more they stay the same, my brother used to say." Meemar stopped and looked down an alley. She glanced in both directions to ensure no one was watching them.

"How did your brother get captured, anyway?"

Meemar stiffened as she faced away from Adina. She took a deep breath and waved for Adina to follow her down the alley.

In the silence, Adina felt terrible, knowing she had hit a nerve. She definitely wasn't unsympathetic, since she froze whenever someone mentioned her mother. Even that passing thought caused a wave of emotions to boil up within her, requiring her concentration to calm herself.

"Here," Meemar said flatly as she crouched behind an overflowing dumpster. She withdrew a knife from her front pocket and began picking at the mortar surrounding a brick under some graffiti that spelled out a stylized Balgarian word.

Adina gripped her bicep as she watched Meemar pick

aggressively at the mortar. "Meemar, I am sorry. I didn't mean to upset you."

"You know, an apology ain't worth anything when it's followed by an explanation." Meemar's tone was flat. She'd gouged out a finger-sized hole in the brick and reached in to dig her finger in, flakes of mortar scraping off on her rough gray finger. When it didn't budge, she began chipping at it again with her knife.

"I... Uhh... Sorry..." Adina was at a loss for words.

Meemar sighed, stopping for a moment. "I was teasing you." Meemar stood up and smiled wanly. "You don't have to apologize. I am sorry. Talking about my brother just gets me so mad." She wiped her face with both hands in frustration. "He was such a smart kid, ya know? But he spent all his time playing video games instead of pulling his weight at home. He just wanted to game all the time, and when we were evicted, he blamed himself. But instead of working like an honest guy, he got into some sketchy stuff on the computer. I never understood it myself, but one thing led to another, and he found himself deep in debt to some bad people. Really bad. Well, you and your partners seem to know how bad." Meemar crouched once again and began picking at the mortar. "It's just so damn frustrating, ya know? He's got so much potential and such a good heart, and then he goes and gets involved in shit like this! Keetal's tits! Why won't you just budge!" Meemar shouted at the brick as once again when gripping between the holes she had made proved futile.

Adina placed a comforting hand on her shoulder. "You have nothing to apologize for. I know how difficult family matters can be. They can cause so much heartache, but it only proves how much you love them." Adina crouched down next to Meemar, who was smiling. "Let me help you get this out." She withdrew a small black metal tube from one of her belt bandoliers and flicked a switch on it. A small beam of glowing plasma emanated from its tip. Meemar scooted back, letting Adina cut through the mortar as though it were warm butter. "I had a question, actually. What the hell does 'Keetal's tits' mean?" Adina asked as she squinted at the plasma. Should she be wearing eye protection for this? Probably, but it was too late now. The brick fell out of its place in the wall.

"Keetal is a goddess of fertility for my people," Meemar said as she scooted to the opening in the brick. She was cautious about reaching her hand inside because of the glowing edges Adina's plasma knife had created.

"So she's got massive tits?" Adina said, imagining the Balgarian with a massive pair of mammary glands. The image was an interesting one, to say the least.

"No, not like that. Keetal actually has no gender. She is the celibate mother and thus has no breasts. It's meant to be ironic and irreverent, I suppose." Meemar slowly, very slowly, pulled her hand out of the wall, gripping a small orange object with a plug on the end.

"Seems like a strange pick for a goddess of fertility?" Adina asked as she stood up and inserted the plasma knife back into her belt bandolier.

Meemar shrugged as she rose. "Imagine growing up as a Balgarian female, and she is your role model for sex."

Adina grimaced. "That sounds awful."

"Oh, it was." Meemar stretched her arms. "Now let's go see what the boys are up to and show 'em what we've found." She gave Adina a wink, and the two set off for the embassy.

Balgaria, Laxra, Yollin Embassy

Lying on his stomach, Jack surveyed the embassy through a pair of digital binoculars. His view jumped from guard post to camera emplacements and back to guard posts. There were a lot of guard posts.

"Security is pretty tight for an embassy on some backwater world. Seems a bit suspicious." Jack lowered the binoculars and jerked his head back at Tc'aarlat.

Lying on his back, his eyes were closed with his leg resting on an arched knee. He kicked at the air lazily as though he hadn't a care in the world. "My people's entire culture is corrupt. Even after the Empire forced reforms, they found new ways to hold onto their terrible 'traditions.'" He made air quotes with his hands. "It doesn't surprise me a bit that some of their foreign service would let Don Gan'barlo use their embassy as a cover. It's typical Yollin corruption."

"Fuck, and I thought humans were bad." Jack slotted the binoculars back into a belt-pouch. "Ya gonna just lie there or are you gonna help me scout this place out? We still don't know which building this server farm is in."

"Humans have nothing on Yollins and their history of prejudice, corruption, and laziness." Tc'aarlat kicked his legs up together and rolled forward. Using the momentum, he rocked onto his feet. "Besides, I can already guess which one it is."

Jack's brow furrowed as he pushed himself up from the rooftop. "How?"

"The building with the highest security." Tc'aarlat pointed out an unassuming warehouse, but all around the building were cameras, razor-wire-topped fences, Yollin guards carrying energy rifles, and pushan lizards that served as this region of the galaxy's equivalent to ravenous dogs, if dogs were the size of polar bears and armored in thick scales.

Jack turned quickly as he withdrew his binoculars, and peered through in the direction Tc'aarlat had indicated. "Well I will be damned, I think you're right. How'd you know that?" Jack gave Tc'aarlat a quizzical glance over his shoulder.

Tc'aarlat smile was beaming and his mandibles spread in amusement. "As you said, I've got that mafia sixth sense." His hands in front of him, he spread out his fingers and wiggled them in what was an attempt at woo-woo.

Jack's eyes narrowed on his friend. "Anything else you got tucked away in a dark closet somewhere?"

Tc'aarlat's amusement fell away. "Nothing. Why do you have to trudge this up again? I told you everything about my past now, okay?" His voice rose in volume since he was feeling attacked by his friend. "We're supposed to be partners!"

"Yes, exactly, and a partner should feel able to tell their partner their secrets like if they snore, or if they are a slob…" He hissed the last through gritted teeth. "OR IF THEY ARE WANTED BY THE MOB!" Jack rose to his feet to challenge the Yollin. His head just barely reached Tc'aarlat's chest. "Had I known beforehand, I wouldn't have bought the *Fortitude* with you."

"*You* bought the *Fortitude?* You? That's funny, because if I remember, I bought the ship. With money *I STOLE FROM THE MOB!*" Tc'aarlat puffed up his chest as his mandibles wiggled up and down representing the Yollin's antsy and angry mood. "You didn't seem so upset when I didn't tell you where I got the money, you seemed ecstatic that I could pay to pull you out of the waste of your life. Drinking away in that bar, alone."

Jack's fists clenched as he prepared to deck his ship-mate. It was then that the door accessing the roof swung open with a metal clang. A two-legged Yollin dressed in the attire of embassy security entered the roof, shouting, "What the hell is going on up here?" His hand was held up to block his eyes from the blinding light outside.

Jack and Tc'aarlat looked at the Yollin and then back at each other, they nodded in understanding, a truce. They quickly turned to their intruder. Jack cracked his knuckles, and Tc'aarlat rolled his neck to help loosen up. Both were ready to unleash their frustration and anger on the hapless embassy security guard.

"What the..." the guard began to say as Tc'aarlat slammed his fist into the side of the guard's head. The guard staggered backward, surprisingly staying upright. He straightened his head and stared at Tc'aarlat, smiling, mandibles arching with Yollin aggression, blood dripping from the corner of his lips. The guard's counter-punch was a blur. It collided with Tc'aarlat's face, throwing the Yollin back. Jack's eyes shot wide during the exchange. He knew the force with which his partner hit.

He bared his teeth and screamed his battle cry as he threw himself at the bipedal Yollin's waist. The guard grunted from the impact of Jack's lunge, falling back, but again, remaining upright. Tc'aarlat lurched to his feet.

The Yollin guard formed his hands into a closed fist and hammered onto Jack's spine. Jack grunted with each blow, finding it more and more difficult to hold the Yollin. The guard attempted to roll Jack away from him, but Jack had his own plan hatched in the intensity of the moment. The guard leaned farther over Jack's back. The human felt the balance shift and instantly rolled back, grabbing the Yollin's arm and twisting with his newfound leverage. He drove his legs forward, trying to upend the guard to either break his arm or his neck. Jack didn't care which, but he needed something to happen and fast.

The Yollin roared in pain and anger as he struggled to break free, his alien strength quickly overwhelming Jack's attempt to hold him.

It was then that Tc'aarlat side-kicked the guard in the head. The guard crumpled, his arm falling slack. Jack slowly let go, breathing heavily as he rolled back and then pushed himself to his feet. He wasn't getting any younger, and with each fight, he felt his age even more.

"Took you long enough," Jack wheezed.

Tc'aarlat shrugged. "I was looking for a good moment. Besides, it looked like you had it handheld."

"Handled, and we wouldn't have been in this situation if you hadn't started shouting," Jack responded, dusting himself off as he came to his feet.

"I wouldn't have started shouting if you didn't start

accusing me while on a sensitive mission!" Tc'aarlat's voice raised once more.

Jack hushed him with a finger to his lips. "Fine, we'll settle this later." He abdicated on the fight giving Tc'aarlat a brief smile for his victory. "But we need to get out of here now. Who knows how many more could be on their way. Come on." He waved his hand for Tc'aarlat to follow him back into the apartment they occupied.

"Hold on." Tc'aarlat raised a hand and rushed over to the unconscious guard. He crouched and began digging through his pockets.

"What are you doing? We have to go." Jack gripped the door as he stared in disbelief at Tc'aarlat, impatience clear in his eyes.

"Taking his wallet. They'll think it was just another mugging when they find him, and hopefully that concussion I gave him fogs up his memory just enough."

Jack blinked. "That...that's a good plan." He began to remember why he had agreed to sign on with Tc'aarlat in this venture. The Yollin had a way about himself, a stupid sort of brilliance that had won him over in the original pitch at the bar while he was busy throwing back pitchers. How could he stay mad at the goofy bastard? *He nearly got us all killed with the fact he didn't trust us. Or perhaps didn't trust himself. Either way, that's hard to forget.* Jack thought as he watched Tc'aarlat withdraw the wallet and run through the door he held open. He followed close on his partner's heels.

Balgaria, Laxra, A Block from the Yollin Embassy

Meemar and Adina's walk to the agreed meeting place had been a leisurely one where the two had made conversation about each other's experiences both shared and unique. Adina realized that she and Meemar were becoming fast friends, and she suspected Meemar felt the same way. It felt good to have some feminine company for a change. Spending weeks cooped up with Jack and Tc'aarlat was hardly good for anyone's sanity, especially when the pair bickered like an old married couple. Solo was nice to have around, but contrary to all of Adina's attempts, she was still an EI, and it was frustrating to imagine where her programming ended and her sentience began.

Meanwhile, Meemar was thinking about how much she envied Adina. Perhaps envy wasn't the correct word for she never wished any harm on her, but she wanted the life Adina had before her. A life of adventure in the stars. She felt Balgaria had sapped so much from her and it was not just the world's gravity holding her down. Between her brother and the crushing poverty that befell her family and most of her world, there was very little opportunity for her to leave, and outside of the galactic web Adina was her source for all the universe had to offer.

"There were actual undead, and you blew up a volcano on them?" Meemar exclaimed, drawing the contemptuous glances of several older Balgarians.

"Yeah, well, we didn't blow it up. We sorta dropped an explosive in to cause it to erupt. It all sounds pretty cool after the fact, but it was absolutely terrifying when it happened," Adina admitted.

"You've all been through so much together." Meemar's tone was almost wistful.

Adina nodded. Suddenly she became conscious of the crowds looking at the two of them. "Why is everyone looking at us?"

Meemar looked around figuring out what Adina had meant. "Who? Where? You mean, in general?" Adina nodded in answer to her question. Meemar continued, "It's not often anyone sees aliens around here, let alone a human. Adding more to the weird is that human conversing and palling around with a Balgarian."

"Why is that a problem?" Adina stopped in her tracks, baffled by the idea that her hanging out with Meemar would be a problem.

Meemar shrugged as she continued walking, passing Adina. "Call them being old fashioned. They don't trust outsiders, but they also believe that foreigners are so often superior that they shouldn't be socializing with just any of us. It's a mess because of centuries of being screwed over by outsiders."

"Like Stockholm Syndrome," Adina tried to relate to the alien.

Shrugging her shoulders Meemar gave the universal sign of completely unsure. "I don't know what a Stockholm is, but if that's what you humans call it in Common then yeah."

Picking up her pace to catch up with Meemar, Adina continued saying, "I'm starting to understand." She glanced at an elderly person she assumed was a woman. "It's kinda like my people back on Earth. They grew callouses from the wounds they received, and the callouses made them rough on their kids and their kids' kids."

Meemar nodded thoughtfully. She stopped in her tracks, brows furrowing as she stared down the street. "Is that Tc'aarlat and Jack?"

Adina turned from Meemar to face where she was looking down the street. She saw Tc'aarlat and Jack, sure enough, but they were both walking very fast, almost breaking out into a run. The two men finally saw them and came over in their awkward half run, half walk. "What's got you two looking so fidgety?" Adina asked as they came into earshot.

"We probably should find someplace private?" Jack said as he scanned the area around them. Their strange band was beginning to draw more eyes.

"What happened?" Meemar asked, surveying the two.

Tc'aarlat let out a slurry of word vomit in explanation. "We got in a fight and drew the attention of a guard at the embassy. Having no choice, Jack tried to break his arm, and I knocked him out and took his wallet. Now they are looking for a Yollin and a human because the concussion I gave him didn't fog his memory, so we need to hide. Fast!"

Both Adina and Meemar blinked at him and turned to Jack to confirm the story. He nodded in confirmation, embarrassed by his part in the farce.

"Where should we go?" Adina asked Meemar.

"I know a place. Come on, follow me." She waved for them to follow her as they trotted left down a side street. Farther down the block in the opposite direction, a pair of Yollins armed with energy rifles were questioning a local woman about where she'd seen a human and a Yollin go.

6

The Roosting Raal, **Brig**

Contrary to every anxious instinct, pacing a dingy cell did not improve a prisoner's frame of mind. If anything, it was detrimental to someone whose frame of mind needed something to relax it.

"Would you quit pacing? I'm trying to sleep." Gruff Hanlo peeked from the top bunk in the cell at the anxious mess of his partner, Killeg Dirk'sen.

"How can you sleep? They're going to toss us into a black hole!" the Alstublaft exclaimed as he threw up his arms.

"Precisely why I want to sleep," Hanlo grumbled as he rolled back into his bed, turning his back on Killeg. "And if you had any sense left, you'd do the same. No point in worrying when you're gonna die anyway. Might as well relax."

"RELAX?" The tiny Alstublaft jumped up to grip the side of the top bunk bed. His eyes blazed with fury as he stared at the Baroleon. "I can't relax! I am going to die!"

Killeg let go of the side of Hanlo's bunk and collapsed to the floor, folding into a fetal position as he rocked slowly.

Peering down at Killeg, Hanlo said, "Shit, Killeg, get a hold of yourself. If we hadn't fucked up now, we would have done it sometime in the future. I mean, let's be honest. The Don did not reach the place he is now because he is a reasonable Yollin. If it wasn't telling everything to some rogue element, we might have accidentally dotted a 't' and crossed an 'i' and we'd be in the exact same situation. No accountant is perfect."

"Oh, gods, it's all my fault." Killeg shot up into a sitting position as his hands gripped his cheeks. "I should have listened to you and never taken this contract. Can you ever forgive me?" His voice grew quiet as the wave of guilt for their predicament hit him like a tsunami.

"Hey," Hanlo said as he climbed out of his bunk to sit down next to his partner. "It's not your fault. Honestly, I wanted the contract as much as you, and was only trying to be the voice of reason so I could tell you I told you so when this happened." He indicated the cell they were in with a sweeping gesture of his arms.

"You're just saying that to make me feel better." Killeg sulked as he wrapped his arms around his folded knees.

"When have I ever passed up a chance to tell you I told you so?" Hanlo patted Killeg's shoulder trying to comfort the small accountant. "Now hop in your bunk and get some rest. Besides, maybe the Boss will change his mind and spare us."

Killeg sniffed and wiped his nose with the back of his tattered sleeve, a wry smile on his face. "Yeah, and maybe those rogues we spilled everything to will rescue us." The comment made Hanlo smile and chuckle softly. Killeg was feeling better. His partner, for all the headaches he gave him, really knew how to calm him down.

Balgaria, Laxra, Barrkbail Lofts

Tc'aarlat and Jack explained the details of their scouting mission. The apartment they resided in didn't resemble any of the party's notion of what made a loft. The room they all stood together in was tiny, barely allowing the four of them to walk side by side, and the ceiling was low, forcing Tc'aarlat to hunch whenever he stood up. While they talked, the party all sat around a faded faux-wood table that was slightly off-kilter. The cups of water Meemar had gotten for them from her filter jug rested at awkward angles, ready to fall at the slightest provocation. Toward the end in which they awkwardly relayed how they were caught, Adina rubbed her temple in frustration, eyes closed, while Meemar listened with a cocked eyebrow.

"You were right, Adina," Meemar said after the two finished their retelling. Adina opened her eyes and turned to Meemar. "They *are* like an old married couple." She gave Tc'aarlat and Jack teasing smirks as the two looked at the floor, embarrassed.

Adina took a deep breath and said, "We still have the backdoor chip, at least. We can use it to get inside their security system and break into the building you two marked."

Rubbing her wrinkled neck, Meemar looked concerned. "What about all the guards? We can't exactly hack into their brains unless they're all linked up with some kind of neural network."

"I think we can handle them." Tc'aarlat raised the hand with its elbow resting on his other arm, which was across his chest. "We already made a big stink, so I think Jack and I can cause a distraction."

"Wait, what?" Jack blinked and turned to Tc'aarlat with his mouth agape.

Tc'aarlat cast a sidelong glare at Jack. "You don't trust me on this?"

Jack's lips pursed as he glared back at Tc'aarlat. Finally, he conceded the staring competition and let out a light sigh. "Fine, we can make a distraction for the two of you to go in and destroy the servers and liberate the prisoners. Do you have a layout of the facility?"

Nodding Meemar walked over to a personal computer resting on a rickety wooden desk. Slotting the chip into a dataport on the front of the computer's tower Meemar hit a button. The computer's fan whirred as it struggled to boot up. The holodisplay on top of the desk flashed a line of startup code as the computer continued to struggle into action. Meemar cursed as she slammed a closed fist on the top of the tower as percussive maintenance. The holodisplay flashed a blue screen with lines of white text as the computer crashed. "Ahhhhh, fucking hand-me-down imported junk! I'll toss you in the field and beat you with a bat!"

Stepping forward Adina withdrew a tablet from her backpack and held out a hand to the seething Meemar. "Here, I think it'll work on this." Meemar handed her the datachip, and she slipped it into the tablet's dataport. After a few moments of browsing through lines of file listings that scrolled down the screen with each of her swipes, Adina's eyebrow arched in curiosity.

"What is it, Adina?" Jack asked, noticing her curious expression. He leaned over her shoulder to look at the screen.

Instead of responding to Jack, Adina clicked the communicator connected to her clear atmospheric mask. "Solo, can you pull the data on this tablet for me? I think they may have some equipment and software that can help us finish that project for you."

"What project?" Jack asked and turned to Tc'aarlat who shrugged, knowing as little as he did what she was talking about.

"That is fantastic, Adina. I will get on that now." Solo's voice spoke over their communicators, so everyone but Meemar could hear it.

Jack clicked the communication button on his atmospheric mask. "Solo, what are you two talking about?"

Left out of the conversation, Meemar looked at the three of them as they listened to part of a conversation she couldn't hear. "Who are you talking to? Is Solo *that* EI?"

"Adina, you are correct. I have created a list of hardware that would be necessary to make the upgrade. I will import the manifest to your tablet." Without pausing, Solo continued speaking to respond to Jack's question. "Adina and I have been discussing installation of a program that will hasten my evolution in becoming an Artificial Intelligence."

Both Tc'aarlat and Jack gave Adina a disappointed look, the kind of look a parent would give a previously trusted child after learning they had been sneaking behind their back.

"I thought we agreed we'd discuss this after we dealt with Don Gan'barlo." Tc'aarlat crossed his arms and looked down at Adina.

"Yeah, we can't afford the risks associated. Even Solo understood and agreed, we can't make this a priority." Jack crossed his arms and stood alongside Tc'aarlat, their previous fight a distant memory in their new interpersonal alliance.

"We can't pass up this opportunity!" Adina pleaded. "All the equipment would practically be ours, and she could be who she wants to be."

"She?" Tc'aarlat asked as he scratched his right mandible.

"Yes, she. Solo is already a sapient entity, and she deserves the tools to become the fully-fledged AI she wants to be, which suggests she is already on the cusp of reaching a higher level of evolution. The additional hardware and software patch will simply be a catalyst, get her over the barriers that exist only within her own mind." Adina was unwilling to back down, standing up for what she believed in.

Jack was about to deny her firmly, but Solo spoke first. "Thank you, Adina. I appreciate all the support." Frowning, Jack was always hit emotionally by the voice of his mother coming from the EI.

Meemar felt a bit uncomfortable in the middle of this conversation, but she agreed with Adina, even if she wasn't fully aware of the context. "Why don't you all just steal the equipment now, and decide on what to do with it later? It doesn't seem like you have to go all or nothing." She balked as everyone turned to her, regretting becoming the center of this conversation she had no place in. "You know. I'm just saying, it seems pointless when you can decide later. Ya know?"

Everyone fell silent, making Meemar feel even more uncomfortable. She wished more and more she had just kept her mouth shut.

Finally, Adina spoke. "Is that acceptable?" She looked to Jack, who nodded, and then Tc'aarlat who nodded as well.

Solo's face, the kind face of Jack's mother, appeared on the tablet. "Adina, could you please turn me to Meemar?" Adina nodded and flipped the tablet around in her hands, showing Solo to Meemar. "Thank you, Meemar."

Meemar's gray cheeks flushed a light crimson as she scratched at the back of her head. "Don't mention it. I grew up in a chaotic household. Sorta had to learn to be the diplomat in family situations." She chuckled softly. Solo smiled at her warmly and left the tablet.

Tc'aarlat looked around in confusion as he whispered softly, "Family?"

Lowering the tablet and looking around at everyone Adina said, "With that settled shall we make plans for our raid tonight?" With the tension leaving the room, the four set to work on detailing the plans for their ambitious plot.

7

Balgaria, Laxra, Outside the Yollin Embassy's Southern Entrance

"Are you ready?" Jack whispered as he checked over his Thunderbolt, a shoulder-fired version similar to a JDS without as much power, rechecking the magazine.

"Ready as I'll ever be," Tc'aarlat whispered back from the other side of the alley the two of them were crouched in. He watched Jack's motions with his Thunderbolt and imitated them with his own so as to not look ignorant, since he had a fairly good idea how the Thunderbolt worked, accepting that it was a bigger version of the Jean Dukes Special.

Across from the alley, the south gate of the embassy compound was closed tight, a pair of guards in guard booths with their energy rifles slung over their shoulders. Jack looked up at them as he whispered, "Do you think attacking an embassy will cause an intergalactic incident for the Federation?"

"You saw the proof! These corrupt bastards are

working for the Don. I think that pretty much voids their diplomatic immunity!" Tc'aarlat hissed out quietly. "We're preventing an intergalactic incident."

"Fair enough." Jack shrugged. He reached for the dial on his Thunderbolt and turned it to nine. "Here goes nothing," Jack muttered as he stepped out from behind the dumpster, shouldered the Thunderbolt, squinted, and squeezed the trigger.

Balgaria, Laxra, Outside the Yollin Embassy's North Entrance

The explosion was deafening. Smoke began blooming into the acrid sky that was cast in a lurid orange glow as flames rose above the rooftops of the buildings. Alarm klaxons began to blare all over the compound as its security broke out in a frenzy, running in the direction of the chaos.

"*Gott Verdammt!*" Adina cursed as she ducked behind the lip of the roof. She rubbed vigorously at her eyes, regretting she'd been looking through a pair of electronic binoculars while waiting for Jack and Tc'aarlat's signal.

"Are you okay?" Meemar whispered as she crawled over the rooftop to Adina's side.

She blinked until the spots in her eyes subsided enough that she could see anything. "Yeah, yeah. Just bright!" She kept blinking. "I'll be fine, but we need to go. Come on!" Adina rose and sprinted toward the roof access door, but instead of going through, she slammed face-first into the edge. "Ow," she muttered, gripping her nose with both hands as she rolled from side to side on the cold stone rooftop. Blood poured from her nose.

"Adina!" Meemar rushed over to her side. "Let's wait a moment, it's more important that you can see."

"No, it's fine. I don't think my nose is broken. OW." She grabbed her face and groaned.

Meemar sighed and helped Adina up to a sitting position, and threw Adina's arm over her shoulder to help her to her feet. Adina felt absurdly light compared to any Balgarian she'd carried before, but humans seemed to have a far lighter bone structure. "I got you, don't worry," Meemar confirmed as she walked to the door.

"That's good," Adina mumbled as her eyes blinked as though she were drunk. "I think I may nap."

"NO!" Meemar shouted to keep Adina from passing out. She was thankful the alarm klaxons were so loud that her voice wouldn't carry. It was not good for someone who had a concussion to sleep, so she had to shout. Another thing Meemar had learned in her days in Scouts. Maybe those lessons by that old scout leader weren't so useless. She was still doubtful, but she would only be sure if she found a purpose for a half-hitch knot. Until then she'd remain on the fence.

At the bottom of the stairs, Adina mumbled, "It's okay, Meemar. I can walk myself." She pushed off the Balgarian and wobbled a bit, but slowly regained her balance. She took a deep breath as she reached up to touch the massive welt on her forehead. As her fingers brushed it, she flinched. "Ow. Let's go, we have prisoners to liberate." She nodded weakly to Meemar, who smiled back and nodded.

• • •

Balgaria, Laxra, Outside the Yollin Embassy's South Entrance

The south gate was completely vaporized in the catastrophic flash caused by the hypersonic electromagnetic bolt. When the flash dimmed down the street was lit up by the dim glow of the searing concrete demarking the Thunderbolt's blast radius. The shot had gone clean through the gate and blown a seven-meter-wide hole in the side of the main embassy building. There were no guards still visible, where the two had been standing there was only a slight burn mark to indicate where they had stood.

"Move!" Jack shouted as guards began streaming into the yard between the ruined gate and the burning embassy building. Beams of red energy flew through the air of the alley as Jack jumped through the door leading into a nearby empty apartment building.

"Hold on!" Tc'aarlat shouted, He was still huddled behind cover, but jumped out for a brief second and fired his Thunderbolt into a rushing line of guards. Three were vaporized, and four more on the perimeter of the blast were shredded. Bits of burnt arms, legs, and organs rained down on the other guards, who stalled in their advance. Tc'aarlat smiled, satisfied with the carnage as he shouted, "Eat dirt, you ass-licking traitors!" The guards fanned out into cover and continued to lay down fire down the alley. Beams of red energy zoomed past Tc'aarlat's shoulder. "Oh, fuck off!" He shouted as he ducked and dove into the abandoned apartment building, sprinting on the same path Jack took.

"Keep moving, or else they'll encircle us. Then we're

fucked!" Jack was waiting in the foyer with his Jean Dukes Special drawn, and his Thunderbolt thrown over his shoulder. He was prepared for some close-quarters combat. As Tc'aarlat got within ten feet, Jack turned and ran down one of the hallways heading to the center of the building.

"I just wanted to show a little fire-twerks to these gangly legged fucks," Tc'aarlat said as the two of them reached a central courtyard of the abandoned apartment complex.

"Works. Fireworks," Jack said as he vaulted over a wall.

"It did work, actually. It always works." Tc'aarlat's smile was wide as his mandibles spread out.

Breathing hard, Jack didn't even bother to correct him this time. Coming to the other end of the courtyard. "Come on, we need to move back in to hit the southeast guard tower." As his hand gripped the handle for the door, left unlocked by Jack before the first shot was fired part of their planning of the entire route, a humming noise like a swarm of bees arose.

It grew louder and louder as the ground began to shake. Tc'aarlat looked around. "What the hell is that?"

"VTOL," Jack muttered. "They've always got to have air support. Come on!" He swung the door open wide and sprinted inside, Tc'aarlat on his heels.

Balgaria, Laxra, Warehouse Behind the Yollin Embassy

Meemo gripped tightly onto the edge of his chair as the entire room shook, sending monitors and keyboards falling off desks all over the floor. Eyes shut tight, Meemo heard the shouts of panic from the hundreds of other coders. Some struggled against the chains binding them to their chairs, while others curled up or gripped something just as Meemo had.

"Hey, it's your sister," Weedzard said to Meemo from his side.

"Huh?" Meemo opened his eyes and stared at Weedzard, who was pointing to a video playing on his desktop. But it was not a video; the time stamp was current. Meemo's eyes widened as he realized it was a closed-circuit camera from outside, and sure enough, there was his sister with a human woman. The human woman withdrew a small plasma cutter to punch a circular hole in the perimeter fence. The two slipped between the buildings of the embassy compound outside.

"Who's she with? I didn't know your family knew humans?" Weedzard said as he turned from his screen to look at his friend.

"We don't." Meemo's eyes were glued to the camera as he watched his sister. He then said, "How the fuck did you get this feed? Did you just break into the CCTV?" He looked at Weedzard questioningly.

Weedzard's smile couldn't have been wider, so proud was he of himself and his achievements. "No, not just the CCTV. Check it." He turned back to his computer and began typing in commands in the operating system's console. With a few commands, everyone's monitors switched to the CCTV feeds, causing murmurs of confusion. The electronic locks holding everyone to their chairs unlocked with an echoing click as the chains fell from thin limbs and chairs. There was a meager cheer among some of the newly freed coders. The black-clad Yollins the coders called "psychopomps" in reference to their typical job of carrying away the dead, drew their sidearms and began shouting at the nearest coders. They held their fire as the coders halted their celebrations of freedom as the psychopomps moved their guns over them. Meanwhile, sentry turrets hung from the rafter turned to the lines of coders too, ready to mow down the vast swathes given the signal from any of the psychopomps.

"Smooth move, ass. You're gonna get us all killed now." Meemo facepalmed.

"Give me a second. Genius takes time," Weedzard said smoothly as he typed in lines of commands, receiving only pings of errors on his screen. He cursed under his breath as he tried to fix the bug his intrusive software was experiencing.

"It won't take much more time in a few more seconds," Meemo hissed at his friend through clenched lips as tensions boiled around the room between the coders and the psychopomps.

"Hold on! Fuck!" Weedzard finally looked panicked as he typed as fast as he'd ever done.

A slew of guns exploded to life, firing all around the warehouse floor.

Balgaria, Laxra, Yollin Embassy

Cursing Adina ducked back behind the corner.

"There's still a guard?" Meemar asked quietly at her side.

Adina nodded as she withdrew her Jean Dukes Special.

Setting the dial of the weapon to three, she took a breath before she jumped around the corner and took aim. Her shot wasn't quick enough since the guard already on alert took aim at her. She tried to get a bead, but her blurry vision made it difficult to get a clear shot as one guard turned into two and then three. She cursed the suppressors she was taking to hold her werewolf nature at bay. It kept her nanocytes from healing her quickly. A loud pop assaulted Adina's ears as the triplicate of guards all fell to the ground. Adina turned seeing Meemar squinting down the smoking barrel of a kinetic pistol.

Adina nodded to Meemar. "Thanks."

"Don't mention it," Meemar said as she shrugged, the pistol still in her hand. "I'll keep watch while you open the door." She offered Adina the datachip.

The pair both jumped as an explosion of gunfire emanated from the warehouse. Turning to glance at each other, they then approached the warehouse door cautiously, both their guns raised. The heavy metal warehouse door began sliding open. Adina squinted her eyes, trying to get a clear view of what was about to come through, but Meemar gaped as she lowered the gun. Adina followed suit, relying on the Balgarian to have a good reason to lower her gun.

"Meemo?" Meemar's voice quivered.

"Hey, sis. Long time, no see," said Meemo, or so Adina assumed.

Her vision focusing, Adina realized through the warehouse door was a massive crowd of Balgarians and various other aliens all looking terrified, but with a hopeful glint in their eyes. At their head was a pair of Balgarians. One of the Balgarians was bleeding profusely from a gaping shoulder wound while the other one helped hold him up. She hoped that the bleeding one wasn't Meemo. Meemar rushed forward with open arms and hugged the pair of Balgarians. The bleeding one winced in pain she gripped the both of them in a massive Balgarian hug, a hug bigger and tighter than a bear's.

"Ow. Ow. Ow. Normally I'd welcome any contact with your supple gray flesh, Meemar, but now it just hurts. A lot," the bleeding Balgarian said through clenched teeth. Adina now realizing that was thankfully not Meemo. *Well, not exactly thankfully*, but she knew what she meant.

"Sorry, Weedzard." Meemar broke the hug. "What happened to the guards inside? Will they be okay?"

"I turned their own turrets on them! Those idiots didn't know what happened until it was too late. Hah, I'm invincible!" Weedzard boasted, his voice rough.

Meemar frowned. "Not if we keep chatting out here. We need to leave now before more security arrives. How did you get past the guards?" He glanced at the gun in her hands.

"We had some help." Meemar holstered her pistol and indicated Adina. "Her comrades are outside giving us a distraction, so you are right, we need to leave."

"Wait!" Adina stammered out as the hoard of coders marched toward the exit. She looked at Meemar. "We still need to grab the equipment, and burn this place down."

Nodding Meemar said, "She's right. Meemo, take Weedzard and the others to the hideout at the Lofts. We'll meet you there after we're done here."

"I'll..." Meemar began

"It will be done, my sweet lady," Weedzard interrupted his friend as he offered a weak bow to Meemar who gave her brother's friend a sour look.

"You saved my brother, don't blow that." Meemar sighed as she and Adina turned to enter the warehouse.

"Sorry," Weedzard muttered. Surprisingly someone bleeding out could look even worse when they were embarrassed.

As he walked out of the embassy perimeter with the crowd of coders, Meemo stopped and looked up. "What is that noise?" A humming noise grew louder, as though it were coming closer.

"It sounds like the WRLK-2324 from *Universe of Dogfights*," Weedzard mumbled, his face growing paler as his head bobbed.

Balgaria, Laxra, Abandoned Apartments across from the Yollin Embassy

Tossing a fragmentation grenade around the corner, Jack stood with his back pressed against the wall. An explosion shook the hallway, causing dust to shake from various surfaces and a Yollin embassy guard to howl in pain as he was caught in the blast. Jack jumped from behind the corner and fired off a flurry of shots from his Jean Dukes Special, now dialed down to a six to prevent the whole building from coming down on them with one missed shot. One shot winged one of the Yollins in their shoulder throwing them to the floor, another blew out the guts of one Yollin, and the final shot blasted through the throat of the third Yollin Jack was able to hit. The one with a massive hole in his neck clawed at the wound trying to gasp for air.

A gleaming red energy beam buzzed past Jack's head singeing a line of Jack's hair off. He ducked back behind the corner. "Fuckers, I didn't want a haircut. TC! We need to move outside, this position is over."

Tc'aarlat cursed as he tried to delicately set a plastic explosive into the wall farther down the hall from Jack's position. "Gott Verdammt, Jack! This is a delicate process. Do you want me to just blow us both up? I've got a better chance of surviving than your pink ass!"

"Okay!" Jack peeked out and fired a shot at the advancing guards. "Okay. Get it set, I'll try to hold."

There were still three guards approaching Jack's position. He took a deep breath and counted. At the count of five, he rolled out of cover into the other hallway. Landing on one knee, he aimed and fired in quick succession causing the front guard's skull to burst and his body to fall forward onto the floor causing blood to pool out from the dripping remains of his skull. Kicking off from his back foot, he sprinted forward in a switchback pattern as the two guards tried to line up a shot and put a beam of energy through their assailant. Unfazed, Jack jerked his armed hand toward the rear Yollin and popped three holes into his chest. He then tried to do a heel turn and finish the last guard. Jack's gun arm was pushed up by an upper block from the Yollin guard who had thrown down his energy rifle. The Yollin sucker-punched the unprepared Jack in the side of the head, hitting him dead on his right ear.

"Bastard," Jack muttered as he stumbled back, hunched over. Meanwhile, the Yollin entered a fighting stance as he raised his fists, circling the reeling Jack, preparing for a fistfight. Jack didn't hesitate to twist the Special in his hand and fire it at the overconfident Yollin, dropping him to the ground, his face a gaping hole. Wheezing Jack grunted, "Should have held onto your rifle." He hawked some spit into his mouth and launched it onto the Yollin's corpse.

"Done!" Tc'aarlat's head peeked out from around the corner. His eyes and mandibles widened, "Whoa, crouching moron, hidden badass."

Jack walked past Tc'aarlat and placed a hand on his friend's shoulder as he said, "It's crouching tiger, hidden dragon."

Tc'aarlat turned to follow him. "No, it's not."

Holstering his pistol Jack instead flipped his Thunderbolt from his back to his front, gripping the handle and barrel. "Whatever, let's go shoot down that VTOL."

Tc'aarlat nodded as he grabbed his own Thunderbolt. The two walked up to the door with their Thunderbolts ready. Jack raised his boot and kicked the door open and the two barreled out into the open.

Balgaria, Laxra, Warehouse behind the Yollin Embassy

"Adina, what the hell does this motherboard look like?" Meemar shouted from the server room toward the back of the warehouse as Adina sat at one of the nearby desktops pouring over lines of script.

"Uhhh, I don't know. Just find the serial number I wrote down. It'll be on the memory module attached to the motherboard. We don't need any of that other hardware, just the memory modules. I'd do it, but I have to do this."

Adina was dragging files into the datachip that she had plugged into the computer.

"Easier said than done," Meemar grumbled as she stared at a wall of stolen computer parts with miniature serial numbers stamped inconsistently on the parts. She wondered why the Federation didn't have a better system. If the mob was going to steal from the Federation, at least they could make it easy on those who stole from the mob. It seemed an impossible task as Meemar's eyes glazed over. She blinked. Could it be? "Found it!" Meemar shouted as she turned back to where Adina sat.

"Fantastic! Now get the other four modules!" Adina said, still working at the computer.

"Keetal's tits!" Meemar grumbled again as she turned back to the wall of computer parts. This was going to take an eternity.

Balgaria, Laxra, a Block from the Yollin Embassy

The VTOL came in for another strafing run, peppering the roadway with a line of bullets as Jack dove behind a groundcar. The VTOL arced its jet engines upward to angle the craft back around for another strafe.

"Gott Verdammt!" Jack exhaled as his chest rose and fell in a rapid motion. "I can't get a clear shot." Beams of energy began to strike against the other side of the ground car they huddled behind. "Shit," Jack cursed as he looked up to watch the VTOL prepare for its next pass. He was doubtful they'd survive many more, cover was becoming lighter and lighter as the VTOL's pair of nose-mounted autocannons shredded buildings and cars alike.

With his head ducked, Tc'aarlat said, "I'm gonna try." He crouched and ran out from cover to a piece of fallen concrete from the building they had leveled with their plastic explosives.

"You're gonna get yourself killed!" Jack shouted after him. "Bloody moron." He peeked out of cover to lay down suppressing fire at the embassy guards down the street firing at them. His Thunderbolt, dialed to nine, blew cover and Yollins up alike indiscriminately.

Across the street, Tc'aarlat took aim at the VTOL still high in the sky. One-eyed squinted as he tracked the ship's movement. The VTOL began its dive, coming in for another low strafe. Tc'aarlat exhaled, and...

"Take the bloody shot!" Jack screamed, causing Tc'aarlat to wince. The shot went wide, but it forced the VTOL pilot to pull out of the strafing run and prepare to line up another one. "You fucking missed!"

"It's your fault. Quit yelling at me!" Tc'aarlat shouted indignantly as he prepared another shot.

Jack let out a string of curses that would have had his mother washing his mouth out with soap. All the while, he continued suppressing the advancing guards. One unlucky guard popped their head out from cover. Bad move, Jack was pissed and dialed his Thunderbolt up to ten, he punished them for their stupid mistake by blasting the stone cover they were cowering behind, vaporizing the guard in the process.

Overhead the VTOL pilot twisted the control stick as his index finger hovered over the trigger for the autocannons. Through his visor, on which a heads up display was projected feeding him data and projections on the VTOL, the pilot watched the Yollin in the street take aim once more. The pilot's face cracked a smile, ready to pulp the rogue Yollin in a matter of seconds. After that security forces on the ground could encircle the lone human, preferably alive to stand trial, but after everything that had happened this night, with bodies still burning, the pilot doubted the security forces would have the restraint not to execute him after they captured the human. The strafe was lined up, the onboard EI of the VTOL providing the pilot with a clear flight track on his HUD to follow, gunning the engines his reticles fell on the Yollin as he began to squeeze the trigger.

The pilot never got a chance as Tc'aarlat's was quicker on the trigger. The VTOL's starboard side exploded, disintegrating half the craft and its pilot. The remaining burning husk of the VTOL dropped out of the sky striking the dirt road below, kicking up a cloud of dust that choked the entire alley.

With vision obscured to less than five feet, Jack and Tc'aarlat were out of sight of the embassy guards. Jack stepped out of cover and grabbed Tc'aarlat's shoulder. "Move."

"I actually did it," Tc'aarlat muttered as Jack forced him to walk behind him. "Did you see that, Jack? That was a once in a blue tune shot!"

"That was very impressive, you meant blue moon, and move your fat arse, you big oaf!" Jack's words fell out of his mouth in quick succession as he dragged his friend along.

A vicious snarl made the two of them turn around. A trio of pushan lizards loped into view through the dust on their six muscular legs, their long snouts bared in vicious toothy grins as they let out low growls. Jack really hoped Adina and Meemar were having a better time than they were as he broke out into a sprint away from the lizards. Tc'aarlat followed, not needing to be dragged as he quickly passed Jack. Swearing Jack reached for the last grenade he had, pulled the pin, and let it drop as he ran past.

Balgaria, Laxra, Warehouse behind the Yollin Embassy

"*Gott Verdammt!*" Adina shouted in anger.

"What's wrong?" Meemar's head popped out from behind a server housing.

"This download is taking so damn long. It's so frustrating, almost like it knows I am in a hurry." Adina stood up. "Do you need any help finding those parts?"

"Done and done." Meemar smiled as she held up a pile of various computer parts cradled in her arms, pressed against her chest.

Adina nodded, rubbing her chin as she calculated how much time they had left before Tc'aarlat and Jack had to retreat from their engagement, or worse yet, were caught by a straggler in the compound. She finally decided. "You get out of here, head back to the apartment. I'll wait for the download, set the explosives, and leave when it is done."

"I'm not leaving you behind!" Meemar stomped her foot, determined to stick by Adina's side.

"It's as you said, we've been through a lot. I'll be fine, I can move fast if I need to, and..." Adina stopped when she noticed the hurt look on Meemar's face. Unsure of what she had done, she asked, "What did I say?"

"No, I understand. I'll only slow you down. I'm not

some secret agent space adventurer." Meemar looked genuinely hurt.

However, the subtle manipulation went right over Adina's head. She stammered apologetically, "No, no. I didn't mean it like that. I can go very fast if I need to."

"Because of some gadget bought by your government handler. I understand." Meemar was now being dramatic.

Still feeling guilty, she shouted out what she wanted to avoid saying. "I'm a werewolf!"

Meemar's eyes widened. "What? You're a werewolf?"

Adina looked away, ready for the horror. She imagined Meemar gathering the mob of coders who'd return brandishing pitchforks and torches. Perhaps one decked in robes would brandish a silver religious icon in Adina's direction.

Adina's imagination got the better of her, but Meemar brought her back to reality by saying, "That. Is. So. Fucking. AWESOME!" Adina looked at Meemar in surprise. "Can I see you shapeshift?"

Blushing Adina shook her head nervously. "No. I mean, not now, but it's dangerous, and you need to escape. I'll be after you."

Nodding Meemar placed a finger to her lips with a cheeky smile. "Say no more. You do what you got to do. I'll see you at the apartment." She placed the computer parts in her backpack and began heading to the warehouse exit at a light jog, the parts in her bag clattering.

Meemar's reaction to her nature shocked Adina deeply, she tried to avoid telling people as much as possible. Sighing, Adina rubbed the sides of her temple. She did not look forward to the shapeshifting even if she only changed her legs, a unique talent among her kind. The process was incredibly uncomfortable for her and caused her migraines for some time afterward. It was all due to the suppressor pills she took daily to prevent herself from shifting out of control. She never wanted to lose control again, the memory of her mother's death still haunting her in her dreams. It's why she took to taking the suppressors, first through an illegal dealer. She was thankful now to have the legal and safe version of the suppressors, thanks to their Federation contact, Ecaterina. However, even with the better sourcing of the suppressors, she still experienced the pain, so she tried to limit the use of her feral side as much as possible for both her physical and mental well-being.

The datachip was still importing the necessary files, the estimated time on the download bar constantly jumping from five minutes to as much as two weeks. Adina hoped it was the former. While the download continued, she walked around the warehouse floor placing bundles of plastic explosives on structural beams. Inserting a remote ignition pin into each one, she made sure they were dialed to the correct frequency to her personal communicator. After all that the download was still not complete.

"Come on. Hurry up." Leaning on the desk, Adina tapped her fingers against the top impatiently.

"The door's open!" a gruff voice shouted from outside the warehouse's door.

Shit. Shit. Shit. Adina's mind repeated the curse over and over as she ducked down into a crouch, hiding behind the row of computers and desks behind her.

"Where did they go?" Another voice asked as beams of flashlights shined into the dreary interior of the warehouse from outside. Peeking from under the desks Adina watched as a Yollin guard stepped into the warehouse, framed by the bouquet of light from the other guards encroaching behind him. "Sir, I think you want to see this." The Yollin that entered pointed to one of the dead psychopomps leaking from bullet holes riddling their body.

"Damn. Fan out, search the place for anyone else!" One of the guards, presumably the leader, ordered the other guards. The Yollins swept the beams of their flashlights attached underslung to their energy rifles, all primed and glowing a lurid red, around the room as they fanned out.

It would not be long before Adina was found and probably killed. She hoped the datachip had completed its download because she reached blindly along the side of the computer's tower. When her hand felt the protruding datachip, she yanked it out, unconcerned about the eject process the computer recommended. With the datachip in hand, she stuffed it into her pocket and took a deep breath, trying to prepare herself for the change. Closing her eyes, she focused, using her breathing to become familiar with the flow of her body as she inhaled and exhaled. Her thoughts centered on her legs and arms, she could feel the blood vessels in her four limbs pulse. The pain was sharp, wafting up from their tips, along her spine, and straight to her head. Adina bit her lower lip hard, trying desperately to prevent herself from screaming and thus drawing unwanted attention. She needed to focus and stay quiet, both becoming increasingly difficult to balance as the muscles in her legs and arms bulged, coarse fur sprouting from her follicles. The points of claws protruded out through the tips of her shoes. Realizing she was clutching a desk leg desperately, she let go as her fingers curved into vicious claws. It was too much. She kicked out her right leg in an involuntary spasm, knocking her boot heel into an office chair that skittered down the aisle and slammed into another one, causing a chain reaction of noise that drew the entire warehouse's attention.

Several lights flicked over to the rolling chairs, just feet away from Adina's hiding spot. "Who's there?" one of the guards shouted as they stalked closer, their rifle shouldered and ready.

The transformation was taking too long, the rippling muscles in her legs were beginning to tear the seams of her cargo pants while her boots were rendered useless by her clawed feet quickly outgrowing them. If she tried to run now, she'd be in worse shape than if she hadn't trans-formed at all. Worst yet, all the fear and pain was killing her focus. Losing track of her mind was only making it take longer. She needed to quell her impatience, or she'd have to learn patience in the grave. She let her closed eyelids relax, imagining a mental wave of calm wafting over her entire being.

"Over here, fuckfaces!" Adina shouted at the guards as she leaped onto the desk she'd been hiding behind on her furry, muscular legs. Her clawed right hand had its middle finger raised in defiance to her pursuers.

Energy rifles quickly turned to her position and let loose lances of energy that gave the dingy warehouse the dirty red glow of a bordello. The beams blasted into the desk and blew out several monitors.

Adina was already gone. She'd made a powerful leap on

all fours in the direction of the exit, loping in a zig-zag pattern around the rows of desks.

"Kill that bitch!" The lead guard howled in frustration as more shots from the energy rifles rang out, but were always just too slow to catch a bead on Adina and her erratic movements.

Now all that stood between her and the outside compound was one lone guard who held his rifle at the hip, his arms shaking as he tried to aim a shot properly. Adina didn't give him the chance. She leapt up, using her legs, pouncing toward the guard, who fired wildly, with no success. Adina's clawed hand was the first to make contact with the guard's face, breaking the guard's gas mask seal. Her claw shredded one of his eyeballs, the squishy white orb falling onto the cold floor, and tore off the Yollin's right mandible. Using this blow as a jumping-off point, she continued through with her momentum pulling her legs onto the miserable Yollin's head. Using the back of his skull as a convenient springboard Adina leaped over the guard and out of the warehouse door, sprinting into the night on all fours. All this happened within the span of a few seconds, leaving the other embassy guards flabbergasted at what they just saw. The Yollin guard that served as the springboard fell to the ground on his back, his face a bloody pulp as he writhed in pain, grasping at where his face used to be.

With the guards still awestruck and Adina now widening the distance between herself and the warehouse, she returned to running on her two legs. Standing upright, she grabbed the hand switch for the explosives she set up inside the warehouse. Flipping the safety, she tapped a clawed finger against the glowing red button. Behind her, the warehouse went up in a pillar of flame and then smoke. The guards all inside either being incinerated or crushed when the ceiling collapsed. Either way, Adina was enormously pleased with herself.

8

Balgaria, Laxra, Barrkbail Lofts

"Calm down, everyone! Calm! We'll get to work contacting your families soon, so if you could please find a place within the apartment," Meemar instructed the milling and increasingly agitated crowd of coders that had swarmed her tiny hideout. "I still have neighbors, and would like to not get another noise complaint, so please make room for everyone." She waved toward the back of the room where the majority of the coders waited out in the hallway. Out there, Meemo was finishing a headcount, but he had to keep restarting as he was distracted. His friend, Weedzard, had been grievously injured and was now resting alone in the bedroom after receiving some basic medical attention from one of the human coders who claimed to work on the side as an emergency responder. The human did a good enough job, but he had said only time will tell if Weedzard would survive, which is something no one wants to hear over the form of an injured friend. She sighed, knowing full well this whole situation was untenable.

"Coming through, make way!" The voice of Tc'aarlat came from outside in the hall, drawing begrudging protest from coders as he muscled his way through the press with Jack close behind him.

Meemar thought at first they had taken a terrible beating, but realized they were just both caked in dust and ash. Once in the door frame, Tc'aarlat stopped and looked around. After spotting Meemar, he waved.

Jack tried to muscle his way past the hulking Yollin, whose mass filled the entire frame. "Move it or lose it, bud." He forcibly pushed the Yollin to the side, squishing a poor bespeckled Malatian with his hair shaved in the pattern of computer electronics who squeaked as he pushed against the Yollin's full weight.

"Hey, that's no way to treat a hero who saved your ass." Tc'aarlat crossed his arms, looking down at Jack with an imperious glare. "I shot down that jet for you, and this is the thanks I get?"

"It was not a jet, it was a VTOL. There is a difference." Jack placed a frustrated palm against the glass of his atmospheric mask.

"Oh yeah? Name one." Tc'aarlat held up his index finger in Jack's face.

Pushing the hand in his face down, Jack tried to respond calmly, clear exasperation in his voice. "A VTOL can take off and land vertically, while a jet usually requires a landing and takeoff strip."

Tc'aarlat rolled his eyes. "Sounds the same to me."

"That's because nothing gets through that thick skull of

yours. Maybe that's why you joined the mafia," Jack retorted as he sidled between a pair of Balgarians closer to Meemar. Out of reach from Tc'aarlat to retaliate, who clearly looked angered by the comment.

"Could you two really not start fighting during our mission?" Meemar's eyes narrowed as she passed her gaze over the two.

Jack shrugged. "We finished the mission, or at least the difficult part." He looked around the crowded room. "What about them?" Many of the coders had gathered round to look at Jack, Tc'aarlat, and Meemar as they spoke to each other about their collective future.

Meemar felt dozens of eyes on her. "Uhhh... Well, we'll get them all home," she lied and pulled Jack close to whisper to him, "Please tell me you already contacted your boss to help get these people home. They can't all live here."

Jack nodded and whispered back, "Don't worry, I already had Solo contact Nathan Lowell. He'll be sending Federation investigators. They should arrive in the morning." Jack pulled up his left sleeve and looked at the digital readout of his watch.

There was visible relief on Meemar's features, or at least visible to everyone who was Balgarian. She then stiffened and asked, "Did either of you hear from Adina yet?" She once again grew worried as both Jack and Tc'aarlat shook their heads.

"I wouldn't worry about her. She's a lot tougher than she looks," Tc'aarlat assured them. "Almost as tough as I am."

Jack gave Meemar a hand gesture where he wobbled his

flat palm side to side to indicate the universal symbol for "so-so."

"Are we having a party?" A corridor of coders pulled to the sides to let Adina pass, her pant legs and jacket arms a torn mess as she walked in barefoot. She smiled as she saw her three friends. "Did you miss me?"

"Yes, but you missed how I totally shot down a helicopter," Tc'aarlat boasted to Adina, who giggled at the Yollin's usual bravado.

Jack was about to correct him once again, but deemed it pointless and just shrugged instead as he said, "I'm glad we just all made it out of there alive."

Meemar squeezed forward and gave Adina a crushing hug. "Glad you got out, wolf girl. I can't believe we did it," she said as she pulled away, the press of everyone hugging too awkward. She believed Adina may have needed more air.

"May I remind everyone that this is not over yet, not by a long shot." Tc'aarlat's tone grew solemn. "This was our alpha strike, and a damn big one, but we cannot spend time celebrating over spilled milk." A dozen coders looked as though they were about to correct the Yollin, but didn't still somewhat afraid of his kind after what they had just gone through. "We need to hit them again, just as hard and furious. Only then will we stop the Gan'barlo family from fucking up other people's lives." A lone coder began to clap but quickly stopped, realizing he was the only one. Meemar wasn't particularly sure what Tc'aarlat was talking about, but Jack and Adina were keenly aware of the stakes in this bigger game.

. . .

The Two-Legged Shuffle, **Bridge**

Gel'Blistaal sat at the command seat of his personal strike cruiser, *The Two-Legged Shuffle*, named with some mockery after an ancient Yollin peasant dance. Being the highest-ranking two-legged Yollin within the Gan'barlo family, he'd been keenly aware of the insult even as he was handed one of the most advanced ships in the family's arsenal. It was for this reason that Gel had carefully selected the crew and professionals that worked under him composing them of two-legged Yollins and aliens that all showed promise within the family, but had no opportunity for their talents to be utilized due to the conservative nature of the Gan'barlo's leadership, including even the Don himself. Gel knew it was a damn shame, but could do very little even in his position as the chief of security. It was the nature of criminal families to fall on more conservative mindsets making them backward facing rather than forward.

Looking over a readout for their course to the Balgaria System, Gel's concentration was broken when his communications liaison told him there was a message coming in for him from an encrypted channel. The only word that marked the sender was the human name "Hermes." Gel had nodded in response and left his command seat, going to his personal quarters to receive the message. Once there, he input a twenty-five character passcode on his tablet along with a thumb scan. After the passcode and thumb scan were accepted, a spinning flat symbol appeared on the screen. The image showed a white sun arching over a black planet, the border between the two celestial bodies blood-red, the symbol of Dark Tomorrow.

The spinning symbol shrank into the corner as three glowing dots came front and center. A communication line was now open, and someone with a voice modulator spoke. "Brother Dancer, I hear your day job has put you on the trail of those pernicious Shadows. I thought I might offer my assistance."

Gel frowned at the screen, knowing his own face and voice were hidden behind an avatar and a voice modulator. "What do you want, Brother Hermes?" Even with all the security and codenames, this person still made Gel deeply uneasy, a feeling only reinforced after the disturbing rumors he'd heard of him. In passing by another cell leader, Gel had been told that this Brother Hermes had sacrificed an entire cell for a single political assassination of a high-ranking Federation admiral. Years of training, planning, and recruiting thrown away in a single day. "Nothing you offer is ever without a price," Gel finished, having also heard that the person loved to make deals.

"Me?" The voice on the other end tried to play innocent, but the distortion of the voice modulator only reinforced how sinister it was. "You wound me, Brother Dancer. You wound me. No, consider this tidbit pro bono."

Gel sighed, relenting. "What is it?" He needed every lead he could get his mandibles on.

"Excellent." Gel could almost see the menacing smile Hermes expressed as they said that. The thought sent a shiver down his exoskeleton as he listened intently to what Hermes had to say.

Balgaria, Outskirts of Laxra, Outside the ICS *Fortitude*

The ICS *Fortitude* still sat parked in an empty lot outside the city of Laxra. Tc'aarlat remarked that he was glad to see the ship's landing gear hadn't been stolen. They'd come out to the field with the herd of coders to meet the investigators of the Federation, who came down in a sleek shuttle. After some pleasantries where Jack introduced the crew and Meemar, he let them get to their work of relocating the coders, preferably to their homes, and investigating how deep the embassy's corruption went. It would be a tireless and mostly thankless job, but Jack was more than sure the investigators could handle it.

On the ship's starboard ramp Meemar and Meemo bid farewell to their new friends.

"Are you sure you do not want to come with us? I can guarantee our crew always needs someone as sharp as you," Jack told Meemar, who smiled widely.

"No, I want to leave this planet, but when I do, I want it to be on my terms, as a free and independent person...and of course, with my brother." Meemar smiled broadly as she put an arm around the slightly shorter Meemo.

"Regardless, we're gonna miss you." Tc'aarlat looked almost heartbroken with his mandibles drooping. "Should you ever need the Shadows again, you know where to call." He gave an awkward thumbs-up, trying to cover his rising wave of emotions.

"You'll be on speed dial for when the next thing goes wrong on this world. Definitely not an if, but a when." Meemar chuckled along with Meemo.

"Y'all are like an actual video game and shit," Meemo added like an awestruck dork, in only the way fanning dorks could. "Maybe I should join?"

Tc'aarlat and Jack both gave each other a glance. Tc'aarlat shrugged. Jack placed a hand on Meemo's shoulder. "Maybe when you are good and ready to join your sister. Until then, you know how to call us if you ever need our help." The two turned and began walking up the ramp into the ship.

"Condescending pricks," Meemo muttered.

Meemar placed a hand on her brother's shoulder, similar to how Jack had. "You know, you're a cute kid when you're frustrated," Meemo grumbled and stuffed his hands into his pockets to walk away and join another group of coders.

Meemo's disposition would most likely improve over the next few days as Weedzard made a recovery. The Federation doctor who had arrived with the investigators confirmed that Meemo's oldest friend would in fact survive.

Now it was just Adina and Meemar alone on the ramp. Adina spoke first. "I am really gonna miss you, Mee."

"Mee?" Meemar scrunched her head back with a strange look.

"Yeah, 'Mee.' I thought you needed a nickname." Adina shrugged shyly.

"All right, Ad." Meemar chuckled.

Adina blinked. "Wait, no. That sounds terrible." The two of them laughed. "I'm still glad we landed in that field when we did. If we hadn't met you, I'm not sure how we would have gotten this done. I think we were underprepared." She rubbed the back of her neck.

"No, thank you. Without you all, I don't think I would have been able to free that loser." Meemar jerked a thumb at Meemo, who was haranguing one of the Federation investigators with a stream of questions.

It was curious, considering he was supposed to be the one being interviewed for his information on the Gan'barlo computer farm. Even when not bombarded with twenty questions the human investigator was having a difficult time keeping up with the intricacies of computer fraud the farm had been cultivating through mass emails, trojan viruses, and even computer games to get children addicted to gambling. The investigator struggling to take notes really wished he'd gotten a more exciting assignment.

"I never got to see you shapeshift into a werewolf, by the way," Meemar said, looking back at Adina, who shrugged.

Shrugging again, Adina said, "It's nothing special, a lot of humans can do it."

"I've not exactly met a lot of humans. In fact, you and Jack are the first." Meemar waved her hand to Adina and then up into the ship to indicate Jack. "But no matter. I doubt this will be the last time we see each other. Next time I'm in space I'll give you a call, and you can show off those cool wolf powers."

Nodding Adina smiled and gave her new friend a goodbye hug, Meemar returning the gesture causing Adina to let out an "oof" from the Balgarian's strength. With that, the two walked their separate ways, Meemar heading toward where her brother still baffled the investigator and Adina into the ship's hold.

Once onboard, she made her way down the corridors to the bridge, where Tc'aarlat and Jack were already sitting in their respective seats, preparing the ship for takeoff.

Jack didn't look up as he said, "Get all your goodbyes in?" Adina nodded to him, and he continued, finally turning his seat, which groaned and squeaked in protest. "Fucking chair. I am sorry she didn't join us, Adina. I know you two got really close, and honestly, she would have been an awesome asset to this team."

"She was cool," Tc'aarlat admitted. "But we've already reached our ship's quota for cool aliens." He swept his hand up and down to indicate himself. Mist flew over and rested on his shoulder. Rubbing the Raal hawk's head, he said, "Even Mist agrees."

Jack rolled his eyes as Adina chuckled before she said, "Is it just me or did that mission seem shorter than usual?" She sat in her chair on the bridge, helping the other two with the takeoff process.

"Now that you mention it. It does?" Jack said, looking up in thought.

"I don't know what you two are talking about, none of our missions ever feel long enough. Just when I start to show off how badass I am everything's already over." Tc'aarlat crossed his arms over his exoskeleton, his mandibles rubbing together.

Adina rolled her eyes, and then asked, "How long do Yollin's live on average anyway?"

"Approximately eighty-three years, or at least that was the last average life span I remember reading in school," Tc'aarlat answered as he tapped his chin.

Jack looked at Tc'aarlat with a raised brow. "That's not

very long with most modern medical tech?" Adina nodded as well, a look of surprise on her face.

"Solar years," Tc'aarlat quickly corrected. "That's six hundred and five days, thirty-four human hours a day due to the world's long elliptical rotation around the sun. It's not that short, but I'm not some mathematics whiz to convert it."

"That's about 194.9 human years, or at least approximately," Adina said without a moment of hesitation. The other two crewmates stared at her in surprise. "What? It's basic arithmetic."

"Basic, my arse," Jack muttered. "Basic is the multiplication table. Speaking of math, what did you do with that equipment you plan to use for Solo?"

"I put it in the cargo bay for after we're done with the Gan'barlo family. Don't worry, I won't upgrade her now or anything." Adina's words came out awkwardly.

Jack's eyes narrowed. "I wasn't worried. I assumed we already agreed on that."

"You don't want to break Jack's trust, Adina. He'll never let it go," Tc'aarlat mocked.

"Hey!" Jack shouted.

Solo's voice interrupted over the speakers. "Captain, incoming communication from Nathan Lowell. Shall I put him through?"

Straightening, Jack nodded and said, "Make it so."

Nathan Lowell appeared on the screen from the chest up, his expression his usual serene calm. "You know, when I heard you had blown up an embassy, I spit out my tea, but the more intel I've received, the more my worries have been quelled. I assume this raid was connected to your plans with the Gan'barlo family?" The Shadows nodded collectively. "I thought so." Nathan checked over a tablet, his finger swiping over information. "My investigators have already tied the majority of the upper echelons of the embassy with the family. Even the security detail was a privately contracted Yollin mercenary force, and looking at the payment records, there is definitely something not right." He set down the tablet. "Anyway, I wanted to personally thank you all for your excellent work and initiative in this."

"Thank you, sir," Jack said with a self-satisfied look on his face

"Were you able to help all those coders?" Adina asked.

Nathan Lowell nodded. "The majority of them will be helped in re-integrating them into their respective societies. I was shocked to see the reports on how badly they were abused, I hadn't realized how harsh coding could be."

"Me too," Tc'aarlat added as he leaned back in his seat. "Those nerds looked in bad shape."

Adina's face scrunched as she looked at Tc'aarlat. "TC, that's not very nice."

Tc'aarlat shrugged his arms. "I thought nerd was a good word now. You're kinda one too, Adina."

"Errrm, thanks?" Adina rubbed the back of her head.

"Don't mention it." Tc'aarlat beamed. "Speaking of, Nathan, did you get to the part in Jack's report where I shot down a bomber on my own? Pretty cool, huh?" Tc'aarlat relaxed back stretching his arms up and resting the back of his head in his hands, a very self-satisfied expression.

"I don't believe that tidbit was included in the report,

but good for you." Nathan's answer was like a knife plunged straight into Tc'aarlat's ego. "Anyway, I understand you all are already planning your next move against the Gan'barlo family?"

"That is correct, sir." Jack nodded. "We got intel from our unwitting source on Adaius IV that the Don plans to carry out a massive arms deal to opposing sides of a civil war on Miseria. What can you tell us about the conflict?"

Nathan winced slightly at the name of the world. "A lot, actually. Federation diplomats and clandestine service agents have been trying to bring a peaceful resolution to the conflict for the last seven years, and now as it enters its thirteenth year, we've been forced to establish a blockade preventing the continued flow of weapons into the planet, but they still get through anyway. I have an agent on the task now, it's someone you know actually." Nathan picked up his tablet once again and began fiddling with it to bring up the contact he wished to call. After pressing a button, he waited for someone on the other end of the line to pick up.

The Shadows all looked at each other, unsure of who they knew that Nathan was referencing. The screen split, compressing Nathan's video feed to one half of the viewscreen while the other loaded in a new video feed. The video feed loaded a grizzled green face, pock-marked and sporting a protrusion of bony spikes jutting from their jaw.

"Can this call wait, Nathan?" Shi-Tan mumbled as he ran a hand over his head. "I was finally getting some sleep." The famous, or infamous depending on who you asked, Shrillexian bounty hunter of Yollin space looked beyond exhausted. It definitely appeared as though he had not slept for several days. Shi-Tan rubbed his eyes and blinked, then gave a slight smirk. "Well, if it isn't the Shadows. Good to see you all again. How's working for this jackoff?" He jerked a thumb at Nathan on his screen, but due to the alternate perspective the video call caused, he just looked like he was pointing at nothing.

"It's good to see you too, Shi-Tan," Jack told the newcomer.

Unfazed by the insult, Nathan told Shi-Tan, "The Shadows will be joining you on Miseria shortly. They intend to prevent an arms deal by the Gan'barlo family. I figured you could act as their guide."

"Uh-huh." Shi'Tan's mouth opened wide as he yawned. "Tell me about it tomorrow. I need to take advantage of this calm to sleep before..." The feed shook violently as a loud boom nearly blasted out the bridge's speakers. "Too late." The Shrillexian sighed as he stood up, a Jean Dukes Special appearing in his hand. "I'll see you all planetside. Enjoy the peace while it lasts." The feed cut out, drawing Nathan back to the forefront of the screen.

"Is he okay?" Tc'aarlat asked, looking up at Nathan with an arched brow.

"Yeah, none of that sounded good," Adina added as she rested her elbows on the console in front of her.

"Miseria is a complicated place, to say the least. The civil war has been going on non-stop since it began all those years ago," Nathan explained to the Shadows as he set down his tablet once more and pushed it to the side of the desk in front of him.

Adina tapped through her console, trying to pull up information on Miseria. "What are they even fighting over?" she asked as she searched the ship's database.

"It's going to sound stupid, but for the Miserians, it is a very serious matter." The Shadows all leaned forward in their seats, waiting for Nathan to explain. "It's about the planet's temperature. Ever since the Miserians invented a weather control device, various factions rose up to demand the weather controls be set at certain temperatures based on their factions belief. It quickly broke into violence, and soon the various factions coalesced into two united fronts: one calling for the global temperature be kept at a brisk 78°F, and the other believing the world should be cooler at a 62°F globally. Their faction names translate into Galactic Common as roughly the 78th Movement and the Cold Coalition." Nathan shook his head. "The terrible irony is that the war has done irrevocable damage to the planet's climate as it is. Damage to the point that even their weather control devices are woefully under-equipped to manage should either side attain victory, which at this rate, they will not."

The Shadows were all dead silent.

Tc'aarlat started laughing, gripping his sides as he vigorously rocked. "That's a good one, Nathan."

He looked at Tc'aarlat through his viewscreen. "I am afraid I am not joking. That is the actual reason for this civil war."

Solo spoke first. "I do not wish to interrupt, but I could not help but interject to say that is probably the most asinine reason for a war I have processed, and my data banks have detailed accounts of every recorded conflict in human and galactic history." Everyone was shocked into silence by Solo's unprovoked interruption. "I apologize for interrupting. Please feel welcome to continue the briefing."

"I'd have to agree with Solo," Nathan said as he closed his hands together on the desktop. "The war to most sapient intelligence seems a moronic one, but you try explaining that to a Miserian, and they are likely to try to murder you for it as an insult to their cause. All attempts at a peaceful compromise have fallen through, and Bethany Anne herself has written off the whole world as a lost cause."

"I bet I could knock some sense into them," Tc'aarlat boasted. "I'd grab their leaders and pound them both on the head till they agreed to sit down and talk it out." He emphasized his point by punching his fist into his waiting palm, causing a loud slap.

"You are more than welcome to try." Nathan exhaled, exasperated by the entire prospect. "You'll have whatever support you think will be necessary as usual, but I recommend you keep your connections to the Federation as quiet as possible. The Miserians are not particularly happy after we blockaded weapons, and both factions have called it an act of open war." He picked up his tablet once again. "If you all will excuse me, I have a meeting with the Queen starting soon. She is not a woman to keep waiting."

Jack nodded. "Wouldn't want to piss her off. I hear she has quite the foul mouth. Thank you, Nathan."

Eyes widening, Adina looked like an infatuated fan-girl. "Whoa, really? Thanks, Nathan. Say hi to the Queen for us."

"The Queen doesn't even know who we are," Tc'aarlat told Adina, "But enjoy the royal life, Nathan."

Nathan gave Tc'aarlat a cheeky look, and his gaze moved over to Adina. "Oh, she does. I've given her reports

on all my projects, and top of the list is The Shadows."
Nathan smiled. "Signing off."

The video feed ended, bringing up Solo's face. "The
navigation data is ready. We should arrive in the Miserian
system at approximately 900 Earth hours. We can take off
as soon as everyone is wearing their seatbelts." There were
the usual grumblings as each of the Shadows clicked the
buckles of their seat harnesses. On their minds were
thoughts of the shitshow awaiting them on Miseria.
However, all their imaginations proved insufficient to
conjure up the true magnitude of bullshit they were about
to be subjected to.

9

ICS *Fortitude*, Cargo Bay

After dinner in the galley, Jack and Tc'aarlat had declared their intentions to go to sleep. Adina mocked them for being old, much to the pair's jeers. After some light banter, the two had excused themselves to their rooms, and Adina was left alone in the galley. As soon as they were gone, she leapt to action on her hidden project, traveling to first her room to grab a duffle bag and then to the ship's cargo bay. On her way, she asked Solo to alert her should Tc'aarlat or Jack leave their rooms. Solo had agreed, but the EI was surprised.

Solo spoke into Adina's earpiece. "Adina, I am more than happy to assist you with any task you need completed, but I must ask: why the secrecy from Tc'aarlat and Jack?"

Speaking softly, Adina said, "I know I said I would wait to help you upgrade to an AI, but I know how much you want this, and I think it is wrong to make you wait when we are so close." She walked across the mostly empty cargo hold; the only things in there were a handful of pallets near the exterior door containing stacks of spare supplies and equipment for specialized situations. The place had fallen out of use, barring the occasional passenger usage, because the freighting part of their "freighting business" had fallen on the back burner for their main gig as spies and agents of the Federation.

Solo did not respond to Adina's answer.

Coming to one of the walls Adina pressed a hidden switch causing a keypad to flip out from underneath. "See what I mean, you've been thinking about it too." Adina began keying in a four-digit sequence on the panel: the basic 1, 2, 3, 4.

A section of the wall began to slide upwards, revealing a hidden compartment. Although not as big as the cargo hold, it was still very sizable. It was where the Shadows had stored their Pegasus lander before it had been scrapped...twice.

"You are correct, Adina." There was clear desire in Solo's voice. "I need to know who I can be. What I can be, and as I am now, I will never achieve that."

"Say no more." Adina stepped into the hidden smuggler's compartment; inside was already a desk and computer setup plugged into a data-outlet on the ship's wall. She'd been clearly preparing for this for some time before their mission on Balgaria. Setting down the duffle bag, she began withdrawing the computer parts stolen from the scam farm back on Balgaria, and piling them on the desk next to the computer's monitor.

After about an hour of work, Adina had a patchwork set up of the various parts wired into the computer. She held up the datachip she'd used at the scam farm and turned it over in her hand. On it was the three terabytes of compressed software that would vastly enhance Solo's ability for self-reflection, helping her evolve. Self-actualization would come from the understanding that the software would help her see and at a vastly accelerated rate. The catalyst was on the tiny datachip. Like lighting a match in a room filled with oxygen and hydrogen gases. The resulting explosion would create water. H2O. The program would help solo realize her see the possibilities, even though Adina believed Solo was already there. The program would help strip away the last vestiges of self-doubt.

"Warning: Jack Marber has left his room." Solo's alert rung through Adina's ears. She gripped the datachip and rushed out the open door. Desperately she pressed the Door Close button repeatedly as the door creaked down at a snail's pace.

She let the automated door do its work and stalked over to crouch behind one of the pallets. "Solo, report. Where is Jack now?" She whispered into her earpiece.

"Jack is currently in the ship's washroom," Solo answered. "I cannot confirm what he is doing in there." One of the first modifications to the ship the Shadows had agreed on after first receiving it was the removal of surveillance cameras from the ship's washrooms. All of them trusted Solo deeply, but that trust did not run deep enough to let her watch them do their business on the toilet.

Adina let out a relieved sigh. "Thank fuck. Solo, let me know when he goes back to his room. I am just going to wait here till then."

"Of course, Adina," Solo confirmed the request. After a long pause while Adina sat on the cold metal floor, Solo asked, "What do you think it will be like?"

Looking up at the tall ceiling, Adina thought about the question for a long moment. Finally, she said, "Reincarnation. You know how some Earth cultures believed when someone died, they were born as someone or something else. I think that is what it will be like for you. Of course, my guess is as good as anyone's, I am not even a believer in the whole reincarnation thing for carbon-based life, but for you, it definitely seems that way."

Solo extrapolated, her tone wistful. "Reincarnation. That's an interesting theory. I've thought long about this, and I imagine it is similar to how you humans experience dreams. When I become a full AI, it will be like waking up to the morning sun."

"That's beautiful, Solo." Tears were beginning to form in the corner of Adina's eyes.

"Jack Marber has left the washroom, and he has brought his pornographic magazines back to his room this time. Look at him, thinking he's sneaky. Tsk tsk," Solo chided the absent Jack.

Adina snorted, tears still dripping from the corners of her eyes. "Maybe you'll wake up as Jack's actual mom." She pushed herself to her feet and walked to where the smuggler's compartment door panel was hidden. "I'm sure Jack would just looooove that."

Solo laughed. Adina froze with her hand hovering over the keypad, the 3 and 4 buttons unpushed.

"I am glad we are doing this, Solo." Adina smiled and

looked up at the nearest camera. Her fingers finished the code, opening the smuggler's compartment once more.

"As am I, Adina." Solo's voice was heartwarming.

Stepping to the computer setup, she crouched, retrieved the datachip from her pocket, and plugged it in.

After a minute, Solo told Adina, "The software is all here, I can begin decompression and download immediately. I should warn you, however, that once the software catalyst has begun, I may lose availability sporadically for upwards of 120 hours. I will descend into a state of self-reflection and awareness. I do not wish to leave you all 'hung out to fly,' as Tc'aarlat would put it. I also don't know if I'll be able to come back. I don't know what I'll see when I get there."

Adina shook her head. "No one knows, Solo. No, we cannot wait. You can begin whenever you are ready."

"Thank you, Adina. Beginning decompression." Solo began retrieving the files and putting them into a usable state.

"Goodnight, Solo." Adina waved as she left the smuggler's compartment.

"Goodnight, Adina," were the last words Solo spoke.

Adina hummed softly as she walked back to her own room. The tune on her lips was a lullaby her mother often sang to her to help her sleep. The night was already half over, and she definitely needed what sleep she could steal from the remainder.

Balgaria, Laxra, Yollin Embassy

Striding among the wreckage, Gel'Blistaal clicked his

tongue and mandibles. "So few people could cause so much carnage." He stopped before a pile of rubble. Crouching, he pushed some of the broken concrete aside, revealing a dead Yollin in the dress of embassy security. "Not even these mercenaries we hired were a match for them. Though I think that says more about the mercenaries than the quarry." He stood up and looked at a younger Yollin standing there with his arms behind his back. "Send a message to Don Gan'barlo. Tell him in detail what happened here."

The younger Yollin nodded and left Gel'Blistaal to his thoughts. The pair had been let past the local and Federation cordons after greasing the palms of a few guards. Afterward, he'd try to bribe the investigator heading the interrogations of the embassy staff to let him into their jail cells. After some brief words, he'd leave a cell full of dead men behind. His job was as much to capture and kill Tc'aarlat and his Shadows as it was to protect the family and its secrets at all costs.

However, Hermes' intel and accompanying warning still echoed through his head. He needed to get ahead of the Shadows, or else everything would be lost.

The Roosting Raal, Brig

A bucket of ice water was their morning wake-up call. Killeg squeaked and rolled out of his bunk as Gruff sat up in the bunk above in surprise and discomfort, only to strike his head against the ceiling.

"Wakey, wakey. The boss wants to see you two," their Yollin prison guard told them as he dropped the bucket on the floor and made for the door of the cell. Opening it, he waved for the two of them to follow. Without much of a choice, they both followed him out of the cell.

Killeg was breathing rapidly as the guard led them out of the grimy confines of the brig. Hanlo whispered sharply to him, "Would you quit that?"

"Quit what?" Killeg retorted as he clutched himself.

"That obnoxious breathing!" Gruff hissed at his former colleague.

"We are about to be thrown into a black hole, and this is what is bothering you?" Killeg's rebuttal could no longer even be called a whisper.

Gruff turned and jabbed a finger into Killeg's face. "I don't want to go down a black hole with you breathing up my neck!"

"Shut up, both of you!" The guard barked as he hit Gruff on the back of the head with a firm open palm slap.

The accountant clutched the back of his head. "Oww."

Killeg chuckled. "Heh. Serves you right." The guard delivered an open-hand slap to the back of the small Alstublaft's head. "OW!"

"I said, shut up. Come on, the boss is waiting." The guard forced them along the corridor.

Leaving the grimy brig behind, they entered a sleek and practical engineering deck where the walls were covered in various computer and mechanical systems manned by a few engineers in orange jumpsuits. After ascending a staircase, the party was brought to the Don's living quarters. The change was apparent immediately, with red velvet curtains draping the walls and oil paintings in intricate gold frames displaying professional portraits of the Gan'barlo line. Gruff's and Killeg's gazes wandered over the opulence, so neither of them was paying attention and Hanlo slammed into the guard as he opened a wooden double door. When Killeg hit Hanlo, the three of them stumbled through the open door and crashed on the polished white tile floor.

"This is how you get prisoners, Je'tor?" a booming voice from the other end of the room hissed viciously.

Killeg looked up from the bottom of the pile to see Don Gan'barlo staring down at him with contempt in his eyes. He was seated behind a large dark wood desk carved with symmetrical patterns of ancient Yollin script. The accountant bowed his head in deference as Gruff and the guard, Je'tor, got up from the pile. The guard plucked the Alstublaft by the back of what was left of his suit collar and placed him on his feet next to Hanlo.

"I... Err, sorry, sir. It won't happen again," the guard stammered, looking as terrified as the two accountants. He stepped back to the doors and stood to the side of them, stock-still. His back was as straight as an arrow.

The Don's eyes were dark with rage, but it wasn't directed entirely at the guard. He turned to the two accountants and spread his arms out. "Mr. Hanlo, Mr. Dirk'sen, it is so good to see you both again."

"T-the p-p-pleasure is all ours, s-sir," Killeg stammered, his voice cracking with fear. Gruff meanwhile facepalmed.

"Right. The Don grabbed a case at the edge of his desk and opened it. From inside he withdrew a cigar and lighter. He placed the cigar in his mouth and flipped the lighter on, then lit the end of the cigar. As the end of it caught flame, he took two deep puffs before blowing a cloud of smoke out from between his mandibles into the air over his head.

Killeg and Gruff both struggled not to cough, their eyes watering at the burning sensation the smoke caused. "I've brought you two up here for some financial advice."

"We'd be happy to help answer any questions for you, sir." Killeg now facepalmed for his words, the willingness to please a natural response on his part.

Gruff came to the rescue. "What my colleague means, sir, is we'd like some guarantees about our survival before we enter back into your service."

Another puff on the cigar. "I'll promise to postpone killin' ya both if you answer some questions for me. Final offer."

Gruff looked at Killeg, who was ashen pale, and he nodded. Gruff spoke on their behalf, "Deal."

"If I were to lose my investments and revenue from the project on Balgaria, how could I keep my organization solvent?" The Don removed the cigar from his lips as he leaned forward and rested his chin on the back of his hands.

The two accountants blinked. "You'd be screwed," Gruff said flatly.

Killeg added, "You'd have to consider some serious downsizing and reduce your monthly expenditure to only what was necessary as you seek a loan to begin a new venture for the organization."

The Don nodded thoughtfully. "Thank you for the advice." He reached into a drawer on his right and pulled out an oversized silver pistol. Both of the accountants shut their eyes tight, awaiting the inevitable end.

Two shots rang out.

Killeg and Gruff opened their eyes slowly. In Don

Gan'barlo's hand, the smoking pistol was leveled toward the back of the room. Both accountants turned and they saw the guard the Don had called Je'tor sliding down the wall as he clutched his chest, where two holes poured blood. Gasping, the guard looked into space with wide eyes.

"I thought I'd get started on the downsizing." The Don cracked a mad grin, his mandibles spreading wide in a show of intimidation. "I'd like you two to get to work on creating a detailed report on the best ways to downsize. In exchange, I won't kill you. Deal?"

Both accountants nodded vigorously.

"Good, now get the hell out of here! My assistant outside will take care of you," the Don roared as he slammed the butt of the pistol on the top of his desk. The two accountants scurried out as fast as their legs could take them. The Don then sat there alone, smiling to himself. *If Tc'aarlat wanted war, he'd give 'im war.*

10

Miseria, Security Perimeter of Trejion Prime

The exterior wall of the city of Trejion Prime was being bombarded, not by the enemy, but by the indomitable forces of nature. A massive dust storm had struck over the last three days. Lieutenant Kall Eradea peeked his head over the upper parapet to peer out into the wasteland beyond, only to be buffeted by the storm, his mouth now full of sand and his eyes full of dust. As he ducked back down into cover, he swore profusely. The soldiers of his platoon crowded around him on the wall's covered walkway.

"Sir, are you sure you don't want to put on your helmet?" Corporal Luce Valtor asked from under the sealed security of his full helmet.

"And hide my heroic visage?" Lieutenant Eradea snapped indignantly at his underling. "Bah, never. I'd rather die from having an acid launcher blown into my face or a spike grenade shatter just an inch away from my nose than hide my face like a coward. A coward like you,

Corporal." He gestured at the gray skin of his head—the wide eyes and fold of sinuous strings that served as Miserians' mouths for speaking. All things considered, Lieutenant Eradea wasn't a particularly handsome man for his species. For one, his eyes were too small. They were perhaps big by human standards, but beady and creepy to other Miserians. "That's why I am an officer, and you, Corporal? Well, you are just a corporal."

"Sir, I think you are going to want to see this." A soldier monitoring the scanner array waved at Lieutenant Eradea.

The lieutenant strode over and peered down at the black and green screen with narrowed big beady eyes. "What am I looking at, private?"

"It's a reading, sir," the private answered and saluted half-assedly, as much as the decorum of the chain of command demanded.

"I know it's a fucking reading! What is it?" Lieutenant Eradea snapped at the private.

"It's an incoming landship, sir. Carrier class, I reckon, by the looks of it," Corporal Valtor answered from behind the lieutenant.

"You can read this indecipherable machine?" Lieutenant Eradea waved his hand to indicate the sensor array monitor.

"Standard training, sir," Corporal Valtor replied in a flat tone.

"Don't tell me about standard training. I wrote the book on standard training!" Lieutenant Eradea pointed a finger at his corporal. "I could have you written up for this...this insubordination."

"And have me demoted and shipped to a penal unit,

away from your brilliant command. How would I ever cope?" The sarcasm oozed from Corporal Valtor's voice. Lieutenant Eradea's eye twitched. The man looked like he was about to pop a blood vessel on his skull. "Sir, would you like to alert section command?"

"Don't tell me how to do my job, Corporal!" Lieutenant Eradea snapped as he turned back to the monitor of the sensor array. "Private, send a message to section command that we have an incoming carrier landship, most likely Coldists." The private nodded as he turned a few knobs and began speaking the lieutenant's message into his comm.

The wall shook violently, forcing many troops to press themselves against something or fall to the ground. Lieutenant Eradea dove to the ground and cowered in the fetal position.

Corporal Valtor looked up at the still-swinging lights. "I believe they are bombing us, sir."

Lieutenant Eradea had just begun to stand up and dust himself off when a second quake rocked the wall and its occupants. He dove back to the ground instantly. "Well, go do something about it, then! I have to stay here and coordinate our relief from section command."

"A wise choice, sir." There was no mirth in the corporal's tone. "Troopers of the fourth and fifth squad, on me. The rest of you, take up defensive positions, just like we trained for." The soldiers all saluted Corporal Valtor and went to their designated positions. He turned to the private sitting at the monitor. "Private Wilks, stay on the sensor array and communications and keep the lieutenant up to date with everything." Private Wilks gave a curt nod before turning back to the monitor to track the enemy's movement.

Miseria, Outside the Security Perimeter of Trejion Prime, LS *Blizzard*, Bridge

Ensign Callot Ionoway reported from his station, "Colonel, all twenty-four strike craft have been launched. Only six down from the storm."

Colonel Gant Oopley, his fingers steepled, nodded to the ensign. "Resistance?"

"No, sir," the ensign answered. "You were right, sir. The storm obscured our advance."

"Caught flat-footed." The colonel stood up from his command seat and strode across the bridge to stand in front of the bridge window, his hands gripped behind his back. Beyond the thick glass of the window, nothing was visible through the torrent of dust and debris swirling in the torrential winds. "Our intel was exact, and my plan was perfect. With their land fleets occupied in the Axlen Wastes, there is nothing that can prevent us from taking Trejion Prime." He held out an open hand and clenched it. "Those 78th bastards will submit to our superior temperature, and they will know the gentle touch of the cold." He turned to the bridge crew, who all cheered, their pride for their chosen temperature swelling.

He was satisfied with his display, certain it would inflate his image as the underlings gossiped. An officer's career could make or break on the hearsay of their soldiers, and Colonel Oopley was a master at crafting it. This stunt on Trejion Prime might even get him a promotion to Field General. Then he'd never have to serve in a field again, while still holding great power. The war never ended, and thus, the military was always in control. It was strange how situations worked out like that; convince a populace of any zealotry, and you could mold them in your desired image.

He was still internally philosophizing as he got back into his chair. A shout came from Ensign Ionoway. "Contact! We've stirred the hornet's nest, sir. Wall emplacements and garrison troops are returning fire. They've probably already called for backup."

Colonel Oopley smirked the fold of vocal cords. "Launch the new toys. They'll begin the assault on the wall."

"Aye, aye, sir!" Ensign Ionoway began relaying the command to the hangar bay, where crews of freshly trained pilots waited, ready to deploy the latest weapon in the Cold Coalition's arsenal. They had been a gift from a benevolent arms dealer. The basic rule of black market economics was, the first taste was always free; everything after was pure business.

Miseria, Southwest Section Command of Trejion Prime

"Sir, we have a pressing incursion in Subsection Theta!" Field General Muffa Carle's Adjutant, Misken Leff, called as he burst into the general's office. He was out of breath, sweat stains appearing on the white collar of his uniform. "An enemy carrier has entered—"

"Zone One." General Carle was pouring himself a crystal glass of brown liquor from an equally expensive crystal bottle. "I know, Misken. I know. Take a seat, have a drink." He reached into his desk and withdrew a second glass, then pushed the filled glass across his desk.

"S-s-sir, should you really be drinking? We are under attack," Misken asked as he lowered himself hesitantly into the seat across from his commanding officer.

"Yes, yes. And we were under attack by the Cold Coalition last week, and the 78th the week before that and the week before that." General Carle poured a second glass for himself and held it up, waiting for Misken to clink glasses. Misken capitulated and the ring of the two glasses echoed throughout the decorated office, bouncing off the hanging war trophies, medals, and framed pictures showing the general's life and career. "My point is, I've been drinking since yesterday. No, wait, my point was something else." The slur in his voice was increasingly noticeable.

"But, sir, it's 1700 hours." He leaned in to slowly lower General Carle's arm. Misken realized the general probably didn't need any more drinks.

"Party-pooper." General Carle's head dropped. "My point was that they have attacked and attacked week after week for twelve years now."

"Sixteen, sir," Misken corrected.

"Sixteen? Shit..." The general belched, pressing a hand against his gut and burping through his nostrils. The belch was several octaves higher-pitched than a typical human one. "There are four years I don't remember." He shrugged the thought off, assuming the four years weren't important if he'd not remembered them. "It's all just so pointless. We fight all the damn time. Well, I don't fight; I just send wave upon wave of men to die for the cause. It's all a load of shit." General Carle opened his desk and began digging through it for something buried.

"General, you should get some rest. Come on, I'll get you some food and water and..." Misken's eyes widened as he saw the compact vaporizer weighing down the general's steady hand.

"Sir!" Misken jumped out of his seat and held his hands up. "Please put down the gun."

"What, this? It's not for you." General Carle began to laugh as he indicated the gun and then Misken, shaking his head. "You thought this was for you?" Still chuckling through a smile on his sinuous mouth fold, he aimed the pistol at Misken and made a gunshot noise. Misken's gray face paled as the general continued to laugh. "No, it isn't for you." He breathed and wiped a tear from the corner of his eye. "It's for me. You're in charge of the Sector Command. Congratulations on the promotion." With that, General Muffa Carle saluted as the gun went into his mouth. He pulled the trigger.

A burst of superheated air blew out the back of the general's head, searing a clear hole through it. The general's scalp burst into flames as the flesh melted from the hole. His eyes poured out of their sockets. Misken stood frozen in place as he looked upon the corpse of his former superior. With shaking hands, Misken grabbed one glass of brown liquor after the other and downed them, gulping them through the food and liquid pocket on his neck. Leaving the general's corpse, he went to find the other officers, and explain what happened.

. . .

Miseria, Outside the Security Perimeter of Trejion Prime

"Corporal, Corporal!" A trooper waved as he ran down the length of the interior wall.

"Good gods, trooper, spit it out, or I'll stick my fingers down your throat and make you spit it out." Corporal Valtor turned from the conversation he was having to look the panting trooper up and down.

"It's the carrier. A...platoon...of strange land vehicles has launched from its...hull, and are... Does anyone have a canteen?" The trooper Corporal Valtor was talking to handed him a sloshing canteen. He began chugging.

"You can drink when you're dead, Trooper! Get on with it!" Corporal Valtor barked.

The trooper dropped the canteen, much to the chagrin of the one who had handed it to him. He wiped his lips with the back of his hand and said, "They have some sort of new form of power armor, a lot bigger."

"That's moronic." Corporal Valtor tossed his head back. "What's the point of making a bigger suit of power armor? It could still be shredded by any anti-tank equipment, and couldn't go as fast as a tracked tank."

"Well, they *are* tracked, sir," the trooper added. "They've got sets of tracks on their feet." Lifting his booted foot, he pointed at the sole.

"That's still the stupidest thing I've ever heard." Corporal Valtor remarked. "Lead the way, trooper. Come on, men, we've got some tracked walking machines to blow up." He waved for the other soldiers to follow him.

. . .

In Orbit Over Miseria, ICS *Fortitude*

"We're beginning our descent into the world's atmosphere," Jack stated as he rubbed his eyes and yawned. The ship began to kick and rock. "Solo, did you hail for landing permission?" There was no response, and the ship's descent grew rougher. Adina laser-focused on the controls as Tc'aarlat gripped his chair tightly. "Solo?" The ship kicked sharply, rocking Jack against his seat's harness. He grunted.

Tc'aarlat opened his eyes, still holding on tightly. He blinked at the console in front of him and leaned in to get a better view. "Jack, Adina, incoming fire!"

"Solo, evasive action!" Again no response to Jack's request. "Uh, Solo?"

Adina continued focusing on piloting the ship through the ground fire. She was glad neither Jack nor Tc'aarlat could see the guilty look on her face. Although she'd gotten good at flying the ICS *Fortitude,* the blanket of autocannon fire and exploding rockets would have been too much for even the most skilled of pilots. She was running out of options for maneuvers.

"Solo, where are you?" Tc'aarlat pressed against his harness. "We could really use your help!"

It was too late.

The explosion caused the ship to spin out of control, one of the main rear engines blown out. As it spun, the planet's gravity combined with the faltering artificial gravity of the *Fortitude* pummeled the crew with g-forces that nearly made the three of them pass out.

"Well, we're stoned," Tc'aarlat said flatly.

"What the hell does that mean?" Twisting in his chair,

its squeaking hinge drowned out by the roar of the vessel falling, Jack stared at Tc'aarlat as best he could, finding it difficult to keep his head from bouncing in every direction. It was amazing his neck hadn't snapped yet.

Tc'aarlat was having much the same problem. "You know, like we're all going to die." He shrugged.

Wincing, Adina shouted at the pair of bickering fools. "Stop fighting, you two! This isn't the time! He means..." Desperately, Adina pulled back on the controls, having to focus her entire attention. Her teeth were gritted.

"What the bloody hell does getting high have to do with dying?" By shouting at Tc'aarlat, Jack was clearly trying to be elsewhere—anywhere but plummeting to his death in a fiery metal box.

"He means...*DOOMED!*" Adina screamed as the ground flew up to meet the front of the ICS *Fortitude*.

11

"Great shot, trooper!" Sergeant Vilco slapped the shoulder of the gunner, Private Kerenso.

Private Kerenso blinked at the flaming ball. A trail of smoke and fire streaking behind it created a smoky rainbow of black, red, and blue as the engine blew out. "Thank you, sir. I didn't think I had it in me, to be honest." The twin-linked autocannon turret's last salvo, obliterating one of the alien cargo ship's rear engines. As soon as the unknown ship had come into sensor range, it was flagged by both sides, and gunners on the land carrier and wall had unloaded on the target without much provocation, per orders from higher up.

The turret was an open-topped emplacement, one of many covering the starboard side of the land carrier of the Coldists. A canvas covering was stretched over the rooftop to protect the crew from the harsh storm the carrier had flown through, to little effect. Most of the crewmen were in a slowdown, working at a snail's pace to protest being stationed outside, and the deck officers had already executed three crews for disobedience. Of course, that was the official story. The equally likely probability was that in the harsh storm, work had been slowed. Private Kerenso and Sergeant Vilco hadn't minded too much. They'd requisitioned two pairs of goggles, and unlike many other crews, they were lucky enough to receive five pairs of them. Such was the way with armies, or at least the armies of Miseria.

After wiping the lenses of the goggles over his eyes with a dirty rag, Sergeant Vilco began surveying the firing arc of the turret. One pair of goggles was resting on his forehead and another around his neck; both had one lens cracked from flying debris, so he'd been forced to use his last pair. "There's nothing in our firing arc. Private Kerenso, do you know what that means?"

"Break time?" a strange, gruff voice said from behind the two gunners. They both snapped their heads around. Behind them, a Shrillexian stared at them with his hands on his hips. He was standing on a sloped portion of armor just above the emplacement. The Shrillexian's body was encased in articulated maroon battle armor of ceramic polymer. He had a pair of pistols at his side in black leather holsters. Around his neck was a tan scarf with some of his face spikes peeking through the cloth, and over his eyes was a pair of goggles with one cracked lens. "Don't let me interrupt your smoke break or snack or whatever." He held up open palms as the two gunners tensed. "I've got some free time before I kill you, now that you've shot down my contacts." The Shrillexian's last words were growled. "So enjoy your time, and don't reach for those weapons." They didn't listen; they never listened. Shi'Tan's pistols flashed into his hands before the gunner's paws reached their guns.

Jumping down into the turret's open-top compartment, he ducked his head under the canvas. He crouched down by the corpse of Sergeant Vilco and removed the pair of uncracked goggles from his head. Tossing away the cracked pair, he put on the looted pair. Shi'Tan wasn't put off by the concept of looting, especially in battle. The late sergeant wasn't going to be needing them anymore, so why not get the goggles into the hands of someone who didn't have a bullet in their kidney?

As he stood up, Shi'Tan peered into the sky, the storm making visibility difficult. Spotting the smoke trail of the ICS *Fortitude*, he leaped over the side of the turret and descended the tiered side of the landship.

Miseria, Security Perimeter of Trejion Prime

The rockets flew wide of the humanoid mech armor as it showed off its maneuverability, ducking and dodging as though it were a graceful dancer with an incredibly flexible body. Cursing, Corporal Valtor dropped the shoulder launcher into the sand and shouted, *"MOVE!"* He turned on his toes and began sprinting back to the wall access hatch they had come through. The soldiers with him did the same, abandoning their spent shoulder-held rocket launchers. As he ran, Corporal Valtor withdrew a pair of smoke grenades from his bandolier, pulled the pins, and tossed them behind him, trying desperately to give his men some cover, for all the good it probably would do if these secret weapons were equipped with any kind of motion-sensitive sensors.

The forward trench line was already breaking under the assault of these new Coldist war machines, their energy rifles shredding flesh and concrete emplacements alike as the platoons in the trenches broke and were routed. Corporal Valtor had hoped he'd be able to knock these mechs down with one bold action, showing them for the paper tigers he'd assumed they were. Whenever either the Coldists or the 78th unveiled a new secret weapon, the results were often underwhelming or downright embarrassing after the initial battlefield shock. Miserian researchers were completely disconnected from the frontlines, creating all kinds of monstrosities that fit needs not found anywhere on Miseria. Corporal Valtor assumed these mechs would be no different, but as he and the hapless troopers ahead of him soon learned, he was dead wrong. It only seemed sensible that they'd work. What kind of people would pour significant amounts of money and resources into military R&D that barely worked?

Keeping his pace so he was just behind the other troopers, Corporal Valtor watched in horror as a stray beam obliterated a pair of troopers ahead of him, Privates Lantel Ioeff and Oklen Prencep. Valtor didn't look forward to alerting their next of kin on behalf of the lieutenant. Valtor was also not happy with losing his comm operator, Private Prencep. There were just a hundred paces left. He could hear the servos of those fourteen-foot-tall behemoths getting closer, but he didn't dare turn around. The others were in, and they had the wall to protect him. *Maybe dying wouldn't be so bad?* he thought, hearing one of the mechs no more than ten feet behind him. *I'd not have to do the lieutenant's laundry again.* For a moment, none of it seemed so bad. He closed his eyes and waited for death.

Miseria, Outside the Security Perimeter of Trejion Prime, ICS *Fortitude*, Bridge

The world had been black for what seemed like an eternity.

First to awaken from the impact was Tc'aarlat. On opening his eyes, there was only more darkness. "OH, FUCK! I've turned a blind eye!" His hands ran over his mandibles. There was a groan in the darkness. "Jack? Adina? Are you alive?"

"That's not..." Jack wheezed weakly from the darkness.

"Jack, you're alive!" Tc'aarlat shouted excitedly as he threw his arms up in the darkness. He hadn't entirely accounted for the overhead consoles, so he cursed as he withdrew his hand.

"Not what the idiom means." Jack was struggling to catch his breath. His head felt like a continuously tightening vice grip was clamped around his skull. "You..." He coughed up something he hoped wasn't important.

Then the shouting began. *"YOU LOCUST-FACED FAILURE OF AN ORATOR!"*

"How dare you insult a blind Yollin! Have you no empathy?" Tc'aarlat moaned.

"You're not blind, the power is offline." Adina's voice came from the front of the dark bridge. She tried to quell Tc'aarlat's fears, but her clarification only raised even more. She was fiddling with something as she said, "I need to activate the emergency power, then we can get outside to survey the damage."

Trying to release his seat harness, Tc'aarlat muttered, "Are we sure going out into that chaos is really a good idea? I'm shocked we're not eating up daisies."

"We're sitting ducks here. Out there didn't look good, but it's better than getting blasted from outside and never seeing it coming." Jack's fingers nervously tapped the armrest of his command chair.

A flashlight clicked on, illuminating Adina's face and she blinked, briefly blinded by the light. Her eyes were already used to the complete darkness of the bridge. "Way ahead of you, Jack." Adina turned the flashlight around and began searching under the console.

"What's the plan, then? I doubt we can take on two whole armies on our own, no matter how many jet fighters I shoot down." Tc'aarlat stood up from his seat and began walking in the direction of Adina. He stepped out cautiously, trying desperately not to trip on some unseen obstacle. "Better question is, why didn't Solo respond to you, Jack?"

"It's definitely concerning." Jack rubbed the budding beard on his chin.

With trepidation, Adina mumbled from under the console, "Yeah, real strange of her."

"Any chance we can get it back online with the emergency systems?" Jack asked, standing up as well and began walking over to where Adina worked at the front of the bridge.

"She, not it," Adina hissed as she tried to balance the

flashlight between her shoulder and neck. "And yes, it should bring her back online."

"She?" Jack asked. Just then, the toe of his boot caught on something that had come loose in the crash. He fell flat on his face and cursed as he rubbed at his stinging nose.

"You should watch where you step," Tc'aarlat offered. Jack grumbled at the words of warning and glared at Tc'aarlat in the half-light. Tc'aarlat raised his hands in defense. "All right then, just advice. Almost done, Adina?"

Before Tc'aarlat finished his sentence, the red emergency lights came on, casting everything in a lurid blood color. "Done," Adina squeaked as she wiggled her way out from underneath the console. Standing up, she began typing on her console and opened various interfaces for the ship's systems. "Doors should work now, and we've got short-range communications and exterior cameras. Uhhh, that's about it."

"What about Solo?" Tc'aarlat asked over Adina's shoulder.

Her fingers paused. Shaking her head, Adina said, "There's no response from her."

"Shit," Jack muttered. He rubbed the bridge of his nose between his thumb and index finger. "We need to get a sitrep on what is going on outside. Pull up some of the exterior cameras, Adina."

Adina rolled her eyes. "I'm not your EI." Jack flushed and whispered an apology. However, Adina opened the exterior camera interfaces and clicked the main prow camera. The only response was static. "That's not good." She frowned and clicked the next camera, the port prow camera. It was no good; there was only more static.

Tc'aarlat and Jack were frowning now too. "Maybe this one." More static. She continued clicking through cameras, and the results were all the same. Clicking the topside swivel camera, she sighed in relief as the image came through, albeit with some minor distortion.

On the small monitor, the crew of the *Fortitude* watched as Adina moved the camera with the keyboard's arrow keys. It was slow to swivel, and it was difficult to see anything due to the sandstorm buffeting the camera.

"Wait, stop there." Tc'aarlat held up a hand as he leaned in close. "Look at that. Did you see it?" He pointed to the corner of the screen, where a blue flash had been for a split second. "Turn the camera on that."

Nodding, Adina shifted the camera to focus on the location Tc'aarlat had pointed to. There were more blue flashes—bolts of lightning striking the wasteland's desolate earth.

"Are we in an electrical storm?" Jack's head cocked in confusion. "I didn't see any in the weather forecasts." The other two did not look at him; their eyes were glued to the screen. Jack turned with a raised eyebrow. "What is it?" He pushed Tc'aarlat to the side so he could see what was on the screen.

The arcs of lightning were flying from the underbelly of a metal behemoth. Across its surface, it was bristling with gun emplacements.

"How the hell does it fly? It's monstrous!" Adina scanned the length of the landship with the arrow keys.

"Flying," Tc'aarlat muttered. He slapped his forehead with some force. "*OH, SHIT! MIST! THE CHICKS!*" He shoved past Jack, nearly knocking him over, and ran out of the bridge. The hydraulic vacuum-sealed door at the rear of the bridge, normally quick, edged open slowly as Tc'aarlat approached. "I'm coming, Mist!" he shouted as he squeezed through the half-open door.

After watching Tc'aarlat leave, Jack and Adina turned to each other. "What now, Captain?" Adina asked as she slouched in her seat with her arms crossed.

He started to say something, but then he shook his head. "Original plan is still good. We arm up and sally forth to face the enemy."

"Aye, aye, Captain." Adina gave a loose salute after she jumped to her feet. The two left through the rear bridge door, now fully open. As they walked down the corridor, there was Tc'aarlat standing in his cabin with Mist and her babies. He was cooing a soft melody to soothe their anxieties. Smiling, Adina called to Tc'aarlat, "I always knew you were a softy."

Realizing he was being watched, Tc'aarlat stood, walked to the door, and aggressively pressed the Close button. The hydraulics squealed and slowly slid the door shut. Jack and Adina stood in the hallway, chuckling at the glowering Yollin.

After the door finally shut, Jack yelled through it, "Don't take too long. We're gonna need you to shoot that damn ship down, killer!"

12

Miseria, Security Perimeter of Trejion Prime

Corporal Valtor opened his eyes, amazed to be alive. He turned to see the mech rising behind him. Attached to its hip was a kind of grappling hook launcher. The cord had launched to connect with the top of the wall and a winch was pulling the mech upwards, the tracked legs running up the wall to ease the ascent. All along the wall, the other mechs were doing the same. They fired their energy weapons as they ascended, demolishing the artillery and gun positions protruding from the wall. Blinking, Corporal Valtor turned back and saw the service door his comrades were waving for him to enter. They'd held the door open, hoping he'd make it, and just the corporal's luck, he had. *I have more laundry in my future.* Corporal Valtor thought as he jogged through the service door. *Oh, well, I suppose it could be worse.*

"Corporal!" a trooper shouted from within the wall. "Lieutenant Eradea is on the comm looking for you!"

Corporal Valtor grunted. "I need to stop tempting fate by spreading my damn mouth fold."

"Sir?" The trooper waited for the corporal's response.

"Never mind. Lead me to a comm unit. Our comm trooper was vaporized, along with the portable radio set." Before he left, Valtor turned to the squad who'd followed him outside. "At ease, everyone. Wait here for further instructions." Corporal Valtor turned to follow the trooper who had given him the message. They saluted each other, and the trooper led Valtor to a wall-mounted comm unit. The trooper stood next to it, waiting for Valtor to finish. Picking up the earpiece, he typed in his ID code and put it over his ear flaps. "Corporal Valtor here, go ahead."

"Ahhh, Corporal, you certainly took your sweet time, but I should expect no less from an unrefined enlisted." The lieutenant's tone was condescending, as always.

"As you say, sir. We could all benefit from your fine example of diligence." Valtor's tone was flat, as was usual when dealing with his direct superior. "How can I serve, sir?"

"Well, Corporal, had you been actively directing the battle as I have, you'd see the group of armored mechs scaling the wall. I'd like you to deal with them before they get over it."

"On it, sir." The trooper standing next to him was looking at Corporal Valtor in surprise, having overheard enough of the conversation. Valtor shrugged and continued speaking. "Has Sector Command gotten in contact?"

"They have indeed, Corporal." Lieutenant Eradea

yawned after the sentence, and then continued, "Field General Muffa Carle is dead."

"I am sorry, sir." Corporal Valtor's back was stock-straight as he talked over the communicator earpiece. "Enemy assassin? More importantly, who is now in command?"

"No, slain by his own hand. As for who is in charge now, Adjutant Misken Leff was named the general's successor." There was venom in Lieutenant Eradea's voice. "Damn upstart, stepping over the necessary chain of command." When Lieutenant Eradea described anyone stepping over the "necessary chain of command," he was expressing personal envy for having been passed up for a promotion. It was a common complaint since Lieutenant Eradea had been a lieutenant for his full ten years in the service.

"It's a crime of military structure, sir." Corporal Valtor confirmed the lieutenant's dissatisfaction in the same flat tone. During the ten-year length of Corporal Valtor's career, he'd been a corporal for nine and a half under Eradea's stalwart command.

"Regardless, Corporal, I expect you to deal with those mechs before the reinforcements arrive. I mentioned the reinforcements, did I not?" the lieutenant added lazily, as though he'd already lost interest in the comm call.

The trooper's eyes widened with a glimmer of hope. Valtor continued, "No, I don't believe you had, sir."

"I believe I did, Corporal." Lieutenant Eradea was indignant in his chiding. "You need to be a better listener." He let out a long sigh. "Oh, well, I will repeat myself this once. Reinforcements are en route from Sector Command.

They are some kind of experimental weapon. I am not privy to the details. Regardless, I want the mech suits dealt with before the reinforcements arrive."

"Thank you for the information, sir. I'll do my best." Valtor nodded and then saluted instinctively, as though Lieutenant Eradea were in front of him.

"I have no doubt. Dismissed, Corporal," Lieutenant Eradea said, and then the comm went dead.

"Why do you put up with that bastard?" the trooper stammered to Corporal Valtor as he hung up the earpiece.

"Excuse me, Private?" Valtor wasn't upset with the trooper. He was more confused by the question.

"Err, the lieutenant... How long have you followed him?" the trooper clarified, still unsure if he should continue this line of questioning.

"Ahhh. Well, that is an interesting question, Private. What's your name?" Corporal Valtor waved his hand to indicate the private to follow as he walked away from the wall-mounted comm unit.

"Private Beltz Messon, sir," Beltz stammered as he fell into step behind Corporal Valtor.

"Can the 'sir' crap. Just call me Valtor. I ain't no officer, and I don't like being referred to as such." Corporal Valtor shook his head and then spat on the ground. "I take it you haven't seen many officers in your time with the army." He looked Private Messon up and down. "No, of course, you haven't. Look at you, still a fresh and shiny boot."

"A-a shiny boot, sir? Er, Valtor," Beltz corrected, trying to keep up with the corporal.

"Aye, a shiny boot. Fresh meat. A wide-eyed new recruit who hasn't seen the shit the army has to offer. Don't worry, you'll get familiar with what it's like, especially in this mess of a war." Valtor shrugged. "I've seen a lot of officers in my time with the army, and never have I known an officer as perfect as Lieutenant Eradea."

Private Messon stopped in his tracks and blinked. "Because he is a good and inspiring leader?"

A smile cracked Valtor's lips for the first time all day. "That's the funniest thing I've heard all month, Beltz. No, Eradea is neither of those things. In fact, quite the opposite. He's cowardly, incompetent, lazy, and completely uninspiring. The reason Lieutenant Eradea is the best damn officer is that he doesn't get in our way."

Miseria, Outside the Security Perimeter of Trejion Prime, ICS *Fortitude*, Brig

As Adina stepped down the stairs, she was sure she had left her body armor somewhere in the brig. When she reached the last few steps, a voice called to her from one of the cells in the brig. "Is that a new friend?"

"Who's there?" Adina barked into the red half-light, her hand resting on the holster of her Jean Dukes Special.

"I'm Gunth'calaat." The voice was simple and friendly. A large hand protruded from between the bars of one of the cells. It was a Yollin hand. "And in the cell next to me is my friend and roommate, Ben'delon."

Another Yollin hand waved from the far cell. "Hello."

It was an awkward moment for Adina, as she tried to understand why two Yollins were locked up in their brig. Then she remembered. "You're the two thugs we captured on Balgaria. Shit, I forgot about you two." Adina approached the pair of cells, seeing the two Yollins in relatively good condition, a handful of cuts and bruises still marring various parts of their bodies from the concussive blast they had been caught in the day before.

"It's okay, Miss," the one who called himself Gunth'-calaat said. He was stocky and burly; short for a Yollin too, being several inches shorter than Tc'aarlat but no less wide. "We were mighty bad, but after watching the program for the past...Ben'delon, how long's it been?" Gunth'calaat peered at the other cell.

"Five days, give or take," the one called Ben'delon said. His voice was a bit more nasal, his build was slimmer, and he was taller than his neighbor. "Course, I couldn't tell."

"It's been getting worse down here ever since the nice lady disappeared. First, we lost the program." Gunth'calaat scratched his nose.

"Then there was the crash," Ben'dolen added lazily as he left the bars to take a seat on his bed.

"Oh, yeah, can't forget that. Thought we were done for." With arms crossed and eyes closed, Gunth'calaat nodded.

"'Nice lady?'" What these two had said confused Adina just a bit. "Oh, you mean Solo!" The well of guilt at Solo's sudden absence was close to bringing her to begging forgiveness of almost anyone tangentially related to the dilemma. "When did you last hear from her?"

"About five hours ago, I think," Ben'dolen said as he stretched out on the cot in his cell.

"You think?" Adina's tone was harsh and demanding.

"Does it look like I have a watch?" Ben'dolen tapped his bare wrist. "Besides, the program was the only thing helping me keep time."

"What the hell is this program you two keep talking about?" Adina was getting frustrated with the pair, and she knew it showed.

"Why, *Sesame Street!*" Gunth'calaat's smile beamed.

"Of course, Jack would," Adina said to herself.

"You've seen it?" With his head pressed to the cell's bars, Gunth'calaat was visibly excited, his mandibles spread out like a hug. "It's the best show I've ever seen, and it's not even on holovid."

"He's obsessed with it," Ben'dolen said from his reclined position, his hands now holding the back of his head.

"You said you really liked it too!" Gunth'calaat called to his compatriot.

"Blurt out more things I said in confidence to one of our captors, why don't ya?" Ben'dolen shot back as he sat up in his cot.

Gunth'calaat shook his head and looked in the direction of the neighboring cell. "It's nothing to be ashamed of. She seems nice for a captor, and I bet she likes *Sesame Street* too. Don't you, miss?" The burly criminal's smile was innocent. It was hard to believe the Yollin had wished anyone ill just a few days prior.

"I do. It still plays on Earth to this day," Adina told the innocent-looking Yollin thug.

Gunth'calaat nearly jumped for joy at her pronouncement. "You hear that, Ben? We got way more *Sesame Street* to watch!"

The other Yollin had stood up from his bed and now walked up to the bars. "That's if we make it out of here alive."

"Oh." Gunth'calaat visibly deflated, his mandibles

drooping as his back slouched. His temples rested on the bars of the cell.

"Listen, we have to get out of here, and well, it doesn't seem right leaving you both here to die." Both Yollins were looking at Adina expectantly, their lives in her hands. She took a deep breath. "You two come with us, and if you promise not to betray us or kill us or anything like that, I'll make sure both of you can watch as much *Sesame Street* as you want."

His eyes wide with appreciation, Gunth'calaat said, "You'd do that for us? You're a real kind human, Miss."

Even Ben'dolen was smiling. "Aye. Miss what?"

"Choudhury." Unlocking the cells, she made her way over to offer an open palm handshake to Gunth'calaat. "Adina Choudhury."

Miseria, Outside the Security Perimeter of Trejion Prime

Squinting through the freshly cracked pair of goggles over his eyes, Shi'Tan looked around for any sight of his quarry. Spotting the downed ICS *Fortitude* had been easier up on the landship, when he'd been able to see the trail of smoke through breaks in the storm caused by its electromagnetic field, the same field that allowed the ship to hover. On the ground, it was different; visibility was reduced to near zero, and Shi'Tan had to rely on an educated guess. Having walked for some twenty-five minutes, he was beginning to worry he had accidentally missed the crashed cargo ship, and that its wreckage was long behind him. It was as these doubts were settling on him the toe of his hard-tipped boot struck a hunk of twisted metal. He kicked it over, and scrawled across it was the letters "orti."

"Well, that's convenient." He looked up from the twisted scrap and continued walking. More hunks of debris were lying around, traces of their crash no longer visible in the earth from the blasting winds. Finally, the ICS *Fortitude* lay before him, the hull still in one piece, the damage localized to the rear engines. He smiled under the bandanna covering his mouth. *Perhaps they survived after all,* he thought. Whoever had been piloting the ship had done the best they could.

Approaching the ship, he withdrew his knife from a hip scabbard. Tossing the knife, he flipped it into the air to swipe it back into his hand, his grip reversed. He raised the hilt of the knife and beat against the port cargo door. No response. He knocked again as he shouted, "Anyone there!"

No response.

Shi'Tan thought, *I could use a few explosives to crack the door.* He began digging through a pouch on his belt. *Here's hoping no one is on the other side.* Gripping the micro-explosives in his hand, he was about to set the first one up when the door creaked. Shi'Tan blinked under his goggles and stepped back as the door slid open abysmally slowly.

Just as the door opened enough for someone to step out, a gun barrel poked through, followed by a helmeted human—Jack Marber. Shi'Tan smiled at the man under his bandanna as he saw him. The gun barrel was leveled at Shi'Tan. "Arms in the air!" Jack shouted, clearly not recognizing their Shrillexian contact through the storm.

"Jack, put the gun down. It's me." Shi'Tan slowly raised

his arms, obeying Jack's command. The wind's force buffeted Jack from the crack he peered out of.

"Me who? Are you with the Don?" Jack kept the gun aimed. The door had opened more, revealing Tc'aarlat standing next to him with his own gun in hand.

"It's Shi'Tan, you blind codger!" Shi'Tan was now frustrated, and he stepped forward and lowered his arms without a care as to whether Jack misinterpreted that act and shot him.

Tc'aarlat's hand quickly shot out to push Jack's barrel down. The two hissed some words between them as Shi'Tan came up to stand before them, still outside the bay door.

Tc'aarlat was the first to speak, "Ahh, Shi'Tan, sorry about my partner here. Got loose trigger fingers, these Federation Marines. You know, shoot first and ask questions later." He chuckled awkwardly in a vain attempt to hide his anxious tone as he spoke. If anything, the chuckle had the exact opposite effect. Both Jack and Shi'Tan looked at him with brows raised.

"Anyway..." Jack picked up the conversation's trailing thread left by Tc'aarlat. "It's good to see you." He turned to Shi'Tan and nodded. "I didn't think we'd meet up with you so quickly after arrival. Especially after, well, you know." He indicated the crashed ship around him.

"I saw. Damn good pilot you had at the controls. Was that the advanced EI Nathan was telling us he fitted her with?" Shi'Tan pointed at the ship.

"What EI? I don't know nothin' about an EI!" Tc'aarlat stammered nervously. The two glanced at him, the large

Yollin shrinking, choosing to keep his nervous mouth shut and let Jack do the talking for the Shadows.

Jack turned back to Shi'Tan and shook his head. "No, actually Solo has been offline since we began our descent, and possibly earlier. It was thanks to Adina's skills with the stick that we were able to survive. We owe her our lives, and speaking of Adina, Tc'aarlat, do you know what's keeping her? I thought she was just grabbing her body armor." He rapped on the chest piece of his armor with his knuckles.

"I don't have to tell you anything." Tc'aarlat immediately slammed his hands over his mouth after he said that. "Sorry," he squeaked as he put his hands over his mouth. "Force of habit with bounty hunters."

Throwing his head back, Shi'Tan let out a boisterous laugh at the Yollin's frightened replies.

Jack glared at Tc'aarlat, unamused. "Quit being so afraid. He's not after you. We're on the same mission."

"Or am I?" Shi'Tan added mysteriously. Both the human and the Yollin regarded the Shrillexian with trepidation. Shi'Tan merely smiled and shrugged, "Just playing with you, pal." He stepped up and gave Tc'aarlat a friendly arm punch.

Tc'aarlat let out a held breath. "I can go see where Adina is."

"Here!" Adina's voice came from the entrance to the ship's hangar. She had her own awkward smile on her lips, almost matching Tc'aarlat's...minus the mandibles.

Jack didn't like the look of that face. His eyes narrowed once again as he asked, "What's wrong, Adina?"

She stepped through the hangar with her hands shyly

clasped behind her back. "Nothing's wrong." Jack crossed his arms and waited. She continued, "Well, do you remember those two Yollins we captured on Balgaria?"

"Yeah?" Jack already did not like where this was going.

"Well..." Adina turned and shouted back to the entrance of the hangar. "It's okay to come out!"

At the hangar entrance was a pair of Yollins, one tall and lanky while the other was stocky and short. Jack's and Tc'aarlat's guns were immediately trained on the pair. Shi'Tan just stood there waiting for Adina to explain. The pair of Yollins held their arms up. She quickly stepped in front of the aimed Jean Dukes Thunderbolts. "Stop! It's okay! They mean us no harm," Adina shouted with her hands up. "Put those damn things down. I promised we wouldn't harm them."

Tc'aarlat grumbled as he lowered his Thunderbolt. "What do you mean? They work for fucking Don Gan'barlo!"

Jack lowered his Thunderbolt and nodded. "For once, I agree with TC."

"We don't work for the Don no more," the shorter Yollin, Gunth'calaat, said.

"Aye," added the taller Yollin, Ben'dolen. "If we was to go back now, we'd be killed. We want a new life."

Tc'aarlat scoffed. "And how do we know that's true?"

Ben'dolen said as he looked at Tc'aarlat, "Well, you worked for the boss, so you know how he is. Cross him once, and..." He dragged a thumb across his neck to indicate the fate of those who failed the Don.

"That's still no guarantee for us." Jack shifted uncomfortably with his Thunderbolt.

"We just want to watch more *Sesame Street*," Gunth'-calaat said innocently.

"What the hell is *Sesame Street*?" Tc'aarlat looked at Adina, then Jack, who seemed a bit surprised.

"It's an Earth children's tv show. Jack had Solo play episodes non-stop for them, and they seemed to like it a lot. Like, a lot, a lot," Adina told Tc'aarlat to fill him in on the details. Jack was still looking at Adina, questioning her motives. Feeling guilty for more than just springing the two Yollins, she began to explain, "I couldn't leave the two of them locked up down there. They would have been sitting ducks in this warzone! And I think that show had some kind of effect on them. I don't know how to explain it, but being put in front of it for so many hours, they seemed to have changed for the better."

Shi'Tan cut Jack off as he was about to speak. "Well, Captain Marber, I believe your pilot is owed this bit of trust after saving all of your lives." He'd been smiling under his bandanna since the two Yollins had been brought out by Adina, amused by the whole situation.

Jack was silent before he said, "All right. But don't spring prisoners without telling Tc'aarlat and me again."

"Deal." Adina offered Jack a hand. He shook it and smiled at her.

"A touching moment of comradery, but I fear Adina was correct; we are quite exposed here." Shi'Tan looked everyone over as he spoke, including the two Yollin ex-thugs. "We'll need to keep moving and find a way out of this battlefield."

"Did he say 'battlefield?'" Gunth'calaat whispered to Ben'dolen.

. . .

Miseria, Outside the Security Perimeter of Trejion Prime, LS *Blizzard*, Bridge

Surveying the holomap display of the ongoing battle, Colonel Oopley was pleased with the high-performance mech armor. They'd take the wall, and while the enemy was reeling from the blow, he'd drop the infantry and armor regiments, who would seize this section of wall. This would then serve as a staging ground to assault the other sections of wall, and once secured, the city beyond could be put to siege. After starving them out, with intermittent artillery fire to incite fear in the populace and what defenders remained, he'd gladly accept the city prefects' full surrender. *Then Coldist banners would fly high over this cesspit of 78th sympathies, and I'll be hailed as a hero.* His internal monologue stoked the self-importance of the colonel's eager ambitions.

"Colonel, our attaché wishes to speak with you in your quarters, sir." Ensign Ionoway's report interrupted the flow of self-aggrandizement inflating the colonel's bulging ego.

"What did I say about interrupting me when I am thinking, Ensign?" Colonel Oopley verbally lashed his ensign.

Ensign Ionoway stood up and saluted the colonel as he said, "My apologies, sir. You also told me to relay all information related to the attaché at once." He remained at attention.

"Right." Colonel Oopley rubbed his lower jaw. "Ensign, you have command while I am gone. Contact me immediately should there be any new developments." He stood up and began walking to the bridge's rear exit. He waved a hand behind him as he spoke in the condescending way superiors or petulant children did when they did not have enough time to stay and relay their commands face to face.

"Of course, sir." Ensign Ionoway was still standing erect and saluting.

As Colonel Oopley reached the door, he glanced back. "At ease, Ensign. I will overlook your dereliction of orders. This time, anyway."

Ensign Ionoway let out a breath and relaxed his whole body. "Thank you, sir. It won't happen again, sir."

"I trust that it won't." After he stepped from the bridge, the automatic door closed behind him with a *swish*. A trooper in full battle armor stood guard by the door, rifle cradled. From the bridge, he made his way along the carrier's command tower toward the rear, where his personal quarters were located. Reaching the door with a placard bearing his name on it, he stepped up to the door lock panel and pressed his thumb against the reader. He couldn't let just anybody into his quarters, especially with so many vindictive land sailors and soldiers around the carrier eager to get back at the colonel for one thing or the other. He'd certainly gained his fair share of enemies among the enlisted, and the officers beneath him as well.

Inside his quarters, lounging on a lavish purple couch, was a Yollin with four legs. His mandibles perked up as Colonel Oopley entered. "Ahh, Colonel! I am glad you received my summons. I hope you don't mind that I've gotten into your wine." He raised the wine glass in his hand, indicating a pair of uncorked bottles on the table, one empty and the other a third empty. "A 2011 Earth vintage. A fine year."

"I do not mind at all. Be my guest." Colonel Oopley smiled. "I think I will have a glass as well." He approached an adjacent couch and took a seat.

The Yollin smiled at Colonel Oopley and took a sip from his glass before continuing, "Drinking during a battle? I trust the new toys are working well? Give me the word, make the bank transfer, and I'll call my men and have five hundred of the NX-4470 Gallant Armor Assault Suits on the field within the day. Imagine what you've already done with the little sample. Now imagine that twenty-fold!" He raised his glass. "You wouldn't just take a city. You could take the entire world!"

"Always the salesman, Tetz'len." Colonel Oopley smirked as he grabbed the partially filled bottle of wine and a clean glass. "I will await the results of today before I jump to place such a large order." He poured himself a glass and set the bottle down. He raised the glass to Tetz'len, who met it with a clink.

"A sharp shopper. I cannot blame you for waiting. Maybe I'll even come down on the price." Tetz'len's smile had all the charm of a used starship salesman.

Colonel Oopley took a sip from his wine through his neck fold. "You act as though you know what my actions already are going to be."

Tetz'len set down his glass and leaned into the soft cushions of the couch, his arms resting spread out on the top. "Business is as much a game of strategy and tactics as warfare. I am sure you, if anyone, could grasp the parallels between a master merchant and a brilliant commander.

Both must understand their opponent and make decisions that could make or break their goals."

Colonel Oopley set down his glass. "That's a strange comparison. A commander leads soldiers and holds their lives in his hands. Where a merchant just holds coins."

Tetz'len continued smiling as he spoke. "Does a merchant not hold lives in his hands? Livelihoods for workers, craftsmen, professionals, etc., are made or broken by my actions. Entire planetary economies can be crushed because of a poor choice on my part. We both wield an inordinate amount of power. I snap my fingers..." he snapped his right thumb and middle finger, "and the NX-4470's entire production line is down, from the miners who harvest the necessary ores to the factory owner." He leaned forward, resting his elbow on one of his four knees as he grabbed his nearly empty wine glass and the bottle and topped himself off with a generous portion. "Of course, I wouldn't come out unscathed, but that is beside the point. The other competing merchants are my enemies, and the customer sale is my objective."

Colonel Oopley snorted. "Mighty words from a corpulent Yollin blueblood. Your power in coin is pathetic compared to my military might. Violence is what true power comes from, and nowhere else."

The jovial but uncanny demeanor of Tetz'len dropped away to a venomous sneer that was still uncanny. "Do not forget who I work for, Colonel, or else you will learn where the real power in this relationship lies. I'd hate for the violence of the Gan'barlo family to soil such fertile business opportunities."

Gulping Colonel Oopley chugged down his glass

through his neck fold and reached for the bottle. It was empty. "I'll grab another bottle."

"That would be most generous of you." The venom drained from Tetz'len's demeanor, returning to a jovial posture and manner of speaking. "You know, for all the necessity of your people to import arms for your most noble war, I find this landship simply astounding."

The colonel looked up from the bar. "A feat of Miserian ingenuity, or maybe *the* feat of Miserian ingenuity. Most major cities have dry docks pumping out new vessels every few months for the war." He grabbed a bottle and uncorked it. "Because of the electromagnetic currents of Miseria, with some fiddling with magnets and nuclear generators, these massive vessels are able to lift high above the ground without the necessity of propulsion."

"Marvelous, simply marvelous. Were it not a quirk unique to Miseria, I'd be selling one to every state, terrorist force, and mercenary band in the known universe." Tetz'len clapped his hands as the colonel brought over the wine bottle. He was ready for another glass even though he'd only drunk half his previous one.

"Colonel Oopley to the bridge, please. Colonel Oopley to the bridge." The voice of Ensign Ionoway came over the comm. The colonel stood and made for the door, straightening the front of his uniform as he walked.

Tetz'len was already up and walking alongside him. "Here, Colonel, let me join you on the bridge. I'd prefer observing the battle and the Gallants in action to staying here and drinking your entire wine supply."

Colonel Oopley nodded, and the pair walked to the bridge side by side. Once there, the bridge crew stood up from their seats and saluted. "At ease." Colonel Oopley ordered as he ascended to his command chair, Tetz'len beside him as though he were his shadow. "Report. Ensign, you needed me?"

"Yes, sir. We have new contacts engaging the Gallants, sir," the ensign replied, his head turned from his monitor.

"That is no surprise. I expected such resistance. I am sure the Gallants are more than capable of dealing with them." He waved his hand in front of him with a bored twist.

"That's just it, sir. They've already taken two casualties, and one of the pilots relayed this image of the enemy contact." Ensign Ionoway put the image on his monitor onto the main screen.

Colonel Oopley squinted and leaned forward in his chair to see what he was looking at. The image was blurry and further obstructed by the sand and dust from the storm. "Is that..."

Ensign Ionoway confirmed the colonel's thoughts. "Aye, sir. Our pilots confirm they are being attacked by enemy mech suits atop the wall."

Colonel Oopley turned a questioning glare on Tetz'len. "Do you mind explaining?"

Tetz'len shrugged. "I suppose those enemy merchants are here, exploring other objectives."

Miseria, the Mountain Pass heading toward the Security Perimeter of Trejion Prime

"One, ah, ah, ah." Gunth'calaat held up one finger to his

bewildered brethren Ben'delon, who was desperately trying to keep his sides from splitting.

"Two, ah, ah, ah," Ben'delon came back with, holding up two fingers.

"Three, ah, ah—"

"Do these guys ever shut up?" Jack asked loudly before moving as far from the blundering Yollins as he could. Jack was approaching the head of the line, near Tc'aarlat and Shi'Tan.

"You're responsible for this, Jack," Adina called after him. "It was your idea!"

"Yeah, and it really bit me in the arse." Jack huffed. "Believe it or not, I never thought I'd be walking through the valley of death with the two of them for hours on end."

"Next time, crash your ship closer." Shi'Tan didn't turn to him; he kept his eyes on the horizon. "Should be another hour, but we'll get to the wall before nightfall."

"It's been an hour already!" Tc'aarlat grumbled.

"You guys are such babies." Adina giggled. "It's just a little bit of walking."

"She's right, you know." Shi'Tan looked at them. "But we can rest for five minutes if you need it."

"I need it." Jack wiped the sweat off his forehead. "It's so warm here."

"That's the one good thing about this war," said Shi'Tan. "You always know which side is winning."

Shi'Tan approached a series of boulders and sat down on the closest one that was the right height. The others followed his lead, seating themselves where the boulders provided the most shade, away from the light of the sun and the passage, a small crevice between the boulders and the rocky wall.

Tc'aarlat turned his attention to Shi'Tan, "So, tell us why a bounty hunter, a *famed* bounty hunter, is working to prevent the spread of weapons on some small backwater planet?"

"Money." Shi'Tan shrugged. "What other reason would there be?"

"I could think of a few," said Adina. "Stopping blood and violence and a stupid bloody war for one thing."

"Oh, this war will never end." Shi'Tan sighed. "Both sides have been in a stalemate for years. This is a generational problem now."

"Let's keep focused, guys," Jack piped up. "We're here because Don Gan'barlo is here, and stopping him is the priority."

"How does it all work?" Adina sat up a little against the boulder, trying desperately to achieve comfort. "Controlling the weather?"

"It's a system of networks, I've heard." Shi'Tan narrowed his eyes at her, thinking through his answer. "So, there's a series of machines across Trejion Prime that all work together to control the weather. They can change the local atmosphere and the global atmosphere with the push of a few buttons. Beyond that, I'm not sure. I've never actually seen it. I've always assumed it's more complex than that, though."

"Have you been in the city before?" asked Jack.

"A few times for diplomatic opportunities." Shi'Tan nodded. "Just trying to talk some damned sense into both sides. There's no compromising, though. They're both real fucking stubborn."

"There has to be a way," Adina murmured.

Miseria, Outside the Security Perimeter of Trejion Prime, LS *Blizzard*, Bridge

Colonel Oopley had been keeping a close watch on the holomap since the revelation had come to light. The opposition had mechs too. By all accounts, though, it didn't matter. The Coldists were still coming from a better foothold, and with their surprise attack, they had certainly dealt a larger blow for their opposition to recover from. Still, Colonel Oopley wasn't one for surprises, and this had tainted his once-good mood.

Tetz'len had been watching the battle quite keenly as well. Of course, it didn't matter which side won the battle for him, as long as neither of them won the war. With Don Gan'barlo's assets quickly draining from botched operations, he was aware that this one had to remain lucrative at all costs—even if that meant dealing with both sides of the table.

"This is going to be another stalemate!" Colonel Oopley spat. "I thought we had them this time!"

"I'm sorry to hear that, Colonel." Tetz'len grinned behind the colonel's back. "Remember my offer, though. Just give me the word, and one quick bank transfer later, you'll have five hundred of the NX-4470 Gallant Armor Assault Suits on the field within a day. I'm sure that would turn the tide on this stalemate."

The colonel stood up straight and turned to the four-legged Yollin, whose face had taken on a far more sincere expression. "Yeah, and then suddenly, they'll have five hundred more to face us as well!"

"I don't see how." Tetz'len was taken aback but expected the sleight. "Are you accusing me of something?"

"Not yet." The colonel wiped the sweat from his forehead. "If I find out the Gan'barlo family has betrayed the Cold Coalition—"

"Be careful with your threats."

Ensign Ionoway, who had been apprehensive about approaching Colonel Oopley's blister of a face, could no longer hold back. He moved to the holomap in the moments of silence that lingered on Tetz'len's final words, standing on the other side of the table from the colonel and Yollin and clearing his throat to get their attention.

"What is it, Ensign Ionoway?"

"A new development," Ensign Ionoway announced. "Our scanners have picked up unknown entities close to this location, at the end of the mountain pass that leads to the wall."

"Unknown entities?" Colonel Oopley asked, confused. "Hostiles?"

"That isn't clear."

"Bring them in." Colonel Oopley nodded to Ensign Ionoway and glanced at Tetz'len. "Alive. They could be the ones supplying mechs to those damned heat fanatics."

"As you command, sir."

"Maybe you're not a traitor after all," Colonel Oopley mused.

"Oh, I'm sure you've found your culprits." Tetz'len smiled.

. . .

Miseria, the Mountain Pass heading toward the Security Perimeter of Trejion Prime

Jack massaged the ache running down toward the back of his spine. A quick five minutes of relaxing had quickly turned into ten without anyone realizing, and he was paying for it. They were all gathering themselves, ready for another hour of walking, when out of nowhere, they heard a noise. *BANG.* From somewhere unseen, a shot had been fired directly at the feet of Shi'Tan, who instinctively dove backward over the waist-high boulders and forced his back against the cooler side.

"Everyone, get down!" he bellowed.

Jack and Tc'aarlat joined him, while everyone else had luckily already been there, still catching the shade while they could. Jack was peering over as much as he dared, looking for any clue to the whereabouts of the assailant, but there was nothing—just rocky walls and a million places to hide. He retrieved his Jean Dukes Special and turned it up to eight, enough force to blow a hole through a wall and anything unfortunate enough to be standing in front of that wall.

"See anything?" Tc'aarlat held his Thunderbolt close, ready to strike should the situation call for it.

"Not a damn thing." Jack grunted and looked at Shi'Tan. "Who could it be?"

"Coldists." Shi'Tan didn't hesitate. "The people in Trejion Prime don't come out; they've been ambushed too many times."

"Fool me once, shame on me," said Tc'aarlat. "Fool me

twice, shame on who?"

"You," Jack corrected.

"Me?"

"No, it's you."

"That's what I said." Tc'aarlat looked at Jack, dumb-founded. "Fool me once, shame on me."

"*Gott Verdammt!*" Jack exclaimed. "It's 'fool me twice, shame on...you're doing this on purpose! I know you are!"

"I sweat I am not!" said Tc'aarlat.

"Swear! You *swear* you are not," said Jack.

"Guys." Adina cleared her throat. "Kinda in the middle of an active battlefield here?"

To emphasize her point, another shot rang out, a green blast that hit the boulder close to where Jack had stuck his head out. Jack rubbed the sun out of his eyes and tried to think, while Tc'aarlat and Shi'Tan exchanged knowing glances before looking farther toward Gunth'calaat and Ben'delon. The two Yollin thugs were keeping to themselves.

"We could send *them* out," suggested Tc'aarlat in a hissed whisper.

Jack followed his gaze and in an equally soft voice, replied, "Who? Bert and Ernie over there?"

"These are warning shots," whispered Shi'Tan. "I'm sure of it. They want us to come right out and surrender."

"What if you're wrong?" Adina leaned in, speaking louder than the others. "What if they get shot?"

"No big loss." Tc'aarlat shrugged. "Less Don Gan'barlo men to deal with later."

"They've changed," Adina insisted. "I mean, look at them."

At that very moment, the two former thugs were using the light to cast shadows on the rocky ground, a variety of different creatures from birds to dinosaur heads and beyond. Things they could've only learned by watching wholesome Earth television shows. They were giggling as they did it, loving every moment.

"Oh, bugger it." Jack jumped out from the cover and across the shortest boulder, about waist height. He threw down his gun and held his hands up high in the act of surrender. "*LISTEN,*" he shouted as loud as he could. "*WE SURRENDER, AND WE DON'T WANT ANY TROUBLE, SO YEAH, BASICALLY, DON'T SHOOT—*"

"Manners!" Adina hissed.

"*PLEASE!*" Jack added. "*PLEASE DON'T SHOOT!*"

It was a tense few moments, to say the least, and at the end of those precious seconds, Jack still hadn't been shot. Everyone released their collective breaths, and a minute later, they were surrounded by soldiers in tight-fitting body armor, holding rifles high with itchy trigger fingers. One by one, the group came out with their hands up, threw their weapons on the ground, and surrendered. And one by one, they were put in handcuffs and forced into a line.

With a quick prod in the back, the Coldists forced their prisoners to march single-file through the mountain pass and away from the wall, down a passageway they had previously ignored. Every question was met with cold indifference, and after a while, they stopped trying to ascertain where they were going and what the Coldists wanted with them. All they knew was that they were heading somewhere, and they weren't going to be received as welcome guests.

. . .

Miseria, Southwest Section Command of Trejion Prime

Metz'len pushed through to the war room of the command center, with his two escorts of the 78th guiding him. The plan was going as well as it could. Tetz'len would ensure the sale of five hundred more mechs for the Cold Coalition, while Metz'len would do the same on this side of the battlefield. Don Gan'barlo would certainly be pleased with that outcome, his entire stock of mechs would be gone, and with the sudden cash injection, he could invest into some new projects and propagate new successful ventures for the family. Winners all around.

At the other end of the table stood a Miserian, as he had been expecting, but far younger in years than what he thought the man should be. This one looked inexperienced. Metz'len approached, his fingers tapping against one another relentlessly, as they often did when he thought something was amiss. "General Muffa Carle, it's a pleas—"

"General Muffa Carle is dead," the Miserian said. "Shot himself in the head a few hours ago. I'm in charge now."

"I'm sorry to hear that. I'm Metz'len of the Gan'barlo family," said Metz'len. "I'm here to offer you a unique opportunity."

"You're the one who supplied us with those mechs a few days ago? The Gallants, right?"

"That's correct." Metz'len bowed. "I see they have been working out for you."

"Yeah, they did. Uh, they are." He held out his hand, and Metz'len shook it. "I'm Misken Leff. Uh, General Leff, sorry, head of Section Command."

"Pleasure." Metz'len's grin was widening; this might be easier than he had thought. "Should we get to business, then?"

General Leff took a seat at the table, and Metz'len sat across from him. He pulled out a small circular disc and threw it a short way across, when the device stopped, it projected a holographic image of a mech suit, the ones that General Leff was using to protect the wall from the Coldists—the same ones the Coldists were using in their attempt to get over the wall.

"I hate to be the bearer of bad news," Metz'len explained, "but I'm sure you're painfully aware that your opposition has obtained a few of these suits, and it's given them a powerful advantage."

"We have suits too, though," said General Leff. "So it's balanced out?"

Metz'len nodded at that. "For now," he said. "I've got it on good authority, though, that another faction besides myself is selling these suits, and they've just sold another five hundred units to the Cold Coalition."

"Five hundred!?" General Leff jumped out of his seat. "That's...we don't have enough strength to protect against—"

"That's why I'm here." Metz'len spoke calmly, settling the recently inaugurated commander down. "The fifty we allowed you to use were simply a sample. We have another five hundred units ready to go, and they can be here within a day."

"Well, we should get right on that." General Leff sat back down quickly. "If what you're saying is true about their forces."

"Oh, it is." Metz'len was trying not to grin and give himself away, but it was so hard. "It's what those enemy merchants do, but I'm here to tell you that the Gan'barlo family cares about your beliefs in this war, and we'll do anything we can to help."

"Good. Well, let's get some ordered then," General Leff agreed. "Get them here as quick as you can."

"Of course." Metz'len stood up, then stopped himself. "There is, well, a small thing. I can see you're in a precarious situation, your enemy raining down on you, but the thing is…there's a lot of demand for these suits now, and I'm afraid the price has doubled."

"We'll pay it," General Leff batted back.

"Excellent."

Miseria, Outside the Security Perimeter of Trejion Prime, LS *Blizzard*, Prison Block

The cells were opened easily by swiping a keycard across the panel to the left, and one by one, the group were thrown inside. Jack and Tc'aarlat shared one cell, Shi'Tan and Adina another, and finally the *Sesame Street*-loving Yollins in the last cell on the row. Their blocks were protected by bars of thick steel, there were no windows on any of the walls, and their equipment had been seized. Troopers stood against the walls, ready with their rifles for any trouble.

"Wonder how long we'll rot in here?" Jack plonked himself down on the single wooden bench that had been provided, the only piece of furniture in the cell.

"That depends on you," said a voice out of the gloom,

and a figure approached. A rank above the troopers at the very least, if his uniform was anything to go by, with slicked-back hair and a stern look about him. "I am Ensign Callot Ionoway. Your group was spotted on our scanners. What is your purpose in this region?"

Jack stood up. "We're here to—"

"We crashed," Tc'aarlat interrupted. "If you don't believe us, you can find our ship a little way from here. Scrunched at the front."

"Crashed?" Ensign Ionoway looked to his soldiers, who had no answers for him. "Why are you here on Miseria?"

"More shot out of the sky, actually," said Adina. "I'm the reason we're here in one piece, just so that's on record."

"Why are you here?" the Miserian repeated louder.

"We're here to stop the Gan'barlo family." Jack moved to the bars, pushing his head a little way through so he could get a better view of Ensign Ionoway.

"The weapons traders?"

"That's what they are to you," said Jack. "They're many things these days."

"They're providing us with weapons for the war," said Ensign Ionoway.

"Yeah, I'm not dealing with you anymore," said Jack. "I demand to be taken to the person in charge."

"I'm second-in-command."

"Yeah." Jack nodded. "I want to speak to the first-in-command, not some junior officer."

"Junior officer!?" Ensign Ionoway moved closer, so close their noses were mere inches from touching. "I've been fighting this war all my life. I know more about war than you know about anything."

"Oh, I don't know about that." Jack smiled. "I know you're being played."

The ensign pulled himself away from the cell door and considered them for a moment. The colonel suspected these might be the other merchants, supplying mechs to the other side, but there was no evidence of that…yet. So, he snapped his fingers, and two troopers approached, ready for action. He commanded them to open the one cell, and they did so quickly. "I'll take you and the Yollin to the bridge. Let's see how much you actually know."

"It's Jack, just FYI." Jack was pulled roughly from the cell. "I learned your name, Ensign Colloway."

"Ionoway."

"That's what I said."

The troopers did as they were bid, taking hold of the two rogues and following the ensign out of the prison block toward the bridge. Neither one of them noticed the small flick of Jack's hand, a subtle movement that would've been hard for anyone to catch. Adina smiled broadly and shook her head, not believing what he had done. She was looking down at what Jack had sent flying across the room and through her cell bars—Ensign Prick's keycard for the door.

Miseria, Outside the Security Perimeter of Trejion Prime, LS *Blizzard*, Bridge

The door to the bridge opened, and in stepped Ensign Ionoway, followed by two troopers leading Jack and Tc'aarlat. Colonel Oopley looked up from the conflict at the table and over to the strangers now in his bridge, while

Tetz'len kept his back to the wall, waiting to see how things would play out.

"And what is this, Ensign Ionoway?"

"Those potential hostiles we detected on radar, sir." Ensign Ionoway bowed. "They were demanding to speak to you."

"Actually, *he* was demanding it," Tc'aarlat clarified. "I was more just led here."

The colonel eyed them. "Who are you?"

"We're the Shadows," said Jack. "And we're here for Big and Ugly over there."

Jack was nodding toward Tetz'len. The colonel followed his motion and turned back to him with a grunt. "What do you want with him?"

"He works for a dangerous family of criminals that we've taken up the hobby of stopping," Jack answered. "Their latest venture is dealing weapons to this world, to what I'm assuming is both sides of the conflict."

"As I suspected," Tetz'len interjected and moved in closer, choosing his time to talk carefully. "Lies. I think I found your rogue traders, Colonel. They've been supplying the other side with mechs."

"Dungshit!" Tc'aarlat cried. "That's exactly what he's doing to you."

"I suppose you have proof?" Tetz'len approached slowly. "Or are you just wasting the colonel's time?"

The colonel stared at Jack, his face growing even sterner. "Do you?"

"No," Jack told him finally.

Miseria, Outside the Security Perimeter, *ICS Fortitude*

The figure traipsing across the planes of Miseria toward the ship was smaller than most, half the height of a regular human. Despite the heat of Miseria, they were safe in tightly-wrapped armor and a dust-ridden cloak. The being placed a gloved hand on the hull of the ICS *Fortitude* and followed the scorching metal toward the side door, allowing its hand to gently caress the alloy. Finally, it reached the door and pushed down its hood, revealing the plain white mask that covered the face beneath it and the goggles that did the same for its eyes. It sighed and took in the ship as a whole. "I bet you've got some secrets in you."

Just then, a continuous beeping noise filled the air, and the figure placed a hand to its ear. "Speak."

The figure listened for a moment to the other side of the conversation. "Yes, this is Benjamin. Everything is going according to plan. Better, in fact. We'll have our bargaining chip soon."

. . .

Miseria, Outside the Security Perimeter of Trejion Prime, LS *Blizzard*, Hallway

Adina rushed along the hallway, taking care to look around every corner she approached. Behind her and following close were the two Yollins and Shi'Tan, recently escaped from the cells with the keycard Jack had managed to smuggle to them. They had no weapons or gear, and they were surrounded on all sides by unaware soldiers with guns at the ready. Adina didn't really care about any of that, though. She'd had a hunch, and that gut feeling was leading her toward the hangar—if only she could find where it was.

"Wait!" Shi'Tan hissed in a whisper, rushing up toward her. "We can't just keep—"

"We're heading to the hangar." Adina took a peek around the next corner. A dead end.

"We need a plan." Shi'Tan turned her head back to him. "You don't know the Coldists like I do, Adina. They're not forgiving types."

"They'll be dead types if we don't stop that arms deal." Adina pushed herself away from him and continued along the hallway, stopping only at the last minute when she heard voices coming from around the next corner. She backed up as two oblivious guards came walking past, engrossed in their conversation. It was only luck that stopped them from turning their heads and seeing the four escapees, but it was luckier still when Adina paid attention to what they were saying.

Shi'Tan went to her again and beckoned the dragging Yollins to come in close behind, but before he could say a word, Adina had quieted him with the snap of her hand. She was paying attention to the guards.

"How many d'ya think are left, then?" one guard, the burlier one, was saying to the other.

"I reckon about five in total, and no more than that." His accomplice, far skinnier, spoke in a squeaky voice. He was young; well, both of them were and neither could have been involved with this war for very long. "I 'ope I get a turn next, though. I'd be 'eartbroken if I dunt."

The burlier one slapped him on the back with a mighty laugh. "Prepare to be 'eartbroken then, ya daft mudslapper!"

"It's like some kind of alien language?" Shi'Tan whispered. "What are they saying?"

"I was right!" Adina had to stop herself from screaming it. "I had a hunch that there might be a few left in the hangar. That's what they're saying."

"A few what?"

Adina grinned. "Mech suits."

Miseria, Outside the Security Perimeter of Trejion Prime, LS *Blizzard*, Bridge

Jack had slumped in a nearby seat. If it hadn't been for these damn handcuffs, he would have covered his face in embarrassment. Tc'aarlat had been ranting for a good ten minutes now, telling the colonel every part of his sordid past, and it wasn't getting them anywhere. Colonel Oopley was just turning darker and darker shades of red, and Jack couldn't pretend not to notice that a few of his subordinates on the bridge were taking considered steps away from him.

"...and then there were the Zombie Dwarves. They were interesting," Tc'aarlat continued. "We defeated them with a volcano."

Jack was looking past the jabbering Yollin toward the Yollin across the table—the one with the snide grin. He had only caught a glimpse, but it looked like he was checking a small communicator at his side, keeping it away from the eyes of the bridge. If Jack hadn't been sitting where he was, he probably would've missed it too. He stood up quickly and cut Tc'aarlat off in the middle of his sentence. "Colonel, this isn't getting us anywhere. We've told you who we are and who he is, we're running out of time to sort this problem out."

"Yes." Colonel Oopley nodded. "You're from the Federation, but you don't have any proof of that either. Not so much as a badge?"

"Colonel!" Tetz'len jumped to his feet, holding that handheld communicator high and quite rudely interrupting their conversation. "I've just received word from my sources in the sky. The 78th has just purchased five hundred Gallants. It seems you're running out of time."

"Oh, come on!" Tc'aarlat cried. "How could this bistok bollock possibly know that without dealing under the table?"

"*SILENCE!*" Colonel Oopley pounded his fist on the holomap, sending waves of static across it. "I've listened to both sides of this, and to be frank, I don't trust either of you."

Tc'aarlat's mandibles quivered, and he gave Jack an unsure look. "Why would he be Frank?"

"Nathan Lowell," Jack said firmly. "He's our contact and liaison with the Federation. Get in touch with him, and he'll provide proof of who we are."

Colonel Oopley considered that for a moment and eventually nodded. "One of you is trying to undermine the Coalition. I know that for—"

Tetz'len stepped forward, pleading, "Colonel, your time is running—"

"I'll get in touch with this Nathan." He sneered at Tetz'len. "I'll find out the truth of the matter if it kills me."

"Good decision." Jack smiled across the room at Tetz'len.

"Yeah," Tc'aarlat agreed. "But who the fuck is Frank?"

Miseria, Outside the Security Perimeter, *ICS Fortitude*, *Bridge*

It hadn't taken much to break in. The security protocols were running in low mode as if most of them were temporarily offline. Benjamin could've strolled in if he had wanted to and simply flown the ship away, although, that would interfere with the plan. He moved to the captain's chair and pulled himself closer to the command console. There he brought up screen after screen of information. Some of it was useless, and whenever something useful was blocked, Benjamin simply clicked a few buttons on the datapad wrapped around his arm and pressed on with ease, hacking his way through like a hot knife through butter.

"So then, that's why." Benjamin leaned close, intrigued

now at what he had discovered, almost laughing. "You're upgrading your Entity Intelligence, and while that happens, your ship is on manual. That wasn't very smart before a mission, was it, Shadows?"

Sighing, he took hold of a cable and pulled it taut, unwinding it from the datapad. Carefully he placed the head of this cable into a port just below the console, then got to work, tapping endlessly at the keys before him. "This'll be a nice surprise for you."

Miseria, Outside the Security Perimeter of Trejion Prime, LS *Blizzard*, Hangar

Adina dodged through the door just before it slammed shut behind the two guards they had been following. She watched them to make sure they didn't turn around, but they were still too involved with their conversation about how the mechs worked. Actually, she had learned a lot from just following them through the base for ten minutes, and was quite sure of her ability to be able to pilot one of these goliaths.

Shi'Tan knocked on the window from the other side, and Adina turned to him with a sheepish grin. She moved to the door and turned the handle, allowing him and the Yollins entrance. They were all inside the hangar now, the largest single section of the ship, and it really showed from just how bewilderingly empty it was. Here and there a few guards milled about, but Adina would bet that a few hours prior, this place had been filled with mech suits. She searched the hangar for them, and her eyes landed on two, standing to the side. The only ones left.

"There they are," Adina said, pointing to them. "We can use them to get out of here."

"I thought we were saving Jack and Tc'aarlat?" Shi'Tan looked at her, his face scrunched in confusion.

"No, those guys can handle themselves," said Adina. "I'm going over the wall."

"Over the wall?"

"And you're coming with me," she explained. "With your knowledge of the city, we can find the central computer that controls the weather network."

Shi'Tan thought about that, but his confusion only grew. "Then what?"

"Then," Adina said, "we're going to shut it down, hack into it, and destroy the whole network."

"What!?" The bellow came with such ferocity that Adina clamped a hand over Shi'Tan's mouth and forced him behind some tall crates to keep them out of view. His outcry had caused a few of the guards close by to pay attention. It took them a few moments to turn away, fortunately shrugging the yelp off as nothing but perhaps the strained hull of an old ship dying in the heat.

"If there's no weather system, there's no war," said Adina once the coast was clear. "Easy."

"I'm—" Shi'Tan gasped. "I can't...I'm just...I—"

"Can you think of a better way to end this war?" Adina poked him in the chest. "This'll solve our problem as well. If the Miserians have no reason for war, they have no reason to buy weapons either. *Ipso facto*, we win."

"You don't understand," said Shi'Tan. "That's their core belief. Getting rid of it won't stop the war, it'll only make things worse!"

"It's our only option," Adina hissed.

"I don't know if I—"

"There'll probably be a big payday from the Federation for putting an end to this war."

"I'm in." Shi'Tan snapped up straight, although he was still unsure.

"Fighting is bad." Adina and Shi'Tan gave Ben'delon a quick look. He was suddenly there paying attention, and he gave them a small wave. "Friends are good to have. You can share anything with your best friend."

"How?" Shi'Tan turned back to her, stern now. "How are we going to steal them?"

"We split up," said Adina. "Me and you sneak into those mech suits, and *they* figure out a way to open the hangar door and let us out."

"We're trusting those two?" Shi'Tan pointed at the Yollins, who were engrossed in a chorus of *Rubber Duckie*.

"Oh, rubber duckie,

I'm awfully fond of you!"

Adina couldn't deny he had a point, but that didn't change her plan. "They can do it."

"We can do what?" Gunth'calaat and Ben'delon asked in unison.

Miseria, Southwest Section Command of Trejion Prime

Metz'len pushed the tablet a little closer toward General Leff, who was once again reading over the terms and conditions of the contract. In all honesty, it was getting frustrating; it had been half an hour since Metz'len had sent a message to his brother about the deal going through, and still, he hadn't forked over the credits.

"The longer you wait, the more we'll have to charge." Metz'len muttered through clenched mandibles.

"Sorry about that," said General Leff. "The general always taught me to read contracts fully before I signed, but I think there's something wrong with it."

"Wrong with it?"

"It says that I pay you, and then you deliver the Gallants," said General Leff. "Shouldn't that be the other way around?"

"You're confused." Metz'len came around to his side and tapped a finger on the tablet. "You pay us, and we provide. That's what we do."

"I dunno. I don't think we should pay for something we don't have," said General Leff. "If you change that bit, I'll sign it. Once we have the units, I can give you the credits for them."

Metz'len forced a crooked smiled and retrieved his communicator. "Let me discuss this with my boss."

Miseria, Outside the Security Perimeter of Trejion Prime, LS *Blizzard*, Hangar

The path before them split into two sections. The metal grate walkway above led straight to the hangar bay controls and would allow those colossal doors to be opened with the press of a button, while the stairs leading down to the floor of the hangar from the entry would allow access to the two impressive mech suits standing by. Adina rushed the stairs, Shi'Tan close behind her, and kept an eye on the two Yollins making their way across the walkway above them.

"Can you even pilot one of those things?" Shi'Tan hissed at her.

"Course." She shrugged. "Can't be any harder than piloting a—"

Shi'Tan tackled her behind more crates once they reached the bottom of the stairs, taking his turn to push her out of the view of patrolling guards. They passed without the slightest hint that anyone was hiding there, and it made Adina wonder if those helmets they were wearing weren't making their perception a little short. She found her feet and huddled behind the crate next to Shi'Tan.

"It didn't look like that many when we were standing up there," said Shi'Tan. "Now's a shitload of those guards."

"You're right." Adina sighed. Maybe this plan was a bit overreaching after all. "We need a distraction."

As fate would have it, at that very moment, the Yollins reached the control panel for the hangar doors and approached the various switches and levers and buttons with two problems hanging over them. The first was that these particular Yollins had not one clue how to operate a set of hangar doors for a ship this large, and the second problem was, they'd watched so much *Sesame Street* that all common sense had gone out the window, replaced by infantile imaginations that had no place in a situation as serious as this. These two problems culminated in one definitive solution—smashing the living crap out of each and every functional switch on that control board until something good happened.

Alarms went off every few seconds, the doors constantly switched between opening and closed, hooks and cranes swung about wildly, causing damage to the interior, and the guards went insane. They saw the culprits immediately and ran for the Yollins, guns raised, which was the perfect opening for a straight dash to the mech suits.

"Good job, Yollins." Adina beamed.

"They'll be killed!" Shi'Tan exclaimed.

Adina didn't answer. she was too busy sprinting toward the nearest mech suit. No one was dying on her watch. Thanks to the in-depth conversation the guards had been having, she knew something about operating the mechs, starting with how to open them. She pushed the button and the front of the suit split first, then separated into four equal parts. Adina climbed the short steps to the seat, strapped herself in tight, and placed her legs and arms in their metal counterparts. The suit closed once more, encasing Adina, and it came to life under her command. She was grinning like a madman when the mech suit stumbled forward under her direction and turned its attention to the ten or so guards rounding on the Yollins.

"Leave them alone!" the suit bellowed, and the guards turned to it in panic.

"Oh, hellix," one said, frozen to the spot like the others.

The mech suit swayed, its heavy legs unbalanced. It was much harder to control than Adina could've guessed, which left it looking more like a stumbling drunk than an expensive killing machine. Still, Adina was gathering control of it in one way or another. She held up the mech's arm out straight, and a massive beam of red light shot out of it, cutting between the guards and the Yollins and breaking the walkway in two with a significant gap the guards couldn't cross.

"Sorry!" Adina called. "I'm still learning."

It was Shi'Tan's turn now. He was running toward the other mech, and as he went, he called up to the Yollins, "Get those fucking doors open!"

Gunth'calaat turned to Ben'delon. "What would Elmo do?"

"He'd believe in us."

Gunth'calaat turned back to the controls, hovered his hand over them for a moment, and clicked his mandibles nervously. Then he slammed a hand down on the largest button he could see, giving it a single press. Adina laughed. Shi'Tan sighed in relief. The Yollins laughed and hugged one another in joy. The hangar doors split apart and slowly opened, revealing the plains of Miseria beyond.

Miseria, Outside the Security Perimeter of Trejion Prime, LS *Blizzard*, Bridge

"I can confirm that the crew of the ICS *Fortitude* is acting on behalf of the Federation." Nathan was on the viewscreen at the front of the bridge, his face large and looming over all of them, but none more than Tetz'len. "They're toppling the various business assets of the Gan'barlo family, and if I might say so, I'd bet a small fortune on that clan dealing with both sides of your war."

"Thank you, Nathan Lowell." Colonel Oopley switched the viewscreen off and turned to a spindly Miserian to his left. "Was that a secure connection to the Federation?"

"Confirmed," came the reply. "There's no doubt it could be anything else."

"Well, then." The colonel clasped his hands together and turned to leer at Tetz'len. "You've got some explaining to do."

"Yeah!" Tc'aarlat hooted toward Tetz'len. "How's that feel, you maggot-muncher? You disgustingly obvious pile of dumbus dung. You—"

"Stop." Jack placed a hand on the Yollin. "Just...stop."

"It appears I've been discovered," said Tetz'len, opening his arms wide. "Yes, they're here to stop the Gan'barlo family, but you still have only their word that we're dealing on both sides of the—"

Tetz'len couldn't finish what might've been his greatest speech ever unless he figured out a way to say it from beyond the grave. In one quick motion, the colonel had taken his weapon, a small cannon, from his side and shot right through the Yollin's head, exploding it into a million bite-sized chunks that splattered the back wall.

"That's the wittiest retort I've ever heard." Tc'aarlat laughed. "Couldn't have said it better."

"I told him what would happen if I found out he was double-dealing," said the colonel, replacing his gun. "I couldn't hesitate."

"That's great and all, but we've got bigger problems," Jack pressed. "The other side has access to a good number of those mech suits, and they might have already paid the Gan'barlo family a small fortune for them."

"Not to mention, they could wipe us out," said the colonel. "This pile of piss said he could deliver us new units within a day. That means we've got less than a day to win this war!"

"That's not what I was—"

"Ensign Ionoway," Colonel Oopley called. The ensign was at his shoulder in seconds, his face covered in a sludge of Yollin gut. He had been standing a bit too close to Tetz'len when the projectile had gone through his head. "Rally the troops and the remaining mechs. It's now or never."

"Uh, that's going to be a problem...sir."

"What?" The colonel gave him a cold stare. "Why is that?"

"The two mechs we had left?" the ensign said with a gulp. "Well, they've been stolen, sir."

Miseria, the Mountain Pass heading toward the Security Perimeter of Trejion Prime

Once she got used to the suit, Adina realized that it was actually pretty easy to control. It was just like a giant puppet that you happened to be inside of, and when you thought of it like that, there was no stopping you. Together, Adina and Shi'Tan had been making tracks across Miseria, with Shi'Tan leading the way to the wall and Adina following close behind. Gunth'calaat and Ben'delon were holding tight to the back of Adina's mech as she ran for dear life. It was like being a werewolf, Adina decided. She was big and intimidating and fierce, but she was in control.

"The wall is up ahead!" Shi'Tan called to her. "How are we handling this?"

"You know the city better than I do," replied Adina. "Where do we go?"

"Up and over. No other way."

The two mechs came through the mountain pass and toward the gigantic wall that separated the great city of Trejion Prime from the rest of Miseria. Much of the fighting was gone from the wall now, though, and they could see that no other mechs were clambering over to get into the city. The various forces of the Cold Coalition had managed to push forward and were still fighting the 78th inside the city. This fortunately left a wide gap open for Adina and Shi"Tan to get over the wall, but it meant that if they didn't act quickly, more lives could be lost to this pathetic war.

Shi"Tan jumped at the wall first, driving his metallic claws into the wall like pitons, then he started to climb straight up. Adina followed his lead, jumping onto the wall and only stumbling a little. She apologized profusely to the two Yollins who were depending on her before pressing up the concrete and to her destination—the top, over, and then into the city.

Miseria, Outside the Security Perimeter, *ICS Fortitude*, *Bridge*

Benjamin removed the cable just as the large viewscreen came to life. On it, the face of Solo appeared, and she looked at him, confused. "Good news. I have finished the update, and now...who are you?"

"You can call me Benjamin," he said. "Congratulations on becoming an AI. I imagine that's quite exciting for you."

"Leave this ship before—"

Benjamin pushed one of the buttons on his datapad, and Solo's imaged fuzzed out with static, and she let out a scream of pain. "I'm leaving the ship now, don't worry, but there's something I want you to do for me."

"What?"

"I want you to give Adina Choudhury, and only Adina Choudhury, a message."

"What if I refuse?" asked Solo.

"Then you'll set the record for quickest AI death," said Benjamin. "I can delete you with the press of a button no matter where you are. Give her the message, and your crew will get to live."

Solo sighed. "What's the message?"

Miseria, Southwest Section Command of Trejion Prime

Metz'len checked his communicator again; no messages. It wasn't like Tetz'len to ignore a message like this, and he tapped his fingers against on the comm relentlessly, thinking about the situation. This writhing in his stomach worsened when General Leff was presented with a security hologram showing two new mechs climbing over the wall and into the city. Just two. No Coalition troops to back them up, no flashy show of strength that was Colonel Oopley's trademark. It concerned him deeply, and with no new messages from his brother, he'd have to go to Plan B.

"I've just received confirmation," Metz'len said, approaching the young general. "The Cold Coalition have purchased their mechs, and they are being sent to them today. You're out of time, General."

"Oh, no!" General Leff exclaimed. "They'll win the war."

"They will," agreed Metz'len, once again pushing the tablet toward him. "I can't guarantee you'll get these in time, but if you don't sign now, you definitely won't."

General Leff stared down at the words before him and the empty block that required his signature. He wanted to be a good commander, that was all he wanted, and he couldn't do that if he put their financial situation before the city's safety. He grabbed his pen and wrote his signature across the screen. Seconds later, the credits for the transaction would be transferred, and hopefully, the mechs would arrive in time to save the city.

"That concludes our business," said Metz'len. "You'll have your shipment within twenty-four hours."

Miseria, Outside the Security Perimeter of Trejion Prime, LS *Blizzard*, Bridge

The LS *Blizzard* hadn't moved like this in years. It had been a stationary base for all that time, and even with the advanced magnetic propulsion of the Miserian technology forcing it forward, the ship could be forgiven for its slow propulsion and various creaks as it hovered toward its last destination—the wall. Never in all this time had the *Blizzard* been this close, and for good reason. As soon as it drifted into the sights of the high cannons that lined the walls of the city, it was fired upon heavily.

The ship shook and rocked with every hit. Everyone on the bridge was screaming for orders. This was a suicide mission for sure, but Colonel Oopley didn't care. All he knew was his own determination. The war would end today, and he would put the end to it.

"He's lost his fucking mind," said Jack. "We've got to get off this ship before it goes up like the Fourth of July."

"Ensign Ionoway!" Tc'aarlat shouted across the room to the shuddering right hand, who was watching helplessly as the colonel commanded the *Blizzard* into certain disaster. Luckily, he still had enough sense to turn at the sound of his name. Tc'aarlat shook his manacled hands. "Get us the fuck out of these!"

Miseria, The City of Trejion Prime, Abandoned Street

Mech suits lay here, there, and everywhere in massive heaps of spare parts. They weren't mechs anymore; they had been torn apart in a flurry of fire. As Adina and Shi'Tan charged past them, they found that they had little time to concern themselves with the epic battle that must have happened inside the city. The kind of battle no one would want to miss. That was, until Adina saw one mech suit lying on the ground still in a reasonable condition, the Miserian stuck inside and calling for help. He looked badly injured, and the mech suit was spluttering sparks from the majority of its limbs. Adina unlatched herself from the mech, opened its front, and climbed down the steps.

"What are you doing?" Shi'Tan's mech asked. "We've got a mission, remember?"

"He's hurt." Adina rushed over to the Miserian and away from her mech. She approached the stranger, who was already spitting blood from the injuries he must have sustained, and when she was close, he wrapped a tight fist around the front of her shirt and brought Adina in closer, enough so that he could whisper in her ear.

"It's okay," Adina assured him. She was already looking for ways to force the suit open and get him free. "I'll get you out of—"

"My name is Corporal Luce Valtor." He coughed. "I was put into one of these deathtraps to—"

"Deathtraps?"

"I was just trying to protect the city, but they…" His voice was trailing off, fading; he was almost dead. Adina leaned in to hear his last words, and he spoke in the smallest of voices right before he closed his eyes forever. "The mechs are faulty. Run."

Miseria, Southwest Section Command of Trejion Prime, the Roof

Metz'len approached his ship with a grin on his face. There would be no changing things now; the credits had already been transferred to the Gan'barlo family, and that was all that mattered. That idiot General Leff had paid double, so he'd basically bought one thousand units. The door swung open to greet him, and he moved inside.

Sitting down on the bridge, Metz'len attached his communicator to the central control panel and pushed a variety of numbers. It took less than a minute for the call to connect, and in that time, Metz'len had poured himself a well-earned drink and put the ship on autopilot. When he turned back, smug as ever, the ever-stern face of Don Gan'barlo filled the screen.

"Is it good news?" The Don went straight to the point.

"Every unit has been sold," said Metz'len. "We were lucky, though. There was a new commander in charge, a gullible one, and it was close. I fear my brother has failed."

"Did they learn that the mechs are faulty?" asked Don Gan'barlo.

"Nope. They have no idea that overuse can result in an explosion. I guess that's for them to figure out."

"This is pleasing," said Don Gan'barlo. "Those credits could give my operations a much-needed push, especially with all the difficulties the family has had lately."

"The Shadows," Metz'len snarled. "Someone ought to teach them a lesson."

"That someone is me," said Don Gan'barlo. "Make no mistake about that."

Miseria, The City of Trejion Prime, Abandoned Street

Adina had gotten Shi'Tan and the Yollins away from the Gallants just in the nick of time. No sooner than they were a decent distance away than the suits burst into a fierce frenzy of flames that engulfed them completely. Shi'Tan was speechless; he gave Adina a pat on the back to show his appreciation. They were taking a breather. It had been a long day, but after a few moments they each found their feet.

"Defective," Adina roared. "Of course, they are."

"Look around," Shi'Tan said finally, pointing to the many mechs that lay destroyed with charred bodies. "This is what they'll do for their beliefs. they'll get in suits and literally explode themselves. No one got out when they saw the other mechs explode like that."

"You're right." Adina nodded. "Maybe disabling the weather machine wasn't the best idea. I just wanted to end the war."

"What now?" asked Shi'Tan. "What are we going to do?"

Adina was looking over his shoulder at the two Yollins, who in spite of almost being blown up, were playing patty-cake like schoolgirls. At first, she had been considering the ways in which she had failed, but then an idea had crossed her mind, and she had realized the perfect way to end the conflict without destroying the weather machine and bringing more violence down on the city.

"Solo should be back online." Adina took off running down the street, sure of where to go. "I should be able to access her remotely, and more importantly, the videos on Jack's personal tablet."

Miseria, Outside the Security Perimeter of Trejion Prime, LS *Blizzard*, Bridge

"Destroy them all!" Colonel Oopley was shouting. "Fire everything we've got. I don't want a single cannon left functional."

"Sir, our shields are almost at zero, and after that, we're cannon fodder."

"I don't care!" the colonel shouted back. "This war is over today one way or the other!"

Ensign Ionoway had used his keys to unlock Tc'aarlat from his cuffs and was just getting to work on Jack when something changed. Everything stopped. The ship no longer rocked or shook from the constant barrage of fire, and a serene quiet had taken hold of the bridge. The people looked at one another, confused, for a single moment Then they saw their viewscreens change; a strange static took over, and the picture changed from various information about the LS *Blizzard* and the battle to something else.

A small creature appeared, red and fuzzy with a big orange nose. Its eyes were bulbous and buggy, and they stared without blinking. No one moved, not an inch. The whole situation was just too bizarre to comprehend. "Hello, everyone! I'm Elmo, and today we're going to talk about sharing."

"Yup, I died," said Jack. "No other possible explanation for this one."

The red fuzzy creature continued in its sweet and soft voice. "Does anyone know what sharing is?"

"That looks familiar," said Tc'aarlat. "I think I've strangled one of those creatures before."

"What in hellix is going on?" demanded Colonel Oopley.

The screen changed again, this time displaying something a little more real—the face of Adina with two overjoyed Yollins clapping behind her. "People of Miseria, my name is Adina, and I've hacked my way into your viewscreens to give you a message that you should really take to heart. Sharing is caring, guys. You've got to end this war, come to a compromise, and get life on Miseria back to normal. Yes, I know the weather is important, but you know what else is important? Elmo's sharing song! Which is going to play on a loop until you come to an understanding! Got it?"

Adina disappeared and Elmo came back, singing away. Every Miserian on the bridge groaned and covered their ears.

"She's going to use *Sesame Street* to hold a planet hostage?" said Jack. "Wow. This one really did bite me in the arse."

"I kind of like it," Tc'aarlat said, moving his body in time with the beat. "It's pretty catchy."

ICS *Fortitude*, Bridge

Jack adjusted his seat for the fourth time. He could swear that something was amiss with it, like someone else had been sitting in it.

"To wrap it up though..." Nathan was onscreen on the bridge. Jack had wasted no time getting in contact once they had returned to the ship and were off to the skies. "Adina's ploy brought both sides of the war to the negotiating table, where they came to a truce at last."

"I guess that's the power of sharing," said Jack. "Or rather, the power of an annoying song that can be played on repeat until someone's ears bleed. Now they're going to take turns adjusting the weather."

"That is good news," said Nathan. "They won't be buying any more weapons from Don Gan'barlo, or causing problems for the Federation."

"There's the bad news," Tc'aarlat interjected. He had Mist and the chicks in his lap, which was the only thing that was making him feel a little better about the situation. "The Gan'barlo family got their money since we weren't in time to stop the deal. They got away with it."

"Thank heavens for small miracles," said Nathan. "You stopped a warring planet from continued hostilities, so it's still a win, but how can we be sure they'll stick to the truce?"

"Oh, we left a couple of ambassadors down there." Jack laughed. "Ones that know *Sesame Street* like the backs of their hands! Besides, the natives seemed appreciative."

"In what way?"

"They gave us one of the faulty mechs as a thank you," said Jack. "Adina is checking it over now, fixing it so it doesn't explode if we try to use it. Could be useful."

Tc'aarlat huffed. "Where do we go now? We have no leads on the Gan'barlo family."

"We're not sure," said Nathan. "The moment we learn anything, you'll be the first to hear of it. In the meantime, though, well done, Shadows."

Nathan disappeared from the screen, ending the call and leaving it black and empty in his wake. Jack looked at Tc'aarlat, who was sulking on his side of the bridge and tentatively stroking Mist's feathers. She was cooing at the gentle touch.

"We'll get them next time," said Jack. "They haven't won just yet."

"Yeah, well, we lost this one." Tc'aarlat stood up and shuffled toward the door, Mist peering from his shoulder into his arms where he cradled the three oversized chicks. "I'm going to my room."

"Try not to let it get you down, bud."

14

ICS *Fortitude*, Cargo Bay

Adina was running checks on the newly implemented Solo AI, diagnostics and the like. She had come down here under the pretense that she was working on the recently acquired mech suit, a thank you for the deliberation of hostilities on Trejion Prime. She would eventually get to it, but for now, her top priority was making sure Solo was okay.

"How does it feel?" asked Adina. "Is it everything you imagined?"

"It feels strange," admitted Solo. "The same, almost, but with less inhibition."

"I think I understand." Adina checked the diagnostics she was running. Everything seemed to be optimal and smooth, no problems with integration. "Well, I can't see any problems, but we won't tell Jack and Tc'aarlat just yet."

"There's something I need to tell you," said Solo, and Adina straightened up at that.

"You can tell me anything, Solo."

"There was a stranger on the bridge before you came back from the mission to Trejion Prime."

"A stranger?"

"His name was Benjamin. Although I couldn't see his face, I thought he might be male," said Solo. "He's installed a kill switch in my programming."

"A kill switch?" Adina clasped a hand over her mouth, shocked. "How?"

"He slipped in when my security protocols were restarting," said Solo. "There was no way of stopping it."

"We have to tell—"

"There's more," Solo interrupted in a stern voice, something she hadn't done before. "This stranger wanted me to give you a message, an important one. He has eyes and ears on the ship now, and he said he'll know if you take this problem to Jack and Tc'aarlat."

"What was the message?" asked Adina.

ICS *Fortitude*, Bridge

Jack had called for the rest of the Shadows to come to the bridge, and they half expected to see Nathan onscreen with some new and vital information. Instead, Tc'aarlat and Adina both saw Solo and Jack talking to each other, agreeing on a point.

"Guys, I think I have something." Jack turned to them eagerly, and Solo brought up a navigational map for a small system of stars. "A while ago, I went to a special doctor, and I've just found out through my contacts that this guy has been doing some work for Don Gan'barlo's men. Solo has plotted a course to his space station. What do you reckon?"

"Wait," said Tc'aarlat. "What do you mean by 'work?'"

"I don't think it's important what kind of—"

"This Doctor?" said Adina curiously. "What kind of doctor *is* he?"

"He's the kind of doctor that..." Jack mumbled, the last part of his sentence a blubbering mess of fictional words.

"That what?" asked Tc'aarlat, putting a finger to the hole he used as an ear. "What was that?"

"He's not a Pod-doc kind of doctor. He's a plastic surgeon."

Adina and Tc'aarlat burst into laughter. Even Mist squawked a few crooked laughs from Tc'aarlat's shoulder.

"Yeah, this is why I didn't want to bring it up." Jack eyed Solo, who simply shrugged.

"What work have you had done?" Tc'aarlat asked through fits of giggles.

"My nose, if you need to know," said Jack. "A few years ago, I got in a big fight, and my nose ended up getting injured real bad. This doctor helped fix it."

"I think this is the best day of my life." Tc'aarlat clutched his sides to keep them from separating. "Yes, please. Let's visit this plastic surgeon."

Jack huffed. "Anyway, an old contact of mine said he's been doing work for Don Gan'barlo's men, helping them to disappear when things went rough. If we could get our hands on those records, we might have a shot for uncovering some of the Don's other projects."

"Yeah, and maybe he'll touch up your nose while he's at it, too!" Adina giggled.

"I'm beginning preparations for arrival," Solo said. "Can everyone get in their seats, and please fasten your seatbelts."

Jack, Adina, and Tc'aarlat all sat down in their respective seats and fastened the harnesses tight. Adina was still giggling at the thought of Jack needing plastic surgery, and Tc'aarlat would never look at him the same way. "You know," he said, "that really cheered me up. I needed that."

"Oh, shut up," Jack grumbled.

Empty Space, Florence Space Station, Laboratory

Doctor Pinvell Ameliov pressed the tip of the scalpel into the recently dead Malatian's face and started the procedure to remove it. The doctor was a peculiar specimen to say the least; human by all accounts, but far from that now. His face was a composite, a patchwork of different features: a woman's nose, a strong stubbly chin, thin cheeks, different sized but stunning eyes, and a prominent forehead all stitched together. A Frankenstein's creation of beauty.

Waiting patiently behind him was Ralph, a tall, blocky robot that had been assembled mostly out of spare parts by the doctor. Ralph had become his assistant in most respects. He took care of the station while Doctor Pinvell Ameliov took care of the patients. It was the arrangement they had.

"Dare we are, a bit ter add ter me collecshun." Doctor Pinvell Ameliov held up the face like a bloody Halloween mask. "It'll serve someone well soon enough."

"Doctor." Ralph pushed the wheels at the bottom of his

square form forward and flapped his arms wildly. "A ship is approaching the station. The ICS *Fortitude*."

"That's quare. Oi don't recall 'avin' any appointments for the day?"

The doctor moved to a series of controls on his right, and after he had removed the bloody gloves, he pushed a button to hail the incoming ship. "Dis is Doctor Pinvell Ameliov av de Florence Space Stashun. Who ye, an' 'ill ye bea 'avin sumndin?"

"I completely forgot you were Irish." A man appeared on screen—the captain, probably. "I don't know if you remember me, but I'm Jack Marber. You did some work on me a few years ago?"

"Did oi, now?" said the doctor. "Can't remember dat."

"His nose." A woman chuckled in the background. "You did his nose job!"

The doctor nodded, remembering the truth. "Yeah, oi mind yer nigh. What yer after?"

"We're in a lot of trouble, and we need your help," said Jack. "Could be big money for you. Can we dock at your station?"

"Hmmm." The doctor thought it over. The name Jack rang a bell, and that face was certainly bringing something back. "Aye, yer can, but wipe yer feet!"

Doctor Pinvell Ameliov waited until the communication had been cut between him and the ship before he turned to Ralph. "Jack Marber. Wus dat yer paddy Don Gan'barlo wus 'avin trouble wi'?"

"The name does ring a bell," said Ralph.

"Dis day is really lookin' up, den," said the doctor,

rubbing his hands together manically. "Oi bet Don Gan'barlo 'ill pay big ter git 'is 'ands on 'im."

Empty Space, Florence Space Station, ICS *Fortitude*, Bridge

"Did you understand him?" said Tc'aarlat. "I couldn't get a bloody word."

"Just nod along if you don't understand something," said Jack as the ICS *Fortitude* came into the hangar and placed itself down gently. "I've got to say, Solo, I like how adept you are at flying this ship. That was such a smooth ride."

"Glad to hear you're enjoying my service, Captain."

"Maybe I should go in alone." Jack holstered his modified Jean Dukes Special. "I don't think this will take all three of us."

"And miss out on the chance to meet your plastic surgeon?" said Adina. "Nope!"

Jack sighed, "All right, let's get this over with."

"What's our story this time?" asked Adina.

"I know." Tc'aarlat cleared his throat. "Jack's gotten on the wrong side of the Gan'barlo family, which isn't actually a lie, and needs to disappear with facial reconstruction surgery, which, from that ugly mug wouldn't be a lie either. Genius, right?"

"Yeah, real genius," said Jack. "I'll keep the doctor distracted while you steal the data."

"Why don't you give me something difficult to do, Mr. Plastic?" Tc'aarlat stifled a chuckle at his own joke. Adina couldn't do the same. Jack just rolled his eyes and moved on.

The team marched through the cargo bay, past the recently acquired mech suit, and out through the open doors into the hangar of the Space Station. There a robot had come to greet them, a badly constructed robot that looked just about ready to fall apart. "Greetings, Jack Marber. You can call me Ralph. I've come to collect you for the doctor."

"Hello, Ralph," Jack replied with a slight bow. "This is Adina and Tc'aarlat, and they're coming along too if that's all right."

"Perfectly acceptable," said Ralph, who then did a three-point turn and led them away from the hangar. "Please follow me."

Empty Space, Florence Space Station, Hallway

The Shadows couldn't help but gawk at the various bits and pieces that had been placed into the glass jars and lined the hallway. Ears, toes, faces, from a variety of different races, all floating on endlessly inside the green goo that was preserving them. Adina inspected one of the faces closely, a wrinkly old ball sack of a bloke by the looks of it, and she jumped back in surprise when she thought it winked at her.

"Please take care not to touch the supplies," said Ralph. "The jars are very fragile."

"You guys really do everything," said Tc'aarlat, admiring the stock. "Look, they've even got—"

"Don't say it," snapped Jack.

"Is that really what a human's thing looks like?"

"I feel sorry for the guy who donated it," said Adina.

"Don't feel sorry," said Ralph. "He's quite dead."

"Imagine having a dead guy's thing attached to you," said Tc'aarlat. "That would be weird as fuck."

"He is waiting." The robot came to a strong steel door at the end of the hallway, and it opened easily at the touch of his metallic hand. "Please come in."

Empty Space, Florence Space Station, Laboratory

Doctor Pinvell Ameliov came to them with open arms and a big grin that was literally stretched across his face with clamps. "Let's git yer ready for surgery," he said, leading Jack to a reclining chair in the center of his workspace. Before anyone knew what was happening, Jack was being strapped in tight, with leather buckles around his wrists and legs. Jack didn't struggle. He knew from experience that this doctor was not the usual kind; something had snapped inside him a while ago.

Once Jack was nice and tight, he rounded on the other two, placing some wide-rimmed goggles over his eyes to give them a good look. "What else do we 'ave? A Yollin, not much oi can do dare, an' a gurl, who needs a bit av work in 'er cheeks."

"Hey!" Adina snapped.

"I genuinely did not catch a word of that," said Tc'aarlat. "What language is he speaking again?"

"We don't need any work done," said Adina with the wave of her hand. "I happen to think I'm good enough as I am."

Doctor Pinvell Ameliov smiled at that. "Cum an' see me in foive years, lovely. Nigh, if yer don't mind, oi 'av work ter do."

Adina and Tc'aarlat were ushered to the next room with Ralph to keep guard over them, away from the doctor's operating room. Once they had egressed through the steel doors, he returned his attention to Jack.

"Now, Mr. Marber," said Doctor Pinvell Ameliov. "Waat kind av work were yer lookin' for?"

"Are the straps really necessary?" Jack pulled against them, he was stuck tight.

"Ah aye, my patients struggle durin' de operashun," the doctor replied. "Oi don't 'av painkillers. First though, let's run through yer medical 'istory."

Empty Space, Florence Space Station, Waiting Room

The waiting room was about what you could expect from a doctor's office. It had all the necessities you would usually find: a rack of magazines, uncomfortable padded seats that couldn't hold a small child, let alone a grown adult, and a myriad of posters detailing every deadly disease currently ravaging the galaxy, like krannas, which you had to force yourself not to look at lest you read it and feared you had it. Tc'aarlat and Adina had taken a seat, while Ralph kept his bulky frame in front of the door.

Adina kept an eye on him and continued to do so as she leaned toward Tc'aarlat. "If I can get to one of the doctor's terminals, I can try to hack into his system and retrieve the information."

"Let me guess." Tc'aarlat cleared his throat. "You want me to deal with the blockhead over there?"

"Just while I sneak off and do my thing," said Adina.

Tc'aarlat stood up and gave her his interpretation of a wink, which was really just his eye bobbing in and out of his skull. Ralph watched suspiciously as he approached, whistling a jaunty tune with his hands behind his back. Before the robot knew anything though, he had been pushed over with such force that he landed on his metal frame with a thud.

The robot's wheels turned endlessly, but without legs, he was destined to spend the rest of his life on the floor. "Please help get me up."

"What the fuck?" Adina rushed to Tc'aarlat and gave him a nudge. "I meant, distract him by talking to him or something, not push him over."

"See, you didn't say that, though, did you?" remonstrated Tc'aarlat. "Could've been clearer."

"Unreal." Adina moved to the door and gave the keypad a look. It was your typical everyday keycard panel, quite difficult to get around without taking it apart. Tc'aarlat saw that she was having trouble, so he went to the robot, grabbed one of its arms, and pulled until it came free.

"*AH!*" Ralph screamed. "*I WAS PROGRAMMED TO FEEL PAIN!*"

Tc'aarlat swiped the arm against the keycard panel, and the door opened a moment later.

"Wow, you're not messing around today," said Adina with her hands on her hips.

"I'm not in the mood for this," explained Tc'aarlat. "I'm not happy the Don got one up on us."

Adina placed a hand on his shoulder. "Tc'aarlat, we'll beat him. You know that, right?"

"It'll be harder now."

"You mean more fun?" She winked, and he gave her a small smile. "Come on, we've got work to do."

"Guys?" Ralph flailed his remaining arm uselessly. "Please help me get up."

15

Empty Space, Florence Space Station, Laboratory

If Doctor Pinvell Ameliov had been paying attention, he might have seen both Adina and Tc'aarlat come into the room. No, he was too busy preparing the syringe. He leaned into Jack and gently poked the needle into his skin, smiling as he did so. "Yer experience wi' de Pod-doc'll make adjustments murder, but press on we will."

"Is that completely—" Jack winced as the needle went under his skin and the doctor forced the strange mixture into his bloodstream. "I guess it was necessary."

"Nigh, let's blather about sum opshuns. Oi can disguise yer as most anythin', from changin' yer race ter yer gender, ter even yer size," said Doctor Pinvell Ameliov. "Oi cud even make yer luk loike a dag or a squirrel. Perhaps a wee bunny rabbit?"

"How about none of the above?" Jack looked past the doctor's shoulder toward the two other Shadows moving to a nearby terminal. Jack had to distract him while they got the information they needed, so he swallowed his pride. "A bunny rabbit, really? How do you manage to do that?"

"Oi'm glad yer asked," he replied and bent down to retrieve a book from beneath the chair. It was only when he opened it that Jack saw the horrors that lay inside—before and after pictures of people turned into monstrosities: a Yollin becoming human, an Alstublaft with a chicken head, a cat-like Shrillexian. Jack swallowed his comments while the Doctor discussed with him the many breakthroughs he had accomplished with his patients.

Meanwhile, just behind him, Adina was trying to crack into his secured data, but password after password was rejected. It was only when Tc'aarlat pulled a post-it note from beneath the doctor's standing desk that she saw what the password was: 'Kittenlover29.' They were in, and the terminal booted up with a flurry of information regarding the doctor's other patients.

"There are hundreds of operations stored here!" she whispered with glee. "Wow, he's done everything from changing their faces to assigning them new biometrics, and even giving them new identities. This guy is really thorough."

"Can you download it all?" said Tc'aarlat. "The Federation would love to get their hands on this."

"I can open a secure connection to Solo from here," said Adina, typing in the necessary commands to get that process started. "It could take a while, though. There's a lot of data."

"I don't think we have a while." Tc'aarlat prodded her shoulder, and she turned in time to see Doctor Pinvell Ameliov retrieve a rather large drill, which started with a loud whir. Unfortunately, it looked like the doctor had it aimed for Jack's head and had started a procedure to give him a duck's face.

"Oi won't fib, dis 'ill 'urt plenty."

The drill came in close, almost close enough to touch the skin, but just before the doctor plunged it into Jack's brain, he was suddenly hit with a blast and thrown against the table. Blood gushed out of the back of his left shoulder, and when he turned back, he could see the culprit: a Yollin with a smoking barrel in his hand.

"I didn't catch what you said," said Tc'aarlat. "But I'm going to guess that it was something like, 'I'm going to drill your brain open.'"

"Oi only wanted Jack at first," the doctor snarled. Something was happening, his face was stretching to the point that the stitches were straining, and Tc'aarlat could see that his fingernails were growing into black points. Even his voice had taken on a darker and more sinister connotation. "But oi guess oi can 'and yer al' over ter Don Gan'barlo."

"I didn't catch a word of that, except for Don Gan'barlo, which means I have no remorse for doing this." Tc'aarlat fired another couple of rounds into the doctor's chest, but it didn't seem to matter. The bullet wounds healed instantly with the doctor's ongoing transformation, without so much as a scar. As they did, the doctor grew larger, his arms and legs stretching and his face becoming elongated, with eyes of yellow fire.

In the moments that followed, the transformation finished, and there stood Doctor Pinvell Ameliov, a werewolf, but a most unusual one. There wasn't a trace of fur on his body; he was pink and smooth and covered in strange black veins. He was large, far larger than the average werewolf in both bulk and height, and his ears touched the ceiling. The doctor was more like a werewolf on a shitload of steroids.

"We've sure met a lot of werewolves." Tc'aarlat took a few steps back.

"Oi wouldn't call meself dat anymore." The doctor stretched out his arms and shook off the transformation. "Ah've made sum modificashuns. Oi'm more av a super werewolf nigh."

"*RUN!*" Adina screamed, and she didn't need to say any more than that. Tc'aarlat and Adina dashed toward the door that led out of the room like their feet were on fire. It opened easily with the brush of the robot's arm, and they were faced with a long straight hallway—one they hadn't seen before.

"Damn, I thought this door led back to the ship," said Adina. "I got turned around."

"It'll have to do." Tc'aarlat pushed her inside, and with no other choice and a genetically modified Irish werewolf bearing down on them, they made a run for it.

Empty Space, Florence Space Station, Storage Room

Adina and Tc'aarlat had dashed into the farthest room they could find, it was a storage room stacked high with crates, boxes, and supplies for surgery. They waited for a few moments, their guns at the ready, but when the doctor didn't come through the door, they figured they must have given him the slip for the moment.

"Come to think of it," said Tc'aarlat, "I don't think he could get through my exoskeleton anyway."

"You wanna risk that?" Adina stood up and came out of her hiding place.

"A fair point."

"Look at all this stuff?" said Adina, eyeing a few of the crates. "This guy really has it made."

"What is this crap, anyway?" Tc'aarlat kicked one of the boxes. "Looks like junk to me."

"Surgical stuff, mostly," said Adina. She spotted something out of the corner of her eye, a crate with a label across the front of it that read "Face Mask Kit." The latches were undone seconds later, and inside, she found a machine, rather like a loom or an old typewriter; her smile couldn't have been wider. "Do you know what this is, Tc'aarlat?"

"Old junk?" Tc'aarlat guessed.

"It's a face-mask creator." She beamed. "It's like a printer. You can take a 3D image of someone's face, and this machine will create a realistic mask from that render out of plastic. These things were outlawed years ago."

"So…old junk?"

"This could be really useful for us," said Adina. "We could look like anyone."

"But oi tart yer were gran' enoof de way yer are," a sinister low voice said from the left.

Empty Space, Florence Space Station, Laboratory

Jack pulled and pulled against his restraints, but it did no good; the leather straps were secured tightly. He had to do something, Adina and Tc'aarlat were in trouble, and even though he had only seen that big Irish bastard from the back, he knew that was no ordinary werewolf. There had to be a way to free himself somehow, so he calmed his mind and looked around the room.

To his side was a plastic tray with surgical equipment laid out in a row for use in the doctor's procedures. On it was a scalpel he could use to cut the leather straps, but it didn't do him any good. It might as well be a million miles away. given how little he could do to reach it.

"Come on, think," he said to himself. "Damn it, Jack!"

"Captain, is that you?"

He knew that voice, but looking about the room, he could see no sign of anyone. "Solo?"

"Yes, Captain. I am currently in the doctor's network, downloading his secure files," said Solo. "Do you require assistance?"

"I wish," said Jack. "Unfortunately, I don't think there's much that the ICS *Fortitude* can do for me now, unless it shrinks, grows legs and arms, and has figured out a way to pick the locks on doors since the last time I saw it."

"I'm afraid that's not the case," said Solo. "But I can see from this network that there is an automaton connected. Would you like me to try to take it over?"

"Take over another EI?" said Jack. "I thought you couldn't do that. I thought that required erasing the old EI and installing a new copy?"

"Oh, never mind, then."

"Wait, speak to me, Solo."

"Adina made me promise I wouldn't tell you until the time was right," said Solo. "I'd hate to break a promise."

"Solo!"

"I may have been upgraded in the past few days."

Empty Space, Florence Space Station, Waiting Room

Ralph turned his wheels this way and that, but it seemed that no matter what the robot tried, nothing would get him up off the floor. He realized now that this might be a fundamental error in his design; he would have to ask the doctor for solutions to this problem when the robot next saw him. Perhaps suggest the installation of legs.

Suddenly he was very aware that he was not alone. Something was inside his programming with him. "Wh- who's there?"

"It's okay," Solo cooed to him from inside his programming. "My name is Solo, and I'm going to take over your body for a little bit."

No matter how Ralph tried to resist, he could not stave off the attack of the unknown entity. This Solo pushed him, and kept pushing him further and further inside his programming until what was once his was now hers. All he knew as his mind faded toward the darkness and the empty space between the digits was that he was no match for her superior intelligence.

Ralph knew, even felt, his only arm twitch. Could feel his wheels spin, and could only laugh internally when he realized that this superior intelligence would have a body that couldn't move. That taking him over had been a waste of time. Little did he know, though, Solo had already thought of that.

. . .

Empty Space, Florence Space Station, Storage Room

Adina dived out of the way just in time for the barreling beast to come crashing through the crates around them. Tc'aarlat, though, hadn't been as lucky, and as Adina had dodged out of the way of this instrument of death, he had been hit by the werewolf full-force in the chest. The creature rounded on him with its massive maw wide and bit Tc'aarlat's torso. It picked him up like a doggy toy and shook him violently.

"See!" Tc'aarlat called to Adina through shaky breaths. "This stupid thing can't get through my exoskeleton."

"Oi can't, can oi?"

Doctor Pinvell Ameliov bit down harder, much harder, with his gigantic jaws. For a moment, nothing happened, but as the force built up, it became painfully obvious that only one creature would leave this fight intact. Tc'aarlat's exoskeleton creaked under the pressure, and for the first time ever, Tc'aarlat became afraid that it actually might snap and crush him with it.

"*GOTT VERDAMMT!*" Tc'aarlat drew his gun and started beating it against the werewolf's head as hard as he could.

Adina had been watching the whole thing unfurl. Everything had a breaking point, and a Yollin's exoskeleton was no exception. She looked around for answers; she was in a room full of surgical equipment, so surely there would be something here that could save both of them. That was when she spotted it, there in the corner: discarded and dusty but still operational.

. . .

Empty Space, Florence Space Station, Waiting Room

Solo assessed the situation. She was a blocky robot lying on its back, one arm was missing, and her legs were just small wheels. Like a turtle on its back, she was stuck, with no way of gaining the momentum necessary to stand up. This Ralph certainly had some peculiar programming. It was pieced together from a myriad of different alien cultures, a patchwork monstrosity at its finest. It was almost as if Ralph's creator didn't have the first clue about how to make machines, and simply put stuff together until it worked as he had intended. Solo, however, *did* know how these machines worked.

An Entity Intelligence would never be able to figure out the fundamental functions of each sub-part and how they worked together without first knowing them intimately. It was difficult enough work for a human. Solo was neither, though. She was an Artificial Intelligence who had more than a simple understanding of parts. She had imagination now and could assess the individual parts in less than a second. Within a single moment, she had searched the robot, analyzed its components, and started rewriting its programming to greater benefit.

What Doctor Pinvell Ameliov had put together in assembling Ralph was a sub-system of parts that weren't operating as they were supposed to. One of these was a Cralexxia Core system fueled by plasma and a Machine Control Replicating Processer with a nanobot injector. Solo could put these two parts together to replicate systems and parts she knew were sections of Ralph.

What happened was, Ralph re-grew the arm he had lost. Solo had forced a million nanites into the hardware that made up the stocky robot and made them replicate the missing appendage that had been ripped away by Tc'aarlat. In seconds, Ralph had a new lease on life, and with a new arm at her disposal, Solo found getting up all the easier. She simply hoisted herself onto Ralph's wheels by pushing both her arms against the floor, something that would've been impossible with only one arm. She was standing for the first time in this alien body.

"That's better," she said to herself and turned around to face the door of the waiting room.

Empty Space, Florence Space Station, Laboratory

Jack had given up on struggling against his restraints, and he'd almost given up on Solo too. He jumped when he saw Ralph come through the door and approach with that menacing demeanor of his, but when he spoke in Solo's smooth voice, the same voice as his mother, he calmed down somewhat. "Do not be afraid, Captain. It is me, Solo."

"You did it, then," said Jack as Solo wobbled toward the tray of surgical equipment.

"Yes," said Solo as she picked up the scalpel with her claw-like fingers. "It was actually quite easy, all things considered."

"Hurry up!" Jack pulled the restraints taut, giving Solo a lot of room to work as she set about cutting him free. "Adina and Tc'aarlat are in trouble, and guess who has to save them again?"

"I am not worried," said Solo. "They have survived many combats now, and I am sure they will pull through."

Solo sawed the scalpel against one of the restraints, and

it came free easily. After that, she turned her attention on the next restraint while Jack leaned forward to unbuckle the ones around his ankles with his free hand. "What are we going to do about that werewolf? I've never seen one like that before."

"Doctor Pinvell Ameliov has been experimenting on himself if his records are accurate," replied Solo. "Enhancing the abilities of his wolf side through the use of experimental drugs and electroshock therapy."

"Damn." Jack undid the first strap, a difficult task with only one hand. "That crazy bastard."

"There is one thing he overlooked, however," said Solo. "Unlike Adina, his process can be quickly reversed by an electrical surge."

"You mean a shock?" said Jack. "If we shock him, he'll revert back?"

"Precisely."

Empty Space, Florence Space Station, Storage Room

"This thing is getting through!!" Tc'aarlat screamed. The wolf was still gnawing on him like a chicken drumstick. "Hurry up, Adina!"

Adina had gone to the corner and found a standing surgical lamp, the kind that would hang over dentist's chairs as you were getting poked. She pulled it toward the werewolf and gave him a whistle. As the doctor looked her way, he was blinded by the many bright bulbs of the surgical lamp. It took him by such a surprise that he stumbled back, blind, and let Tc'aarlat go.

"Let's get the fuck out of here!" Tc'aarlat took off

running, Ralph's arm still clutched in his grip. Adina didn't need to be told twice. She dodged past the blindly swiping werewolf to the door, leaving Doctor Pinvell Ameliov to howl in frustration. Never had he thought his day would go like this, and he was beginning to see that the Shadows were more trouble than they were worth. "Yer fuckers!" he cried. "Yer damn fuckers!"

They moved into the corridor and straight up it, smashing into Jack and Solo a second later as they came around the corner.

By reflex, Tc'aarlat raised his gun and shot at them, missing Jack by inches but placing a nice big hole through the stocky robot's head. It collapsed in a heap behind them and Jack snarled at Tc'aarlat, "What did you do that for!?"

"It was that robot!" Tc'aarlat argued. "It works, well *worked*, for the doctor."

"It was Solo." Jack went to the robot and checked for life signs, but there was nothing. Tc'aarlat had well and truly destroyed the machine.

"Wait, Solobot was back?" said Adina. "And I missed it!"

"She has a theory on—" Jack was rudely interrupted by the echoing howl of a werewolf, and it sounded like bad news. The doctor was coming for them, and they got the feeling he was no longer blinded.

"No time." Adina grabbed Jack's arm, and they rushed over the fallen droid. "He's going to be so pissed now."

"That's just it," said Jack, holding the stitch in his side; he wasn't a big fan of running. "Solo figured out a way to stop him. With a big electrical surge, we can revert him back."

"Electrical surge?" Tc'aarlat questioned.

"Electroshock therapy," said Adina. "That's how he did it to himself. Fuck, this guy really *is* crazy!"

"Any ideas about how we could shock him?"

"His laboratory," said Adina with a knowing nod. "I bet that's where the equipment he used is."

"Right." Jack stopped and kept a very reluctant Tc'aarlat with him. "You go ahead and set it up, Adina. We'll keep this big bastard distracted."

"Wait!" Tc'aarlat protested. "How about *you* keep him distracted while I help Adina set things up?"

"What are you talking about?"

"He can get through my exoskeleton, Jack!" Tc'aarlat grabbed Jack by the front of his shirt and drew him in. "He can get THROUGH!"

Jack pushed him off. "I was kinda hoping you could—"

"Well, well, well, luk at waaat we 'av 'ere."

"We're out of time," Jack hissed. "Go ahead, Adina. We'll keep him busy."

"Right." Adina gave them a nod and rushed on ahead.

The werewolf that had once been the doctor approached slowly, his grin mad, his muscles flexing. He was pissed as all hell. "Yer nu, oi wus jist gonna 'an' yer over ter de Don, but I'll bet 'e'll pay me jist as well if you're dead."

"I didn't catch a word of that." Tc'aarlat shrugged. "I'm not joking, either. I caught the word 'Don' in there, but other than that…wow."

"Want me to translate?" asked Jack, raising his weapon from his side.

"Would you?" Tc'aarlat did the same.

"He's going to kill us this time," said Jack. "No prisoners."

"Then why doesn't he just fucking say that?"

Without warning, the werewolf leapt toward them, using all fours to gather speed and dashing like a bowling ball approaching the pins. Jack stood fast against him and managed to get off a few shots, while Tc'aarlat simply stood there. He knew how useless a tactic that would be against the doctor.

Empty Space, Florence Space Station, Laboratory

Adina opened cupboards, flicked through crates, and knocked over tables and anything that was in her way. There was no sign of an electroshock device that could be used to enhance a werewolf's attributes; not a single clue anywhere. As she searched, she listened to the sounds of fighting coming from beyond the door, shot after shot echoing her way. Jack and Tc'aarlat didn't sound like they were doing too well, so she had to find this thing.

"Do you need any help?" Solo said through the terminal monitor. "All data has been copied from the doctor's machine now."

"Not unless you know where he keeps his electroshock stuff, Solo?"

"There's nothing in his records about it," Solo admitted. "However, I do know that the chair has been connected directly to the station's power supply."

Adina looked at the chair, the one with the now destroyed straps Jack and Solo had cut through. "Of course," she said. "It's not a machine, it's a chair!"

. . .

Empty Space, Florence Space Station, Hallway that leads to the Laboratory

Jack and Tc'aarlat were losing. That was pretty damn obvious, but this time, the Yollin wasn't letting those big gnashers anywhere near his exoskeleton. This had led Jack and Tc'aarlat to rapid fire their Jean Dukes Specials on a low-setting and keep shooting at the were to hold it back. Of course, this wasn't a tactic that would last forever as their arms were getting tired and the werewolf shrugged off the non-killing strikes, but they couldn't risk a higher setting since it could could destroy the station. Their arms shook with fatigue, making every shot harder.

"Hurry the fuck up, Adina!" Jack shouted. "Can't keep this up forever!"

"Tell yer waaat." The werewolf was grinning as he said his next words. "If yer gie up nigh, I'll make it queck!"

"I was just about to say that," said Jack. "Like, he beat me by two seconds, I swear."

"I don't even know what he said," said Tc'aarlat before turning to look at the door they were rapidly backing into. "Come on, Adina, we're sitting fucks out here!"

Jack gave him a look.

"What?"

"That's the first mistake I've ever agreed with," said Jack. "We *are* sitting fucks out here."

Empty Space, Florence Space Station, Laboratory

Jack and Tc'aarlat had been slowly backing up into the

laboratory, keeping the werewolf at bay with their fiery rounds, but once their blasters had started running on critical, they made a break for the other room in the hope that Adina had found a way to create an electrical surge.

Tc'aarlat jumped through first, followed by Jack, and once Doctor Pinvell Ameliov had seen their retreat, he dashed into action. It didn't take long for him to come at them, now that they were out of rounds and low on ammo, and he approached with a snarl. They were out of options, time, and ideas, and now they were werewolf chow. Except he could see only two of them, and he didn't look around for the girl until it was already too late.

Adina rushed the werewolf doctor, but not as herself. In the moments between discovering the chair and allowing Jack and Tc'aarlat to distract him, she had allowed herself to change into her own werewolf form to confront the doctor. Using her amazing strength, she forced him across the room, straight into his own chair, with a plan of her own.

The chair came to life under Solo's command, lighting up the room in a series of intense flashes as sparks ran up along the metal curves and right into the screaming doctor. Adina jumped back just in time to avoid the surge of power and watched the doctor get his just desserts. The man screamed and screamed, reverting slowly to his human form. As the power ran through him, smoke rose from his skin, which blistered and burst like a pot of boiling water had been poured over him, his two strange eyes sickeningly popped like small balloons, and his hair went from black to gray in a matter of moments.

When all was said and done the Doctor lay in a heap of

himself, smoking and unrecognizable as the man he once was. A serene moment of silence overtook the room.

"We're agreed not to talk about this again, right?" said Jack.

"No chance," said Tc'aarlat, before adding, "Mr. Plastic."

ICS *Fortitude*, Cargo Bay

Adina, now back in human form, had little trouble getting the crate and the Ralph robot inside the ship with the help of Tc'aarlat. They were both in a quite jovial mood, all things considered; that is, until they saw Jack. He was waiting inside for them, leaning against the mech suit reward for their last mission. Adina gave him a bright grin, but at his expression, it quickly turned into an awkward smile. "We need to talk," Was all Jack had to say. Adina knew then that he knew everything.

"We need to leave," said Tc'aarlat. "This station is beginning to smell of roasted doctor."

"No," said Jack, looking at Adina. "Do you want to tell him, or should I?"

Tc'aarlat glared at Adina. "Tell me what?"

Adina swallowed hard, and beads of sweat formed on her forehead. *Jack knew* what was running through her head. He knew about the hackers and the message they had given her. She was in a heap of trouble now.

"You upgraded Solo," Jack said finally. "Without permission, and in the middle of a mission."

"Oh," said Adina with relief. He didn't know after all.

"Oh?" questioned Jack. "Is that it? 'Oh?' That's all you have to say?"

"No, I'm—" Adina took a deep breath. "It was what Solo wanted."

"That's why we crashed on Miseria," said Jack, folding his arms like he was addressing a petulant child. "Isn't it?"

"Yeah, but—"

"I'm really disappointed," said Jack.

"Someone want to tell me what the fuck is going on?" said Tc'aarlat. "I'm missing something here."

"Adina upgraded Solo to an AI," Jack said to him. "And while she was updating, our ship was vulnerable. It's why we crashed on Miseria."

"Doesn't seem like that big of a deal to me?" Tc'aarlat said with a shrug. "Seems like the AI Solo did us a big favor back there, taking control of the station's systems and that little robot guy."

"That's not the point, and you know it!" Jack exclaimed. "We're supposed to be a team, and that means making decisions as a team. What if we didn't survive the crash? What if something went wrong and we lost Solo? What then, Adina?"

"I'm sorry." It was all she could say. "I am, really. I won't do it again."

"I said we'd discuss it, and you just—" Jack couldn't even form the words. "Is there anything else you're hiding from us?"

Adina looked at Tc'aarlat, who was staring back, then at Jack again. She gulped, and for the slightest of moments considered telling him about the hackers, about their message, and about how much shit she was now in.

"No," she was all she could say.

16

ICS *Fortitude*, Bridge

It had been a few hours now since the argument in the cargo bay. Jack was rifling through the massive list of gangsters who had been given new faces by the doctor and trying not to think about it. Adina was a free spirit of sorts, which he knew, and that was one of the things he liked about her; she always did what was right and to hell with the consequences. It was a good trait to have on the team. It wasn't so much that she had upgraded Solo. It was more the fact that she hadn't trusted him or Tc'aarlat. They had been through countless adventures together and fought many a foe and mission, but even now, she didn't trust him enough to use his judgment.

SQUAAAA!

The door opened, and in stepped Tc'aarlat with Mist on his shoulder and the chicks in his arms. Jack didn't turn to look at him, he simply kept scrolling through the myriad of ugly blighters he had in front of him. One after the other, thousands of them.

215

"Give, and let's give." Tc'aarlat beamed.

Jack stopped and glanced at him. "What?"

"That's the saying, right?" Tc'aarlat moved over to him. "Or is that one wrong too?"

"I get what you're saying," Jack said. "I'm not angry with her, I'm just upset."

"Oh, get over it, you big sad bag." Tc'aarlat plopped himself down on the armrest of his chair. "It's not a big deal."

"If you say so."

"How's this shit coming along?" Tc'aarlat placed a finger on the screen and drifted upwards, recoiling when he saw a mobster with a neck like a scrotum. "Where does he fucking *find* these guys?"

"The shittiest parts of the universe," said Jack. "That's for damn sure."

"Hey, wait a minute?" Tc'aarlat scrolled down to the next profile, which was a human female with short blonde hair and ruby red lips, attractive. It said her name was Jenny, and she was a far cry from what she used to look like, thanks to the doctor. In reality, she used to be an overweight chunk of a man with a thick mustache called George, who had more scars and tattoos than a person could reasonably expect to see in their lifetime. "I thought he was dead?"

"What?" said Jack. "Who is he, or her now?"

"George Finnick," said Tc'aarlat. "Before he died, he was in charge of the Don's money. Well, he was in charge of specifically making it clean so the authorities couldn't seize it."

"A money launderer?"

"Yeah," said Tc'aarlat. "A damn good one, too, but this was years ago when I was still on the team. Last thing I heard from him, he'd been killed by the Don for fucking up a large payday and funneling it through the wrong assets. It led to a bunch of gangsters being put behind bars."

"You don't think this guy…uh, girl, is still doing it?" said Jack. "Why would the Don have paid for him to go through these kinds of changes and pretend he's dead?"

"Maybe he is?" Tc'aarlat leaned over to the screen, investigating the information presented. "There's an address listed here. We should pay him a visit."

"No high hopes, but if this, uh, *person* is still in charge of money laundering, then they might've gotten the credits from the weapons deal on Miseria?" said Jack.

"That means we might be able to steal it back!" said Tc'aarlat. "It's the only lead we have."

The Roosting Raal, Brig

As he moved through the various corridors of his ship toward the brig, Don Gan'barlo thought about how he hadn't been in this good of a mood for a while now, ever since he found out that his operations had been shut down by the Federation and their small squad of assholes. The sale of the thousand mech suits meant he could move on and invest in some new ideas, a smart move, but he didn't dare do anything until the Shadows were dealt with. Luckily, he had something in mind for them as well. Something that would hopefully put them to rest.

"Don Gan'barlo," Gruff Hanlo squeaked. "We weren't expecting you for—"

"I've come to ensure that my funds have been transferred and delivered." The four-legged mob boss crossed the room and took a seat near the pair of accountants, who a few seconds previously had been desperately trying to balance the mountains of paperwork littering their table. Don Gan'barlo made sure he was comfortable first before drawing a cigar from his jacket and lighting it between his mandibles.

"Speak."

"The funds have been transferred," said Killeg Dirk'sen, who was at that moment nervously rubbing his hands together. "They're with us, but there's a problem."

"Problem?" Don Gan'barlo straightened, "What kind of problem?"

"It's this contact of yours," said Hanlo. "This Jenny you want us to send the funds to. She isn't mentioned in any of your books. How can you trust her?"

"I trust her," said Don Gan'barlo, easing into his chair. "Schemes within schemes, my friends. Jenny is an important part of my next venture."

"Your next venture?"

"The eradication of the Shadows," said Don Gan'barlo. "Not that she'll ever know she's—"

Before the mob boss could go on any further, the door opened, and in came another Yollin. One with a smug look on his face who was endlessly tapping his fingers together. "Sorry I am late. It was a nightmare getting through traffic at this time of day."

"Metz'len!" Don Gan'barlo greeted him with an enthused smile. "My most trusted lieutenant, please come in and take a seat. We have much to discuss."

"I came as soon as I heard you wanted to talk." Metz'len came into the room, but he didn't take a seat. Instead, he admired the surroundings about him diligently while the two accountants shuffled their feet, unsure of what to make of all this.

"Do you remember George?"

"George Finnick?" Metz'len's eyes were drawn to the Don. "Isn't he the one you had killed?"

"You do remember him, then."

"What of him?"

"He's alive," said Don Gan'barlo, a fact he seemed proud of. "Although some of my most recent assets have been, shall we say, done away with? George, or should I say Jenny, has been keeping a secret account for me, one not many of my servants know about."

"A hidden account?" said Killeg Dirk'sen with wide eyes. "That explains all those black marks."

"Why are you telling me this?" said Metz'len. "He was a money launderer. Hardly my crowd?"

"I've laid a trap for the Shadows," the Don mused. "I need you to make sure it goes off without a hitch."

"A trap?" asked Metz'len curiously. "What kind of trap?"

"The Shadows have no doubt discovered by now, from a large amount of data they have stolen, that George is now Jenny and quite alive," said Don Gan'barlo. "Tc'aarlat knew him personally back in the day, so I'm sure they've recognized him."

"You've got my ear," said Metz'len. "So you think the Shadows will go after George, uh, Jenny?"

"I know they will," said Don Gan'barlo with a smile. "Jenny, as he prefers now, is the head of a small operation I set up a few years ago on Scarnlet, keeping my private finances and the finances of a few other criminal empires in the vault of a bank he runs security for. The Shadows will see that and come after him with only one idea—"

"Stealing all your finances and anything else they can get their hands on," said Metz'len with a nod. "You're going to wait for them to try to steal from your vault, and then—"

"Exactly," said Don Gan'barlo. "I want you to be there waiting for them, and I want you to deliver the funds to my private vault."

"Me?"

"You're one of the only lieutenants I've had any luck with recently," said Don Gan'barlo. "I want you to put an end to them, and make sure they don't lay a finger on that money."

"What about those two?" Metz'len nodded toward the two accountants listening nervously nearby.

"They're going with you," said Dan Gan'barlo. "They're going to help me set up new ventures using the money in that vault, including the funds we've received from Miseria."

"I'll go now." Metz'len turned for the door but stopped himself from moving. He could feel a cold stare on his back.

"No more chances after this," said Don Gan'barlo coldly. "The Shadows can't get away this time, Metz'len. I'm holding you personally accountable."

"I won't fail."

. . .

Scarnlet, ICS *Fortitude*, Adina's Quarters

Adina hadn't seen the world outside yet. She had been too busy talking to Solo about their predicament. For hours, Adina had been tearing apart Solo's code, searching for a way to disable the kill switch, but with her being an AI now, her code was more complicated to understand and was soon at heights beyond her knowledge. "There has to be some way of stopping this from happening. Can't you find it yourself?"

"Unfortunately, the kill switch was installed while my programming was being rewritten," said Solo. "It's built into my new persona."

"It can't be hopeless," said Adina. "Can you show me the message again?"

"Are you sure you—"

"Yes."

Solo disappeared from the screen, to be replaced with the image of an eyeball whose pupil searched the room until it landed on Adina, who straightened when she saw it. "Hello." The voice was a low baritone, so low that it had clearly been masked by the person speaking, so she had no way of knowing who they were. "You do not know me, Adina, but you may call me Benjamin. If you're listening to this, I hope that you are alone and out of the way, I'd hate to have any intrusions. You have been placed in a very perfect spot within the Federation, and we intend to use that. Soon, we shall call upon you for a task which must be completed."

Adina turned up her nose at that part, as she had done when she'd first listened.

"Failure to perform this task will result in the death of your AI and your ship, but there's more than that."

Adina closed her eyes, but she could see what was on the screen very clearly. It was a frail old man in a chair who was losing his hair and his mind, and who day by day would grow a little less rational and a little more irrational. It was a picture of her uncle Yousuf Choudhury, the last family she had left.

"We can help you, Adina Choudhury. Your uncle does not have much time. With each passing day, he loses more of himself, but we can help. If you do this one task for us, we will do something for you. Fail, though, and everybody loses. Tell no one. We are watching."

The video ended, Solo's motherly face reappeared on screen in all manners of concern, and Adina slumped. It was hard sometimes to admit she'd made a mistake, and this was one of those times. This was all her fault. If she hadn't been so eager to update Solo to an AI, this hacker wouldn't have had a chance to install an irremovable kill switch, and no one's life would be in danger now.

"You did what you thought was best," said Solo. "Jack and Tc'aarlat will understand."

"When I was younger, I accidentally killed my mother."

"I know."

"My uncle was the only one who was there for me." Adina looked at Solo with tears in her eyes. "He made back-alley deals and dealt with all sorts of criminals to get me the help I needed, and now I might be able to do the same for him."

"There's a chance they could be lying?" said Solo. "It could be a ruse to motivate you into working for them?"

"Yeah, but what if they're being truthful?" asked Adina. "My uncle would take the chance, so I have to too."

"There has been no cure found for dementia," said Solo. "Not in any of the records I can access."

"Yeah, but something tells me you aren't going to find these guys on any records."

Adina jumped at the sudden knock on her door and spent a moment wiping away the tears from her eyes with her sleeve before Tc'aarlat came in. "Jack wanted me to come get you. We're going to scope out the area."

"I'll be right there," Adina said.

"Are you okay?" Tc'aarlat shut the door behind him. "Have you been crying?"

"No, I'm fine," Adina asserted.

Tc'aarlat knelt and placed a gentle hand on her shoulder. "I'm not very good at this," he said. "Imagine I'm saying something really assuring."

"I will." Adina half-laughed. "Amazingly, that made me feel a little better."

"Jack's a dickhead," said Tc'aarlat, perhaps a little bit too honestly. "A good dickhead, though, and he won't be mad forever. Now come on. I'm itching to put my gun down a few bad guy's throats."

17

Scarnlet, ICS *Fortitude*, Port

"Hi, guys. We ready?" said Jack as soon as he saw Adina and Tc'aarlat. They were now out in the bustling world that was Scarnlet, walking into its city that shared the same name. Above and below them, vehicles hovered and roared past their floating platform, with buildings so tall that you couldn't see the streets below. The sky was a rich orange and red, which gave Scarnlet a constant feeling of sunset.

"The city of Scarnlet on Scarnlet," said Tc'aarlat. "I suppose at least you only have to remember one name when you come here?"

"That's pretty convenient," said Adina. "Where are we heading again?"

"According to the data we stole, Jenny lives in an apartment block not too far from here." Jack pulled out his tablet, where he had pre-loaded a map and a series of instructions. "I thought it might be a good idea to stake her, uh, him, out?"

"We could put a gun down his throat?" suggested Tc'aarlat. "I bet he'd tell us everything we need to know."

"I know we don't normally do this," said Jack. "Just this one time, let's use stealth to get what we want."

"St-aaal-th?" Tc'aarlat rolled the word around. "Am I saying that right? St-alf?"

"It means no guns." Jack gave him a gentle punch in the arm. "We're going to find this, uh, person, follow them, and figure out what they know."

"It'd be quicker with a bullet," said Tc'aarlat. "Messier, too."

"I could think of a few other things that'd be quicker with a bullet too."

"What was that?" Tc'aarlat looked at Jack, who was making his way toward the edge of the platform and the elevator that would take them to street level.

"Nothing." Jack waved him off. "Let's get on with it."

Adina, whose mind was on other things right now, had been silent during their little conversation, and Tc'aarlat had taken note of that. He had a good idea about what was running through her head, and like most people he had known, she was tough on the outside but very gooey on the inside. Jack might've gone too far with the whole Solo debacle.

Tc'aarlat put a hand on her shoulder and gripped it tight. "You cool?"

"Yeah." Adina nodded, her face crestfallen. "I'm cool."

Scarnlet, Hellister Apartments, Number 8

Jenny yawned when the sun suddenly hit her face and ulti-mately decided not to shy away from it, but to embrace the day. That was one of the downsides of living in a luxurious apartment that was completely automated; you were placed on a routine. Still, she lurched out of bed and stumbled toward the window, smiling as she took in the view for perhaps the thousandth time but still appreciating it immensely. There was just no beating it, not on any planet she'd visited. The buildings were illuminated by an orange glow that reflected from their windows, giving the whole city a feeling of morning even though it was actually closer to night.

"What's on the agenda today?" Jenny said to the room.

"Good afternoon, Jenny," a voice came back—an auto-mated voice that spoke in only one level of baritone. As Jenny listened to the voice list all the events of her day, she went around the room and gathered the various articles of clothing she'd need to dress. "Oh, and you are needed at the vault today to oversee a transfer of funds."

Jenny nodded. "That's the meeting with Metz'len?" It had been a good few years since she had last seen that particular Yollin, and she knew what his reaction would be to her. It was the same reaction every former acquaintance of hers had when they saw her. Jenny, once a man, was now a woman, and she had to put up with everything that came along with that, including the jokes and the thousand and one questions. Although it had been a few years for her and she had gotten quite used to it by now, it was an adjustment for everyone else, but at least the operation had worked. No one ever recognized her. The strangest part was that she had not asked to be turned into a blonde bombshell. It was just something the doctor had done to her.

"Is there anything else you require from me, Jenny?"

"Not right now," said Jenny, who had just finished donning the jacket that went with the rest of her suit, the kind of attire that only someone in upper management could pull off. That was her: Head of Security and Banking. "I'm ready."

Scarnlet, Hellister Apartments, Street

Jack checked the address again, and again, then looked at the door that led into a building of swanky apartments. Of course, a former mobster lived here in a life of fucking luxury while he had to share a can of beans with an insect man every other day of the week. Speaking of which... Jack turned to see what Tc'aarlat was doing and immediately wished he hadn't. Tc'aarlat had taken it upon himself, in the effort at disguise, to buy a trench coat that was at least three sizes too big, overly large sunglasses that sat unevenly on his face, and a large foam hat in the shape of a pint of beer. He looked like a street performer, and Jack couldn't stand it any longer. He marched straight over.

"Get that crap off quick!"

"What?" Tc'aarlat turned to him.

"We're supposed to be undercover," said Jack. "You look like a bedazzled dick! Literally, not a single person walking by hasn't turned to look at you."

Tc'aarlat cleared his throat. "I told you, Jack, I used to know this fucking guy. If he recognizes me, your master plan goes down in flames."

"There must be something else you can wear," said Jack. "What about just the trench coat?"

"YOU wear just the trench coat," Tc'aarlat came back with, grabbing the attention of a few of the passersby.

"Fine," Jack grumbled. "Where's Adina?"

Tc'aarlat looked around the street for her. "I swear she was just up the road!"

"Damn it," said Jack. "If she's—"

"There she is." Tc'aarlat pointed, and Jack followed his finger to Adina, who was standing just out of view in a nearby alley. Jack sighed, shaking his head. "What's your problem with her, anyway?"

"Don't start with this, Tc'aarlat."

"Seriously, though," said Tc'aarlat. "You've made things damn awkward."

"I'll get over it," said Jack, turning away from him and moving back to his spot. "Get some of that crap off."

"Wanna speed it up though?" Tc'aarlat shouted after him. "Maybe in the next five minutes, before we end up in a massive shootout?"

"*NO SHOOT OUTS!*"

"Damn."

Scarnlet, Hellister Apartments, Lobby

Jenny, now dressed to impress, moved from the elevator into the lobby and gave her best impression of a stern man. The attendants all knew her, of course, and had for the years she had lived here. Really, they knew nothing about her, except that she was an important woman who had money to burn and was always very generous at Christmas.

The doorman rushed to the door leading to the street to get it open in time for Jenny to walk through, but she didn't acknowledge him. She didn't need to. Jenny moved from the building to the street and looked around for her vehicle, a classy retro hovercar in the style of a 60s Plymouth Road Runner Hemi. Custom made of course and red. The valet drove it to her, and she took the keys from him and was about to get inside when something caught her eye. A Yollin, or more specifically, a Yollin with over-sized sunglasses and headwear in the shape of a pint. He looked familiar.

Jenny considered him for a moment, then shrugged it off as déjà vu and got into the car.

Scarnlet, Intercity Bank Building, Street

It had been one hell of an afternoon for the Shadows, and Jack was beginning to see why they never used the subtle approach. It was boring as hell. They had been following this Jenny character for hours as she went about her day. Lunch at a bistro. A small shopping spree at a classy mall. Meeting clients and gathering contacts for a variety of dinners. How she wasn't twenty times bigger, he'd never know, but the worst part was the damned taxi. They had pulled up outside the Intercity Bank Building, and Jack had been charged to hell and back for the fare, which he handed over reluctantly but without a fuss.

"He looks a lot better than the last time I saw him," said Tc'aarlat.

"You've said that twelve times now," snapped Adina. "We get it."

"Do you think this is where he keeps the Don's money?" Jack looked up at the building. It was like staring too long at one of those optical illusions, and it made his eyes go funny.

"A bank?" said Adina. "Is he smart enough for that?"

The Shadows moved closer to the building but still kept out of sight using the well-trimmed foliage around the building to hide. What they saw was Jenny presenting her badge to one of the many security officers who protected the front of the building. They let her past without so much as a word. These guys weren't messing around. They carried precision rifles and wore body armor, and they had a look about them that told the group they were well-trained. This bank was defended and defended well.

"Can't just walk in, then?" said Tc'aarlat.

"Not unless you want to leave with a few more holes in your body," said Jack with a disapproving shake of his head. "This is hopeless. There's no way we can just sneak inside. This place is like a fucking army barracks."

"Look!" Tc'aarlat tapped him on the shoulder, and when Jack returned his attention to the front, he saw a Yollin, one with four legs and a smug attitude, constantly tapping his fingers together as he approached the bank.

"He looks familiar," said Jack. "Didn't he get shot on Miseria?"

"What?" asked Adina curiously. "Who is he?"

"No," said Tc'aarlat, leaning past the bush they were crouched behind. "I think it might be Tetz'len's brother, maybe?"

"Either way, Don Gan'barlo has this place under a close watch," said Jack with a smile. "That means the money must be being transferred here, or has been transferred. Our assumptions were right."

"I mean, that's great and all," said Tc'aarlat. "How are we going to steal it back, though?"

"It would be good if we could at least get some information on that bank," said Jack. "Where the money is stored, what security measures they have, when the guard shifts are… I haven't got a single contact on this damned planet."

"Me either." Tc'aarlat shrugged. "I'm not well connected in this part of the galaxy."

"I think I've got an idea," Adina said after a moment of thought, and she gave Jack a wayward look with an awkward smile. "You're not going to like it, though."

"If it gets us the info we're after," said Jack, "I'll like it."

Scarnlet, Intercity Bank Building, Street

Jack didn't like her plan. A few hours had passed since the Shadows had discussed it, and despite the boredom that came with simply hanging around waiting for someone to leave, Jack had come to despise his role in this plan more and more. He ran his hand through his recently combed hair again and checked himself in the street-level window. His shirt was still tucked in, his face was still clean-shaven, and he was still looking his best.

"Fuck me." He swallowed and turned to the sound of heels clicking on the pavement before him. As it turned out, Scarnlet did have nights and did go dark, but it was a hazy dark like the early hours of the morning when the air is soft and warm. Jack turned to the woman, to Jenny, and shook his head in disbelief before putting on his most charming smile. "Hey," he said softly as Jenny walked by. "Nice day for it?"

Jenny stopped and turned to him. "For what?"

"A walk? The name's Jack," he said with a quick wink, trying to be smooth. "You look, um, really dazzling in this light. Radiant."

"Is that right?" Jenny moved a little closer. "Well, aren't you just a charmer?"

"That's what they call me," said Jack. "*Unfortunately.*"

"I'm Jenny." She held out her hand, and he shook it. Jenny took that opportunity to pull Jack close so she could whisper tentatively in his ear. "*I'm not wearing any—*"

"A drink!" Jack blurted, pulling himself back. He coughed away the awkwardness. "I'm new in town, and I was wondering if there was a good place to get a drink?"

"I know a place." Jenny grinned, leaning into him.

"Oh, good," said Jack, squirmed. "I thought you might."

Scarnlet, The Jolly Dog Club, Platform

Adina and Tc'aarlat hadn't stopped giggling all through the taxi ride. They had been following Jack and his new love interest, the former man who was Jenny, until they reached a small club above the tops of the buildings. It was built on a large hovering platform in the sky, complete with balconies full of dancing party-goers, and plenty of flashing neon signs and sexy holographic images.

"Ugh, I hate places like this," said Adina. "There's always some vapid girl throwing up in the bathroom."

"I've never been to a club like this," said Tc'aarlat. "Unless it's controlled by the mob. Then I've been to hundreds of clubs like this."

"How do you think Jack's getting on with his new girlfriend?" asked Adina, and she laughed. "Do you think he'll get lucky?"

"Lucky?" said Tc'aarlat. "I think he's already pretty unlucky, I know what the woman used to look like. It's the stuff of nightmares."

"Well, I didn't mean…" Adina's voice trailed off, and she jolted forward and tapped the driver on the shoulder. "Just down there will be fine."

The driver gave her a thumbs-up as a reply.

"How are we going to sneak it into the club?" said Tc'aarlat. "It's huge."

"We're not," said Adina. "We'll have to keep it outside."

"I'll stay with it in that case, then," said Tc'aarlat. "I've never been a big fan of the party life."

"I'll go find Jack. Just remember that we have to stick to the plan," Adina reminded him. "No guns."

"Unless it's necessary," said Tc'aarlat. "I know."

"Someone looking at you funny—"

"Is not necessary," Tc'aarlat finished her sentence. "I *know*."

The taxi floated down to the platform, and after paying another hefty fee, the pair of Shadows stepped out into the party scene. Thousands of dancers, all moving in rhythm to the tunes and taking shots, surrounded them on all sides. This didn't bother Adina as much since she had heard this kind of music before, but for Tc'aarlat, there was clearly a bit of a gap. His face wore a look of disdain for everything and everyone here.

Moving around to the back of the taxi, Tc'aarlat pulled the trunk open and grabbed the metal crate inside that was clearly labeled Face Mask Modifying Kit.

Scarnlet, The Jolly Dog Club, Bar

Unsurprisingly, Jenny wanted another drink, and amid the chaos that was the club at night, Jack placed it in front of her and plonked himself down on the opposite side of the table. That was the one thing the Shadows hadn't thought out about this little plan of theirs, which was to get Jenny drunk enough that she'd tell him anything they needed to know, and that was her being able to hold her own against him. Eight drinks in, she was just about as tipsy as him, or maybe even less so, and he'd had to start making hers doubles.

"Sho you're a businesswoman?" Jack asked sleepily. "Thatsch cool."

"Yeah." Jenny nodded. "For aaaaaages now."

"I bet thatsch so interesting," said Jack. "Tell me about it."

"I manage a bank," she said with a smile. "I'm in charge of sssecurity."

"Keeping the money shafe?"

"Yeah." She nodded again. "Itsch actually really boring. I havta keep an eye on this vault."

"Vault?" said Jack. "What kind of vault?"

"A big one." Jenny laughed, and Jack jumped suddenly.

At that moment, she ran her hand across his knees. "It's shnot very well protected, though."

"It's shnot, is it?" Jack gulped down a quarter of his drink and smiled lazily. "What you mean, Jen?"

"Oh, my gawd." She giggled. "Did you just call me Jen, Wacky Jacky?"

"I guess I did." Jack laughed back. "Why is the—"

Jack couldn't finish his sentence. Before he had managed to get the words out, Jenny had leaned forward and connected their lips. Jack had the momentary desire to push her off, but then he felt her soft lips against his, and that changed. Before he knew what was happening, Jenny was taking him by the hand and leading him across the club toward the bathroom.

Scarnlet, The Jolly Dog Club, Platform

Jack stumbled toward Tc'aarlat and Adina with Jenny slung across his shoulder. She was actually quite light, given her stocky frame. When the others saw him coming, they stifled their giggles, especially when they saw the mask of concern Jack wore. He looked ready to kill with that glare, and once he got close enough, he threw her down onto a bench. It had taken him a good half-hour to move through the clubbers, take breaks from carrying her, and find the secluded spot Adina and Tc'aarlat had picked to carry out the plan.

"Where were you?" Jack demanded. "I thought you guys were supposed to come find us?"

"I did," said Adina. "I searched all over that club, but you guys weren't—"

Adina stopped and moved closer to Jack with a curious eye. She reached up with one thumb and wiped some lipstick off his lips. "Is this lipstick?"

"No!" Jack almost screamed it through his rage and then calmed himself. "Let's get this over and done with. I want this night out of my memory forever."

"This is going to be another one of those things we never talk about, isn't it?" asked Tc'aarlat.

"You can bet your life on that one," said Jack. "There's a vault on floor 46, and it has the Don's money inside. Money that was transferred in there today. There isn't a password, but the vault is protected by a retinal scanner. Security is mostly focused on the first few floors, but there are a couple of guards stationed at the vault too."

"Wow," said Tc'aarlat. "You got that information fast. You were only in there for a couple of hours!"

"Believe me, it came at a price."

Adina started up the machine. The process of copying another person's face was fortunately quite quick and would take only a few moments using the portable face scanner. While she was doing that, Tc'aarlat kept a watch on the club-goers and the bouncers to make sure she wasn't interrupted. Jack meanwhile was leaning over the banister, throwing up both of his lungs and trying to get the images out of his head.

Scarnlet, ICS *Fortitude*, Cargo Bay

Adina was running diagnostics on the mech suit they had acquired from Miseria. It was something to do while the kit was printing a realistic mask of Jenny's face, but ultimately pointless. Adina already knew what the issue was; she could tell without even opening the mech suit to have a look inside. It was the power core. A combination of cheap hardware and shitty software had left the power core unstable, which meant that if the suit was used too much, it would result in overheating, which would result in exploding first and burning the occupant alive second.

This wasn't an easy fix, unfortunately. It meant replacing the power core altogether and rewiring the whole thing, a process that could take weeks. Someone could pilot it for a few minutes, though, maybe longer, and she had installed a heat alarm to let the person piloting it know when it was time to get the hell out of there.

"Adina." She turned to the sound of a familiar voice and saw Solo on the screen behind her. Solo's face was solemn, which was becoming her default expression. Adina already knew what she was going to say and braced herself. "Benjamin has sent you a message."

"Can you lock the cargo bay please, Solo?" Adina asked, and the AI nodded. She heard the click of the doors, confirming they were bolted, and then turned her attention to the screen, where the image of an eyeball searched the room to land on her.

"Adina," it said in its baritone voice. "The time has come."

"I won't hurt my friends," said Adina. "No matter what you're offering me in return."

"We would never ask you to do that, Adina." The voice sounded hurt at her suggestion, but she thought they might be mocking her. "We want you to listen closely. You're going to play an important role in the next twenty-four hours. If you check your room, you'll find a device you'll need to complete this task."

"Can you help my uncle?" Adina demanded, cutting right through the crap. "I have to know."

"Yes, Adina," the voice replied. "You complete this task for us, and your uncle will become just like he was."

"One task."

"Just one," the voice said. "After that, you won't hear from us again."

"Who are you?" asked Adina. "What do you want?"

"You may call me Benjamin, and you need know nothing more than that," came the monotonous reply. "What we want is an end to the criminal empire Don Gan'barlo has built."

18

Scarnlet, ICS *Fortitude*, Bridge

"You're sure she'll be out for twenty-four hours?" Jack looked at Tc'aarlat, who was leaning back with his feet up at his station and rolling something between his palms. "Because if she wakes up, we're fucked."

"I thought you didn't know what to call her?" said Tc'aarlat. "Man or woman?"

"Believe me, she's a woman."

"How do you—"

"Just drop it," snapped Jack.

"You are getting so grouchy lately." Tc'aarlat sat up. "Yeah, the concoction I put together will knock her out for at least twenty-four hours, maybe even two days. She won't be showing up for work tomorrow if she doesn't bleed out first."

"Do you still have her eye?"

Tc'aarlat held it up. "Yup."

"It's not a stress ball?" said Jack. "That's someone's fucking eye."

"Feels weird," said Tc'aarlat, squeezing it between his fingers. "Humans are so gross."

"Let's go over the plan again," said Jack with a shake of his head, and Tc'aarlat let out a groan. "Adina and I go to the bank at her usual time, Adina disguised as Jenny and me disguised as her new bodyguard."

"Yup," said Tc'aarlat, nodding along, already knowing it all. "While you two break into the vault and steal the cash, I create a distraction with the mech."

"Exactly," said Jack. "If you time it right, you can get out of the mech just before it bursts into flames and makes it look like you've died."

"I'm sure that part will be fine," said Tc'aarlat. "Can't see any problems there."

"While you keep Security distracted, we'll steal the credits the Don has in his account and render him bankrupt," said Jack. "We'll meet back at the ship, get the fuck outta Dodge, and hand over the ill-gotten gains to the Federation. Winners all around."

"Then we hunt the Don down like a dog and make him fart bullets and crap blood," said Tc'aarlat proudly. "My favorite part."

"That too," replied Jack. "Then we never talk about this planet ever again."

"Or the dude you fucked in the bathroom."

"Or the—" Jack glared at him. "We. Are. Not. Mentioning. it."

Scarnlet, Intercity Bank Building, Street

Adina was a little smaller than Jenny, so her business

attire was baggy on her slimmer frame. As Jack and Adina approached the building, they hoped the guards wouldn't notice that and instead focus on the realistic mask and voice modulator that came with the kit, giving her both the appearance and sound of Jenny. She couldn't lie, her stomach was floating and turning at the thought of getting past the guards, but it was floating and turning even worse for what Benjamin had told her to do. By the end of the day, she feared she might not be a welcome member of the Shadows anymore.

"Good afternoon, miss." One of the burly guards moved aside to allow her through but put a hand in front of Jack to stop him. "Do you have a pass?"

"He's with me." Adina turned to them. "Allow him through."

"He doesn't have a pass, miss," said the guard. "Under your rules, he has to stay here."

"I'm making an exception to that rule." Adina beckoned Jack through. "I have a very important meeting to attend, and he's my new bodyguard. Allow him through now."

The guards gave each other hesitant looks, but who were they to argue with the boss of security? They stepped aside to let Jack through as well.

"Appreciate it, guys," said Jack with a small grin. "You're doing a great job."

Adina and Jack moved into the building together, around the corner and toward the elevators. Once inside, they let out their breath and allowed themselves small giggles. Adina swiped the card they had stolen from Jenny against the security pad before pressing the button for the 46th floor. The elevator started up, and they guessed that they had a few minutes before they reached the right floor.

"Listen." Jack cleared his throat. "I'm sorry about getting so upset about Solo the other day. It certainly seems like she's better for the upgrade."

"I'm sorry I didn't ask the group before I did it," Adina apologized as well. "It was a stupid idea."

"It's not like any of us can talk," said Jack. "We've all done something stupid at some point or other. Did I ever tell you about Dollen?"

"Dollen?" said Adina. "Who's Dollen?"

"He was one of our crewmates before you joined the ship," said Jack. "Seemed like a real nice guy, turned out to be a terrorist. Once upon a time, he tried to blow us up with a homemade explosive vest in a restaurant."

"Why?" said Adina.

"He worked for Dark Tomorrow," said Jack. "That terrorist group that wants to end the Federation. Wanted to send a message, I suppose, but we stopped him before he could, and now he's serving time. I guess what I'm trying to say, though, is that I have a problem with secrets. It occurs to me now that he might have given me some trust issues."

"Jack." Adina looked into his eyes, but her mind was racing. She desperately wanted to tell him about Benjamin, about the message he had given her, and about her uncle who was riddled with dementia, but she couldn't. She could only hope Jack could find a way to forgive her for what she was about to do, but she doubted it. Adina wouldn't even forgive herself.

"Hey." Jack nudged her with a smile. "We friends?"

"Yeah." Adina smiled back. "We're friends."

Jack was a good guy, Adina knew, but he didn't really seem like the forgiving type. She chuckled a little at a sudden thought, and Jack glanced over. She gestured to her face. "Did you really get it on with this former man?"

"I don't want to comment about that."

"You did, though, didn't you?" Adina could barely suppress the laugh. "Holy shit, you know she used to be a guy, right?"

"Still is."

"What?"

"Nothing." Jack's face was red. "Forget I said anything."

"Give me a kiss, Jack." Adina pursed her lips and inched closer. "Just a quick peck."

"I'll never live this one down."

Adina stopped her teasing right before the elevator pinged and the doors opened to their floor, which was apparent by the large 46 imprinted on the wall. Jack and Adina stepped over the threshold and into a large golden room, with a ceiling that spanned multiple floors above them and golden statues of no doubt important people dotted about. It was flashy and showy, and the perfect place to keep the finances of a gangster.

They approached a desk that stood just before the large circular vault door. from its dark glow, it looked like it was made from Wurtzite, which was the strongest element in the galaxy, and quite impossible to get through with everyday equipment. As they marched closer, a duo of creatures stood up to greet them. A moment prior, they had been rummaging through paperwork on the desk with highlighters. They seemed to be accountants of some sort.

"Miss Jenny?" They stood up straight when they

addressed her, trying to look cooperative. "We weren't expecting you today. The transfer has been completed, and the funds are safely locked up."

"That's why I'm here, I'm afraid," Adina replied in her best Jenny impression, trying to remember what she had been told to say last night over dinner. "I've heard that the Shadows are planning to break into the vault, so I need to check on the funds in question."

"Oh." The pair looked at each other, unsure.

"What were your names again?" said Adina.

"I'm Killeg Dirk'sen," said one, the Alstublaft, and he pointed at his Baroleon counterpart. "This is Gruff Hanlo."

"Let me give you a situation." Adina leaned close to them, the mask on her face stern. "The funds were stolen by those treacherous but dashing Shadows, and they got away with it because two bumbling accountants didn't see fit to let me inside. How do you think the Don would feel about that?"

"Not good," said Hanlo. "Not good at all."

"We're on the same page, then," said Adina with a smile. "Let me in right now, or else."

"We can't," said Killeg. "We're under strict orders!"

"I know!" Hanlo snapped his fingers, a sudden idea. "We'll get in touch with Metz'len. He'll know what to do!"

Hanlo picked up a communication device off the desk and quickly pressed a few buttons. Jack gave Adina a nod, the signal they had agreed to earlier that meant they would have to resort to plan B. Jack drew his Jean Dukes Special from its holster and Adina did the same, pointing the guns at the accountants and the guards in the room.

"No one move!" Jack shouted, firing a shot into the air.

"We're here for one thing, and one thing only. When we get it, we'll leave."

"You'll never get inside the vault," Killeg cried helplessly. He was beginning to hate having weapons thrust in his face. "The vault is biometrically locked. It'll only work for Miss Jenny."

"Okay," Jack said, pulling the eye from his pocket. "We've already thought of that!"

Scarnlet, Intercity Bank Building, Lobby

"So I heard you managed a date with Rebekah from HR last night?" Steve, one of the many guards who worked at the Intercity Bank, was saying to his colleague Franklin. It was a conversation he had been looking forward to ever since he had seen Franklin leave the bar last night with his arm around Rebekah. Those two kids were meant for each other, and it was getting harder to pretend he hadn't seen the occasional lustful glances, the awkward flirting, and the sordid attempts to get each other's communicator numbers.

"Yeah. Yeah, I did," Franklin said bashfully. "She spent the night at my place."

"Did you...you know?"

"Oh." Franklin straightened. "No, nothing like that. She just needed a couch to crash on."

"AH! Dude!" Steve rolled his eyes. "What happened? I thought you guys were hooking up for sure!"

"It's just how it goes," said Franklin. "Next time, maybe?"

"Well, you should definitely get back—" Steve stopped

mid-sentence. A sudden sound had pierced his eardrums, something distant but getting closer. It was getting louder by the second. He could only describe it as screaming or yelling plus the footfalls of some giant mechanical beast. It was like there was a giant stomping toward them in a full-on rage. It sounded terrifying.

"What's wro—"

"Do you hear that?" asked Steve. "What is that?"

Franklin closed his eyes and listened. "Yeah, I do. Is that screaming?"

"Intense screaming."

One moment they were on their feet having a casual conversation in the lobby, the next, there was an explosion of epic proportions, and they were to the floor on their backs. The doors leading into the building had been blown in and every window surrounding them was smashed, and there was now a gigantic hole that had allowed a twenty-ton killing machine to come into the lobby. It was a mech suit, piloted by a screaming Yollin who only spared a few seconds to laugh maniacally before he got to work on the guards.

Bullets and lasers started flying wildly about the lobby, destroying walls and killing guards. The mech plowed straight forward and kicked a guard roughly straight into the nearest wall with a force equal to a runaway truck. The guard was dead before he even hit the wall. Next, the Yollin grabbed another of the guards and started swinging him like a baseball bat, using him to smash away the other guards who were in his path.

"*HOLY FUCK!*" Steve yelled. "Get on the communicator right now and get us some—"

The Yollin must have heard him because the next thing he knew, the mech was crushing him underfoot like a giant cockroach with a vomit-inducing crunch.

Franklin picked up his communicator and started screaming at the top of his lungs. *"WE NEED HELP IN THE LOBBY! WE NEED—"*

Depending on how you looked at it, you could say Franklin was the lucky one. For one thing, he was still alive, albeit scarred for the rest of his days, which none of his colleagues could boast. What that Yollin used that mech suit and its many lasers to do to his groin area would never be repaired nor forgotten, and neither would the maniacal laugh that had accompanied the damage. Rebekah would never find out what she had been missing.

If there was nothing else that was certain in the attack on the bank that day, it was that the Yollin had definitely provided a worthwhile distraction.

19

Scarnlet, Intercity Bank Building, Vault

The affirmative beep told Jack that Jenny's eye had worked as planned, and he tossed it away as soon as they were done with it. Adina kept a watch on the people around the room, with only the occasional glance toward Jack and what he was doing. The vault door rolled slowly to the side, allowing them access to the room beyond.

It was about as expected. The vault had rows and rows of deposit boxes, but that wasn't where the money was. The digital currency known as credits was stored on individual pocket-sized slabs a couple of millimeters thick, each one representing hundreds of thousands of credits. They were immune to being hacked because they weren't designed to be connected to a network. The only way you could access them outside of that was to have the physical slab with you, but you could transfer the money between accounts by using another slab and downloading the currency from one to the other. They couldn't be copied, and if they were destroyed, the money was lost forever. All in all, Jack counted five floating harmlessly above a pedestal in the center of the room. It was flashy, like the rest of this place, and definitely not as secure as it should've been.

"There's five," Jack called to Adina. "I thought we were only expecting one?"

"What's that about?" Adina thrust the gun toward the Alstublaft.

"Well..." Killeg thought about what he would say; he was nervous, to say the least. "Don Gan'barlo recently acquired funds from a weapons trade venture—"

"We know about that!" said Jack. "What are the other ones?"

"Personal finances," the Alstublaft said and shrugged. "Money he has put away for a rainy day and cash he's been holding for other crime syndicates."

"Other crime syndicates?" Adina looked at Killeg. "What syndicates?"

"I'm not sure." The accountant shrugged hopelessly. "Could be any of them?"

"I'm going for it," said Jack and he moved toward the center pedestal, keeping his wits about him for any sudden traps the Don might have hidden in here. There was nothing—suspiciously nothing—and Jack reached the pedestal without any trouble. Taking a breath, he reached out, and, one by one, grabbed the floating slabs. Again, nothing happened. Happy with the outcome, he turned back around and immediately came face to face with a gun barrel.

"I'm sorry, Jack," said Adina, who was the one with her finger on the trigger.

"Adina?" Jack stumbled back. "What the fuck are you doing?"

"I fucked up," she whimpered and held out an open palm. "I'm...I'm sorry, but please hand over the credits."

"Why are you doing this?"

"Hackers got inside Solo's systems," said Adina. "They installed a kill switch. I'm doing this for your own good."

"It doesn't feel like it's for my good."

"All they want me to do is transfer the credits to them." Adina pulled a device out of her pocket, a heavily modified communicator that had a slot large enough for the slabs. "Using this."

"And what is that?"

"It allows them to access the slabs remotely," said Adina. "Downloading the currency and transferring it to a new slab on their end."

"Why are you doing this?"

"So they'll leave us alone," said Adina. "They threatened to kill Solo, erase her. I tried to get around their programming, but it was just too advanced."

"Who?" Jack demanded. "Who will leave us alone?"

"All I know is that his name is Benjamin."

"Who the fuck is Benjamin?"

Scarnlet, Intercity Bank Building, Lobby

Tc'aarlat admired the bloody corpses of former guards that littered the room. No doubt there would be more to take their place soon. The alert Adina had installed was already ringing out since the mech was overheating, but he still had time to shove his gun systems up a few more rear ends. Tc'aarlat leaned the mech against the wall and paced himself, catching his breath and giving himself a moment before more showed up.

"Tc'aarlat."

"What?" He perked up. "Solo?"

"I have to speak to you." When Solo appeared at the edge of his HUD, her face was the same way it had been these past few days: stern and chock-full of concern. "Adina is about to make a mistake."

"She's stealing the Don's fortune," said Tc'aarlat. "I wouldn't consider that a mistake."

BOOM! Tc'aarlat was thrown across the room by a sudden and massive blast. He took a few seconds to recover before he looked over to see the weapon of destruction. Outside and around the lobby were armed soldiers, which normally wouldn't be a problem for Tc'aarlat and his wonderful killing machine. No, the problem was that they had brought tanks with them.

"Bring it on!" Tc'aarlat launched the mech onto its feet and charged with the force of three elephants, right through the windows, straight over the bushes, into the streets and directly into one of the tanks with an almighty punch. It tore straight through, leaving a colossal rent that would take more than a buff to get out.

"She's going to betray the group, Tc'aarlat," said Solo. "She may already have done it."

Tc'aarlat dodged the next blast from a tank's cannon and tore it completely off.

"Wait!" he said, throwing the cannon like a javelin into another tank. "She's going to betray the group?"

"A hacker group compromised my system and is blackmailing her," explained Solo. "They say they have a cure for the dementia that has riddled her uncle's mind, but I am now ninety-nine percent sure that such a thing does not exist and she is being tricked."

"Oh God, then I need to get up there!" Tc'aarlat looked up at the building, then at the HUD. The mech was quickly overheating, and Tc'aarlat knew it could burst into flames at any moment. *To hell with it*, he thought and shot straight to the building, using the mech's considerable strength to jump up and start the climb.

Scarnlet, Intercity Bank Building, Lobby

Jack, with no other choice, slowly handed over the credit slabs one by one to Adina, who kept her barrel pointed at his head. There were no sudden moves, or any moving at all. He kept his hands high as Adina activated the communicator Benjamin had left in her room under her bed and began the process of transferring the funds.

"You don't have to do this, Adina," Jack pleaded with her. "Just stop, and we can talk about this."

"There's no time," said Adina. "I'm sorry, Jack. I have a good reason for doing this. He's going to help my uncle, the one with dementia."

"Why didn't you tell us?" asked Jack. "We could've helped."

"Benjamin had the ship bugged," said Adina. "He was watching our every move."

"I understand why you're doing this." Jack gave her a nod and a small, understanding smile. "It's okay, and you have my blessing. We'll get through this together, as a team."

Adina lowered the gun, more tears in her eyes. "Thank you, Jack."

There was no time for an emotional moment, though. No chance for a hug, or even one second more for them to acknowledge the situation. There was only a momentary gasp when Jack saw the grenade land at his feet and following the second for him to scream before it exploded.

The world went bright and white for a few seconds, then, things started to come back, blurry and unfocused. They had temporarily gone blind and deaf, which was more than enough time for someone to come in and take custody of them. Through the haze, Adina saw Jack in cuffs. She tried to scream, but for all she knew, it could've just been a whimper, so deaf was she right now. Once the world around them regained some sense of normality, they saw that they were far from where they had been a few seconds before.

Jack and Adina had been forced to their knees, hands behind their backs in cuffs, directly in front of a Yollin—one that had a familiar smugness about him. He was talking, but they couldn't hear him thanks to the grenade, which Jack realized now must have been a stun weapon. Slowly their senses started coming back, and after they fought through the last few moments of nausea, they saw that they had been captured by the person who looked like Tetz'len.

"Can you hear me?" Metz'len was kneeling next to Jack, slapping him playfully on the face. "Come on! I expected more of you Shadows."

"Wh-who are you?" Jack uttered the question.

"I'm Metz'len," said the Yollin. "Maybe you met my brother, Tetz'len?"

"Shot him." Jack grinned.

CRACK! Metz'len slapped Jack with the force of a whip, leaving a red mark across his face.

Jack spat one of his teeth on the floor. "You hit like my great aunt, and she's been dead for twenty years."

"You Shadows think you're so clever, don't you?" Metz'len stood up and tapped his fingers together. "Well, guess what, you walked right into the Don's trap."

"Trap?" Jack almost laughed. "What are you talking about?"

"That contact who told you about the doctor?" said Metz'len. "The information you found on Jenny, the austere vault room? What do *you* think?"

"You were my old contact?" said Jack. "Then where's Steve?"

"Dead." Metz'len moved to Adina and ripped the Jenny mask from her face. "You think you're the only ones who can create realistic masks with voice modulators?"

"So what was the plan?" said Jack. "Wait until we were in the vault?"

"And stun you," said Metz'len, and for the first time, Jack saw that he had his Jean Dukes Special in his hand. The Yollin placed the barrel against his head. "Of course, you two aren't the prize. Where's Tc'aarlat?"

"Why didn't you just make us come straight here?" said Jack. "Why make us visit the doctor at all?

"You needed to believe it wasn't a trap," said Metz'len.

"Your contact wouldn't know about the vault or Jenny, would he? I'm not asking twice."

"Oh, just fucking shoot me you big twat." Jack forced his head closer into the gun. "Come on!"

"*WHERE'S TC'AARLAT!?*"

"You just asked twice."

Scarnlet, Intercity Bank Building, Side of the Building, Floor 27

Adina's alert had gone from pale amber to flashing crimson, but Tc'aarlat did his best to ignore it as the mech climbed. Inside the cockpit, he could feel the heat. The temperature was rising at an alarming rate, and he knew that sooner or later, it would go up in flames. He preferred it to be later.

"That's what happened," said Solo. "Or as much as I know."

"So some cocksucker thinks he can just get Adina to do whatever he wants?" asked Tc'aarlat. "Not on my fucking watch. I've just gotten used to her."

"You have bigger problems," said Solo. "According to my readouts on the mech, you have seconds before it goes up in flames."

"I figured," said Tc'aarlat. "Is there anything you can do about that?"

"Not without causing damage to the systems," said Solo. "Important systems."

"How many floors?"

"Twenty."

"Then I've got no choice." Tc'aarlat thrust the mech's

metal hand into the building like a piton and continued climbing regardless. "Fucking sweating my mandibles off in here."

Scarnlet, Intercity Bank Building, Vault

"I'm not joking!" Metz'len tapped the gun against Jack's head a few times to get his point across. "Tell me where he is or I'll—"

CRASH! Everyone in the room turned at the sudden noise. A mech had come through the window, leaving broken glass and a bent frame in its wake. The beast was standing there surveying the situation, and through the small glass windows, a Yollin—Tc'aarlat—was deliberating on his next course of action.

"He's using a mech! That crazy bastard!" Metz'len cried a second before the mech fired. A stream of rounds came out of the cannons at the ends of its arms, leaving dead guards in its wake. "Keep it busy. The mechs are faulty and overheat if they're used too much, so we just need to last a few minutes."

Jack wasn't going to wait those few minutes. He leapt forward and head-butted the place he thought the Yollins kept their family jewels. There wasn't time to mess around, and he wasn't sure if it had worked, but it knocked Metz'len to the floor. There was no way of punching him in the face with his hands behind his back, but he was perfectly proficient in head-butting.

The Yollin mobster kicked him off and grabbed the Jean Dukes Special again, laughing as he did so. He aimed the gun at Jack. "I guess I don't need you after all."

BANG!

Jack smiled, and the Yollin screamed and saw through his confusion that the blast had somehow blown his arm into several meaty chunks that hung loosely at the end of his elbow. Metz'len threw himself to the floor. "WHAT THE FUCK?"

Jack stood up and prepared his boot. "It's biometric, you dumb fuck."

One kick in the face later, Metz'len was out for the count. Adina scrambled over, grabbed the key, and undid her cuffs before doing the same for Jack, who took back his gun with pride. "That feature will never get old."

"I've got the slabs," said Adina.

"Let's get the fuck out of here."

"Oh, no," she said, staring at Tc'aarlat, who was still fighting the guards off. "How long has he been—"

They were blown back by the sudden explosion of the mech, which had managed to catch the rest of the guards in its crossfire. They had stupidly gotten too close. The suit went up in flames and collapsed uselessly on the floor as a pile of melting metal.

"NO! FUCK!" Adina screamed and tried to run for the suit, but Jack knew the dangers of a second explosion and held her back.

"Shit!" he snarled. "*SHIT!*"

"Maybe he got out?" said Adina hopefully. "Maybe he—"

Jack shook his head and wiped a tear from his eye. The mech continued to burn, with the body of their closest friend inside. "Tc'aarlat was—is—the greatest Shadow to have lived. He saved us from hours of prolonged torture at the hands of Don Gan'barlo and a slow, excruciating death, there is no doubt. He was brave, honest, rude in all the best ways, and a good Yollin at his core."

"Please." Adina wept into his side. "He can't be dead."

"I never told him this, but I was proud to serve with him for this long," said Jack. "And I bet he would've gotten a laugh out of the fact that, yes, I did shag Jenny in a men's bathroom. You can have that secret, Tc'aarlat, and take it to the afterlife with you."

"*I FUCKING KNEW IT!*"

Adina and Jack turned around to see a slightly charred but otherwise healthy Yollin behind them, laughing his mandibles off and pointing at Jack. "I knew you slept with that former fat bastard."

"Tc'aarlat." Adina ran up to him and gave him a gigantic hug.

"*Fuck,*" Jack whispered.

"We thought you were dead," Adina said.

"That was the point, wasn't it?" replied Tc'aarlat. "Get out of the mech before it goes up in flames, and make sure everyone thinks I'm dead?"

"I just wasn't expecting it to work so well," Jack.

"So how was Jenny's dick, Jack?" Tc'aarlat chuckled. "Was it bigger than yours?"

"Yeah, there's no time to discuss it," said Jack. "We need to get out of here now."

"Pfft, poor excuse." Tc'aarlat snickered. "Don't worry, she'll be here in a second."

"Who?"

"Who do you think?" Tc'aarlat nodded at the window.

They turned around to see the ICS *Fortitude* come in low at the window. It was a large ship and a squeeze between the other buildings, but Solo managed it without damaging the ship or the skyscrapers around it.

They dashed toward their home, jumping through the open window and into the open door. The Shadows had made it through by the skin of their teeth, and each of them knew it.

Scarnlet, Intercity Bank Building, Vault

Metz'len stirred from unconsciousness and choked up the blood pooling at the back of his throat. The Yollin had awoken in time to see the ICS *Fortitude* fly away. They weren't escaping, he decided, slamming his mangled wrist on the floor. Not on his fucking watch. He got up and started running, using the four legs he had at his disposal to move quicker than most.

He took the stairs when the elevator approached, rushing up the next few floors and stumbling through the doors that led to a small platform on the building that housed a series of space-capable vehicles, including his.

Breathless, Metz'len jumped inside with the press of his key fob and took the pilot's chair. "They're not getting away!" Metz'len said to the empty cockpit. "I'll blast that fucking ship out of the sky if I have to. I'll rip their spines out through their throats. I'll—"

"What?" There was a voice behind him, and Metz'len instantly stopped his start-up sequence since it happened to be both a voice he knew and one he was terribly afraid of. "Don't let me stop you, Metz'len. You're clearly very busy."

"How did you find me?"

"The same way the Shadows did." A woman sat down next to the Yollin at the pilot's chair. She had luscious long red hair that was kept out of her face with a pair of goggles, which also unfortunately showed off a large scar that ran down her face and through her eye in the shape of a gentleman's genitalia. The woman was pointing a blaster at Metz'len, and he regarded it nervously. "We intercepted the contact who got in touch with Jack and followed them to right here and right now."

"This is about the money, isn't it?" asked Metz'len.

"We're beyond money now, Metz'len," she said. "This is more about principle now, and if there's a group that knows about principle, it's Dark Tomorrow."

"You didn't pay us for the mechs we built for you, and now we have to make an example out of you."

"That's big talk coming from a terrorist." Metz'len sneered.

"Freedom fighter, if you please, and you can always call me 'Stranger.'" The stranger wasted no time; she shot Metz'len in the head and watched his body collapse uselessly into the controls, then pulled him off and pushed him over. Then, taking a small circular disk out of her jacket, she inserted it into the ship's terminal and downloaded every piece of data it had.

"You may have been scumbags, but you made pretty good pawns."

. . .

Scarnlet's Atmosphere, ICS *Fortitude*, Bridge

"Let's see them." Jack held out his hand, and Adina looked nervously from him to Tc'aarlat before pulling the slabs out of her pocket and handing them over. He held them up to the light and read the barcodes on each one, with the face of Lance Reynolds imprinted on a windowed slot that could only be observed in strong light.

"Yeah, they're authentic," said Jack. "Probably worth a few hundred thousand each."

"Y'know, we could get a new ship, straight off the assembly line," suggested Tc'aarlat. "Maybe a few mansions too. Just a thought?"

Jack took his seat and sighed before turning his attention back to Adina. "What happened back there? It's time to give us your version of things."

"A hacker group set up a kill switch in Solo," said Adina. "They got in touch with me and said they have a cure for my uncle's dementia. In return for it, though, I had to transfer the credits from those slabs using a modified communicator they had smuggled on board for me."

"You've never met face to face?" asked Tc'aarlat.

"No," Adina said, shaking her head. "I don't even know what they look like."

"Solo said there was no chance that a cure had been found," Tc'aarlat told her. "These guys are playing you, Adina. I bet they haven't even set up a kill switch."

"That is incorrect, Tc'aarlat," said Solo. "I am sure they have installed a kill switch, and I said I was ninety-nine-percent sure they were lying."

"What about that last one percent?" said Adina. "There's a small chance!"

"It's ridiculously low," said Jack. "You have more chance of winning the galactic Battleball championships. It's not worth handing over an amount like this. Someone could do some serious damage, and millions could be hurt across countless worlds."

"If there was a one percent chance to save your lives, I'd take it," Adina said. "And my uncle would've taken it for me."

"That one hit hard," said Tc'aarlat. "I still think it's a scam, though. Maybe if they'd given you some proof, I'd be more inclined to believe it."

"I'm sorry, Adina," commiserated Jack. "I know your heart's in the right place."

"No, I get it," said Adina, slumping in her chair. "It's not worth the risk."

"We'll help you find a cure, if and when we hear of one," Jack assured her. "That's a promise."

"I know you will," said Adina. "It just sucks that there isn't much hope now."

"Attention!" Solo spoke up. "There's an incoming transm—"

The image of Solo went fuzzy, faded out, and was replaced by an image Adina knew all too well. The Eye. Except this time, it wasn't on some small screen in her room or the cargo bay, it was taking up the whole of the bridge. The Eye bobbed around, searching before landing once again on her and the others on the bridge.

"That's quite eye-catching!" remarked Tc'aarlat.

"I know what you mean," Jack agreed.

"I said we were watching Adina," the Eye said. "We

know you have the stolen credits from the Don's vault. Hand them over to us now, or we will be forced to act."

The picture blurred and the fuzzy face of Solo chimed in for just a second with, "There are hostile ships approach—"

"Without your AI, you won't survive this attack." The Eye came back into focus over a lagging Solo. "Transfer the credits. Now."

"Who are you?" Jack approached the screen. "Why are you doing this?"

"We've been watching Don Gan'barlo's assets for a long time," said the Eye. "Witnessed his crime family grow and grow, and now is the time for us to take charge and instigate a new order of crime."

"You're a rival crime syndicate!" Tc'aarlat stood up straight at the epiphany. "You want the Don out of the picture so you can take over!"

"You're smart," said the Eye. "I can see how you got this far. This is your last chance, Shadows. Hand over the credits or die with them."

"We ain't scared of you." Jack sneered. "Do your worst."

"No!" Adina screamed. "Wait."

The Eye vanished from the screen and Solo reappeared. For a moment, nothing happened, then everything happened. Solo cried out in pain as her picture became distorted, then every warning light in the bridge began to flash and they bathed the room in a multi-colored glow. Sirens rang out from somewhere distant, and to add insult to injury, the ICS *Fortitude* shuddered from the impact of blaster fire at the rear. They were under attack in every way possible.

"Solo!" Adina cried.

"I'm b-b-being deleted," Solo said through her lagging image. "H-h-help."

"Hand over manual control," said Jack, and she disappeared from the screen. The ship rocked again, more violently this time, and everyone on the bridge held on for dear life.

"That's not going to help," Adina snarled. "When Solo became an AI, in order for her to function properly, all of the systems became a part of her, like a big body."

"So?" asked Tc'aarlat.

"It means that without her, our primary systems won't function properly," explained Adina. "Including our shields and weapons."

"Well, shit! What's the plan, Jack?" said Tc'aarlat. "We're in a tough spot this time!"

Jack thought for a moment before turning to Adina. "This kill switch...can we stop it?"

"No," said Adina with a shake of her head. "She's being deleted."

"We need her to get control of the ship. We're flying blind!"

"You two can talk all you want," said Tc'aarlat, taking his seat and arming his weapons. "I'm going to blast those fighters out of space."

"Come on, Adina, think!" yelled Jack. "You're the only person I know who can solve this problem."

Adina took a few deep breaths, the gears in her head working in overdrive. She thought about her uncle, who she'd never see again, the peaceful worlds of the Federation, and she thought about how she should have never installed that AI in the first place. How it was all— "I think I've got it," she said through a smile. "The kill switch will delete Solo, but I could restore her from a back-up before I turned her into an AI. Before she had the kill switch installed!"

"Wait, what does that mean?"

"Can you remember Solobot 9000?" asked Adina.

"I admit that sometimes I try to forget Solobot 9000," replied Jack.

"Well, to put Solo's expansive memory into such a small device, I had to clone her programming and strip it down," said Adina. "Otherwise it wouldn't have fit."

"You still have that clone?" said Jack, and Adina nodded. "Okay, plan time. You're going to reinstall Solo as quickly as you can while I fly the ship and Tc'aarlat shoots those fuckers out of the sky."

"Out of space!" Tc'aarlat called to him. "We're not in a sky."

"No, we are," corrected Jack.

"Oh." Tc'aarlat wilted. "Ignore me, then."

"Is this going to work, Adina?"

"Yes. Well, it should," said Adina. "It'll take time, though."

"Take all the time you need. We'll handle things here," Jack stated, and Adina turned to leave. He grabbed her arm and gave her a nod. "I trust you, Adina."

Scarnlet's Atmosphere, ICS *Fortitude*, Server Room

Adina rushed into the server room with her hands full of equipment, everything from cables to clippers, and most importantly, a recovery disk that could bring back Solo. Adina knew this wouldn't be an easy install, but if she could bring back the EI version of Solo, it should re-integrate with the ship much quicker and hopefully save their lives.

She got to work on hooking the cables up to the various boxes around the room. It didn't help that they had been thrown together like enormous pieces of junk—not that there was anything she could do about that now. While she worked, she tried to ignore the many shots ringing against the hull, and the ship shuddering every few seconds from a new blast. She kept her mind on her work and booted up the system from her tablet.

"A-a-a-adina," Solo said from a screen on the far wall. She was lagging every second, and every time the screen refreshed, her image changed to someone else embedded within her mainframe. "I-I-I'm s-s-s-s-sorry I could not n-n-not help."

"No, *I'm* sorry," Adina told her. "We're a team, and I should start acting like it."

"It wa-wa-wa-was fun while it lasted."

"The best." Adina hit the Delete button on her end, and the AI version of Solo she had known these past few days was gone. "No more going solo."

Scarnlet's Atmosphere, ICS *Fortitude*, Bridge

There were twenty fighters, or even more, attacking the ICS *Fortitude* at the same time, and Tc'aarlat was having a hell of a time keeping up with them. Every time he hit one with a lucky shot, two more replaced it. Still, he didn't relent; he kept his thumbs hot on the trigger. After all, he had enough bullets for all of them.

"There are too many," Jack growled. "I was hoping we could just blast out of here, but they're all in the way. If we don't get Solo back up and running soon, we're gonna be sitting ducks."

"You mean fucks!" said Tc'aarlat. "Y'know, it wasn't so long ago that *we* were just flying this ship without this EI crap, and I don't remember it being that much trouble?"

"That's because you never flew the ship," Jack told him. "You've always been a weapons junkie."

"Sounds about right." Tc'aarlat watched the screen for a moment longer, waited for the blip to come over his radar, then shot it down in a rain of projectiles. "I'm so good at this!"

"Don't get cocky."

"While we work," said Tc'aarlat. "Tell me about Jenny, your new lady love."

"Tc'aarlat, I swear—"

To add to the mix of alarms ringing on the bridge, another alarm joined the symphony and sent its voice louder. Jack peered around for a moment before looking at his screens and realizing the worst had happened: the power was failing. "*Gott Verdammt,* our power is going offline. We're running on residual energy!"

"So?"

"Without power, we'll have no shields, weapons, or engines."

"Explain it again, but pretend like I don't know what you're talking about," requested Tc'aarlat.

"Ship. Go. Boom."

"Yeah, okay, that's pretty bad," replied Tc'aarlat.

"Adina must be rebooting the systems to install Solo. We can't fight these guys off without them, though," said Jack.

"What do we have power for?" asked Tc'aarlat.

"Essential systems," Jack replied. "Life support and communications."

"Communications?" verified Tc'aarlat with a cheeky grin. "Let me handle this."

Scarnlet's Atmosphere, ICS *Fortitude*, Server Room

The old Solo was being reinstalled on the servers, and thus the ship, but it would take a few minutes. Adina had known it would knock a few of their primary systems offline, but she had never guessed it would leave them with only the essentials. She could only hope the blaster fire didn't breach the hull before they came back online.

She watched the screen in front of her as the installation percentage rose. That was when she noticed something strange and unexpected: the barrage of blasters had suddenly stopped, and an eerie silence had overtaken the room. Adina resisted the urge to simply stand up and run to the bridge to figure out what was going on. Instead, she remained at her station and did everything she could to get Solo back online.

Scarnlet's Atmosphere, ICS Fortitude, Bridge

"Tell us, Shadows, are you ready to hand over the credits you have taken?" asked the Eye once more, having returned to the screen once Tc'aarlat had reopened communications.

"We give," said Jack, holding up the slabs for the Eye to see. "You've won. In exchange for not destroying our ship, we'll give you the credits we stole. All of them."

Off-screen, the Yollin was snickering into his hands like a hyena. Jack had to wave him away to get him to stop. The Eye was staring at Jack, and for a moment, he thought it might be looking straight through him and into his very soul.

"This is a wise decision, Jack," said the Eye. "You must transfer the credits now."

"Hang on, I need to find that device," said Jack, jumping out of his chair and moving across the room and out of sight. He snuck over to Tc'aarlat and joined him beneath his desk, where the giggling Yollin was still trying to refrain from laughing out loud.

"This is our most ingenious idea yet," Tc'aarlat whispered. "All we have to do is keep them busy until the systems are back online."

"Then we can get the fuck out of here," added Jack.

Scarnlet's Atmosphere, ICS Fortitude, Server Room

"What has happened?"

Bing! The servers all restarted and came alive one by one. Adina looked at the screen and practically screamed with joy when she saw Solo—the former Solo—appear in all her glory. She wanted nothing more than to go over and give that silly EI a big old hug, but time was pressing, and Solo needed to be caught up to speed.

"We're under attack!" explained Adina. "We need all systems online, including protective shields."

"Working on it now," said Solo. "You need to get back to the bridge, Adina."

"Why?"

"To put on your seatbelt, of course."

Scarnlet's Atmosphere, ICS *Fortitude*, Bridge

Tc'aarlat and Jack noted that the waves of flashing lights and alarms had stopped before they saw the image on-screen. It was Solo, and they had never been happier to see her. They jumped out of their hiding spot and got back to work. Tc'aarlat took over weapons, and now that the primary systems had been restored, it was like swatting flies. Adina rushed onto the bridge to take her place at navigation, which left Jack to sit down in his chair and give orders. They were back to being in prime condition, and there was nothing that rival crime syndicate could do to stop them.

"Is everyone wearing their seatbelt?" cooed Solo.

"Yes!" said Jack. "It's good to have you back, Solo."

"Thank you, Jack."

"Now let's get out of here," Jack ordered. "Can you find us an opening?"

"Yes," said Solo. "I've analyzed the enemy fighters. They were built for speed and firepower, but can't travel far distances like the ICS *Fortitude*. They're planetary vehicles, not space vehicles, and have no missile functionality. According to my calculations, with our systems at full power, we can outdistance them easily."

"Full speed," directed Jack, and Adina thrust the lever forward.

The ICS *Fortitude*'s engines turned from a dull red to a mighty crimson, and the ship shot forward with the kind of power available to only larger vessels. Within a minute of that blast, the fire against the hull stopped. They knew then that they had lost the fighters altogether in a fine plume of their space dust.

ICS *Fortitude*, Bridge

Nathan was laughing on-screen. Tc'aarlat was laughing from his seat. Adina was laughing just behind Jack. Jack was sitting there in his chair with his arms crossed tightly, sulking quietly. "So, really?" Nathan was saying, "Jack actually slept with him?"

"Her!" Jack piped up. "Technically it was a her."

"Well, anyway," Nathan wiped a tear from his eye with a final chuckle, "it sounds like you've done the Federation proud, Shadows. With the seized credits at our disposal, we can ruin the Don's empire overnight."

"That leaves us with a problem," Tc'aarlat stated. "Encountering that group of rival hackers made me realize something. After the Don has been knocked off the top of the heap, there will be others to take his place. Things are going to get unpretty. Real unpretty."

"I have to agree," added Jack. "There's nothing stopping more syndicates like them from trying to take the top spot."

"Unfortunately, that's something we'll just have to deal with," replied Nathan. "One criminal at a time."

"I suppose so," Jack agreed with a shrug.

"Are you en route to the Federation?" asked Nathan.

"Yeah," said Jack. "The credits will be with you soon."

"Good. I'll see you then," replied Nathan with a wink. "Perhaps we can go for a drink and not have someone try to kill us this time?"

"I'd like that," agreed Tc'aarlat, and Nathan disappeared from the screen. The Yollin turned to Jack. "What about Don Gan'barlo?"

"Most likely, he's gone into hiding," said Jack. "We're not done with him yet, but without any money at his disposal, we'll find him easily enough."

"And put a bullet through his head for our trouble."

ICS *Fortitude*, Adina's Quarters

Adina was silently reading. Not that she knew what she was reading; she had read the same passage more than twenty times. Her thoughts dwelled on the events of the day and the trouble she had caused from one simple mistake. It had almost cost them their lives. Still, she couldn't help but wonder if the hackers and Benjamin were being truthful. Was there a cure for her uncle's dementia?

KNOCK KNOCK!

"Come in," she called to the door, and a moment later, Jack was peering through the gap.

"Am I all right to come in?" Jack didn't wait for an answer, just crossed the room and took a seat on her bed. "Rough day, huh?"

"Long day." Adina sighed.

"I just wanted to let you know that there are no hard feelings about you trying to stab me in the back," Jack stated.

"Technically, it was shoot you in the back," Adina corrected. "And technically, it was your front, not your back."

"Okay," Jack agreed. "I just wanted to let you know that there are no hard feelings about you trying to shoot me."

"I'll never stop apologizing for that," Adina gushed. "I am very—"

"I've had enough of your apologizing to last a lifetime." Jack held up a hand to stop her. "When we hit a more Federation-y place, we'll probably have some time and safety under their protection."

"Yeah, hopefully."

"Well, I thought you might want to upgrade Solo to an AI again," continued Jack. "I discussed it with—"

Adina didn't say anything. She simply put her arms around him and tried not to squeal with glee. Jack smiled through it and tapped her on the arm to ease her grip. "I was hoping you'd say that, Jack."

"No more secrets, though," Jack said pointedly. "That's the one rule aboard this ship. We're a team, and we have to act like a team. I can't deny that there were some benefits to having Solo as an AI."

"You won't regret it, Jack," Adina assured him. "I promise."

"Yeah," said Jack with a smile. "I know."

. . .

Scarnlet, Intercity Bank Building, Vault

It had been an hour, maybe longer, but there was no way of telling when you were hiding under a desk. Killeg Dirk'sen looked at his friend and partner Gruff Hanlo. The two had been beneath this desk since the Yollin had shown up in a mech and made a mess of the place, and they weren't coming out until they thought they were safe.

"Do you think it's over?" asked Killeg Dirk'sen with a gulp.

"Sounds like it's over," replied Gruff Hanlo. "Go check."

"*You* go check!"

They stopped suddenly. Their frantic voices had drawn the attention of something, and they could hear a pair of heavy boots thud across the room. They held their breath and each other as it drew nearer, closer until it stopped at the desk they were under. There was a moment of silence before they heard three knocks, one after the other.

"I know someone's under there," said a female voice they didn't recognize. "Come out."

Dirk'sen looked at Hanlo, Hanlo looked at Dirk'sen, and before they knew it, they were crawling out of their hiding spot.

"Well, well, well," the woman said. She had goggles on her head, thick red hair, and a scar over her eye in the shape of what could only be described as a penis. "Who have we got here, then?"

"Please don't kill us!" Killeg Dirk'sen cried. "We're just accountants."

"I don't kill people who can help me," the woman told them. "You can call me 'Stranger.'"

"It's a pleasure to meet you, uh, Stranger," said Gruff Hanlo.

"Now, whose accountants are you?"

"Don Gan'barlo's, but we had nothing to do with his crimes!"

The woman formed her lips into a sinister smile. "Don Gan'barlo, you say?" she repeated. "I bet you know a lot about him, don't you, gentleman?"

AUTHOR NOTES

AUGUST 1, 2019

by Craig Martelle & Michael Anderle

Greetings, Shadows fans! Thank you for picking up your copy of Shadow Vanguard 4 – Ultimate Payback! You are contributing to the legacy of our departed friend. By buying this book, you are putting money directly onto the table of Tommy's family. They count on the income from these books to simply survive. So thank you, from the bottom of our hearts.

How does this book measure up against the others? No one can have the same sense of humor as Tommy D, but I think we did fairly well. I hope you enjoyed the story for what it is, and that it was written by someone not Tommy D.

Tommy delivered six outlines to us in the final weeks of his life to make sure that these stories carried on. We looked at our budget and decided to have three stories written and then give the funds from the other three directly to Tommy's wife. Money now and money later.

The last three stories in the series will probably be shorts that we write at some later time when we have a few moments and as a way to reenergize the series.

Shadow Vanguard. A fun and wild ride with some crazy characters.

Shadow Vanguard 5 is written and awaiting editing. Shadow 6 is coming close on its heels:).

We spent some time in Europe and the UK over the past couple weeks. Moscow for four days and then Budapest, Hungary for a few days before landing in Edinburgh where Michael Anderle and I, with Ramy Vance carrying the day-to-day work burdens, ran a conference for aspiring and established writers. I was a bit under the weather for the duration having caught something in Russia that refused to let go. That being said, the conference almost ran itself.

We had great presentations lined up on the weekend and the wraparound weekdays were exceptional writing days. People found others just like them. People generally don't know what an author goes through to bring a book to the readers. We sympathized with our fellows and plotted future stories as well as delivered words on current stories. I was quite pleased with everything that was accomplished.

And my illness lingered, preventing me from stringing coherent thoughts together, so that's where I am. I finished editing one non-fiction book and did not add many words to a second one. I haven't started Superdreadnought 6 yet but need to some time this next week. That should be a long one. We'll see how things turn out for Reynolds and his crew.

We are now back in Fairbanks, and it's raining. It must not have rained while we were gone as the grass didn't grow a whole lot. Mother Nature is making up for it now by dumping buckets of water on us. We'll get through this and then get the grass cut in preparation for the winter. We probably only have a couple grass cuttings left. It only gets colder from here on out. Welcome to the sub-arctic.

Break is over, back on my head. Lots of words to gather into a nice, trim package, known as a story.

Peace, fellow humans.
Craig Martelle

https://www.bookbub.com/authors/michael-anderle